Salter's Creek

To. Mary ann Gone

From Shey lee Scott

Pages 71
72
73
102
11.2

Salter's Creek

A Parable of Life

Terry Lee Vail

To order additional copies of this book, contact:
Xlibris Corporation
1-888-795-4274
www.Xlibris.com
Orders@Xlibris.com
77429

This book is for my wife and daughter. May their lives be richer for they have been enlightening and fulfilling to me. For in them, I have found my treasure beyond the rainbow.

Bring Me No Flowers A Soldiers Pray

*B*ring me no flowers, I say, for I lie in a field near death for days. For no one has come to see about me, I am dying. My body is covered in blood; my eyes are filled with tears of regret and sorrow. For I am a soldier of war, I have fought with my hands and I have killed with them in your name. I have killed your enemies for you. And now I lie here dying in this godforsaken place. No one knows my name here, or even cares. So bring me no flowers when I am dead, I say. For our leaders have said those that oppose us are our enemies and must pay with their lives, for the only thing that our leaders know is for someone else's son or daughter must die for their lies. So bring me no flowers, I say, when I am dead. The enemies of yours, I have made them pay with their lives; I do not see their faces of those that I have killed for you. All that I see is your enemy. For the young man that cried out and begged and prayed to me and pleaded for his life. I saw not his face; all that I saw was the enemy of yours, for my leaders have blinded me with their hatred of that which is different from them. Know that the end is near; I can see now, maybe some of the men that I killed for my leaders and for you, maybe we could have been friends, but in the words of our leaders, those that are not with us are against us, so say our leaders. So bring me no damn flowers. It's getting cold. I can't feel my hands, nor can I feel my feet. My life is leaving me. When I am gone, bring me no flowers, I say. Now that the end is near, I can see the faces of those that I have killed in battle for you; they look at me as to say why I took what I could not give back. I scream out in fear that they might do me harm, but then I realize that I am almost dead and by now, they can do me no harm. So I say bring me no damn flowers. I think of my mother now that I am near the end of this journey, what will happen to her. For I was born fatherless and brotherless, for I had no sister to comfort me, now that I am at the end. I see my mother homeless, for she has no job and no money, for I was her only support. Oh my god, what will become of the one that I love the most? For she was there for me, when I could not do for myself as a child. Again I say bring me no damn flowers when I am gone. So you see, I was only eighteen when your leaders and you put a gun in my hand. You gave me six weeks of training and said, "Go and fight my battles." Now my body goes numb, from pain, for no one has come for me; I still lie in a pool of blood. The flies have come to eat away at what is left of me, for now I have become food for them. So much blood, Lord, I could drown in it. For night has came and I see no one yet; all that I see are the faces of those that I have killed, for they have become my friends in my hour of need. You sent me a thousand miles away to fight, when the real battle was right at my door. I can see clearly now that the end has come; I see now that we have lost the victory in winning the war. For we have lost the youth to the world. The youth is the victory to this worldly battle we fight, and we have won the war and lost the victory, which is the youth, to the world, I say. Because of our denial of seeing the world for what it is. So I say to you bring me no damn flowers; instead bring me an answer. Why. Why was I sent to this godforsaken place to be killed and to kill? Someone please tell me what I would have died for. Bring me this, I ask, instead of flowers. So when I meet the enemies of yours in the afterlife, I can tell them why. So that your enemies and I can sleep forever in the same bed of lies. Oh my god, I pray now, not for myself. But for those that will come after me. Forgive our leaders, Lord, it is as you said, the blind cannot lead the blind. For those that have yet to come to this place their hands are already stained like mine, for they are just as guilty as me. I pulled the trigger and did the deed, but you stood by and said nothing; you did not say to your leaders, "No, send not this young man or any other young man." So you bring me no damn flowers for they will do me no good, Lord, my time is almost here. Now my eyes grow weak and I want to close them, but before I go home, I must leave you with this, for this is what I have learned, my friend. Be not like me, for I asked no question as to why must I go. Nor did I voice my opinion on finding another way to find peace. Those are things I should have asked, but I didn't; I took their word for it, that this was the only way. Be not like me; ask and ask again, for this place is a lonely place. Keep those words with you. Remember this, for if you keep your mind and your heart open to the truth, it will come to you and you will find the real truth. And you will know when to follow your leaders, when they say,

"Come and follow me" or when they say, "Stay." So bring me no flowers. Instead, bring me the truth and someone tell me why.

This little poem is a parable. Some of you will get it, and some won't for those that don't understand right now. When you finish reading this book, I hope you will have learned what was meant in this poem and learn the thing that matters the most; these words you will read again and again in the pages of this book for that is what matters the most. If you do not learn what matters the most in life, then that soldier in the little poem would have died for nothing. For there is a debt to be paid to him and to all of the men and women that have given that special gift of life to help you keep yours; that is the purpose of this poem and this book and to help you find happiness in your life and to help you understand that gift that so many have given. This special gift of life that God has given you. And we hope that you will learn how to repay this debt that is owed to those that have given their lives. Hell, some of you all don't even care. You say, "It is not my problem, no one made them go." You say, "I didn't ask them to go and give their life." Well, let me ask you this if they didn't go would you. Man has forgotten many of things, even how to accept a gift of this magnitude and how to repay it. So they retreat back into their own little pieces of heaven and don't want to see it or hear of it. For if they really looked at what it means, they would not sleep tonight and they would not rest until the debt was paid. Because for every eye that closes tonight, there will be some that won't open in the morning; that's why you must find out what matters the most. And learn how to live your life to the fullest and learn how to repay that debt and raise your children in the eyesight of God. In this book, you will see the things that matters the most in life. What if you were given a chance to go back in time and change things in your life and the lives of others, would you? Would you make everyone equal, would you make yourself rich and powerful and leave everyone else below you, or maybe you would make yourself the president, the supreme ruler of the world? Or would you pass it to someone that could do a better job than you, or would you only change your life? If you said change your life, then just maybe you will learn how to do just that, after reading this book. Do you sometimes wonder if your life would have been different if you would have made a different choice in life? Or would it be worse? This book will help you realize the answer and accept your life and put the question of the past to bed. For the young people, this book will help you appreciate the important thing in life and the things that matter the most in life. And some of you will find that one thing that matters the most in your life in this book. You will see your childhood in the boys. Each of the boys mean something; they represent life and the things that have happened and the things that are going to happen. There is a message in this book; you will have to find it, and in finding the answer in this book, you just might be able to solve this question. It has been around for years: when does a boy become a man or a girl become a woman? Or do some men or women ever reach manhood or womanhood, or will you find out that it was better to be a child, to run and play and to take little thought of tomorrow? To a child, that is all that matters. After reading this book, you will be able to accept your place in life in the real world of man. Remember, in the real world, man does not get the chance to go back in time to change his or her life or to undo a wrong, but we hope that this book will help you to bear this world. And to realize that thing that has kept you from living your life the way your God intended you to live it will be in the past at last. For regret is a hard thing to bear and to live with. We hope that this book will help you to accept the things that has put you where you are today and to know that everything that happens is for a reason even if you can't see it or understand it, because you are too close to it. But I will give you this to help you understand your problem. You must first solve that age-old question. When does a boy or girl become a man or woman? It has been said that when a child loses the innocence and becomes aware, then he becomes a man. After reading this book, maybe you can agree or disagree, and if you are lucky and make the attempt to understand this book, then you too might become aware and become a man or a woman and can accept your place in life and know that in fate or destiny, there are no accidents. And to live for today and hope for tomorrow, but you can rejoice if tomorrow doesn't come because you have done everything that day that your God has ordered you to do. Once you become aware, you will know what God's orders are and know that what your God has done for you is the best thing, whether or not you are ready for it. After reading this book, we hope that you can now start to live because you will have become aware of the thing that matters the most. Now we hope that you can put that unseen feeling to bed and let it sleep forever.

Thank you and may your eyes be your ears. And we hope that you will have more questions than answers, for this book's intent is to make you want to ask more questions and to open the mind to the answers that are right at your footstep. This book is a parable of life. For those of you who will judge this book on whether or not if it is good or bad, I say to you judge it on whether or not if you learn how to live and to enjoy the little things in life that are free and have always been there; you just never saw them in the light that you now see them. This book is fictional, but what happens in this book happens every day. Kids are abused; women are raped and killed. Greed and lust and hatred are raising our youths. Our politicians can't agree on what color the sky is; they are self-absorbed in their own egotistical ways, stuck in their own selfish pride instead of our needs and wants, while people are dying and suffering. So what is important is that you read this book and open your ears and mind. Now in realizing this entire thing, what are you going to do about it? That is the purpose of this book, to open your eyes and to give the world a chance to save mankind, as these boys in the pages of this book save their friend. So I ask you, my friend, when you finish reading this book, I hope you will realize what is important and what matters the most, and you will hear those words throughout the pages in this book. And remember, it does not take an army to change things, and remember this also, if an ant can move a mountain, surely you can make a change in things. This book is slow in the beginning just as life is in growing up. So I ask you, my friend, read this book and take the time to think and ponder what you have learned and you will see all four sprits of evil in action, then you will be able to solve the parable of this book. The blinders will be removed from your eyes and that protective cover will be removed from your heart and you will be able to feel the pain of the innocent ones, the ones that you have been able to ignore. After reading this book, you will see those evil spirits that have corrupted man and have made them do things to one another, things that you and I would never imagine, but yet man still do those things. In closing, I pray and hope you are one of the lucky ones and understand the purpose of this book and one of the ones that can solve the parable of the book. Thank you. Your friend for life, Terry Lee Vail.

On a late summer evening with nothing to do but to sit around and talk, Paul, Tim, and Peter decided to build a clubhouse down by Salter's Creek, not paying any attention to the rumors of all the kids that had gone missing down by the creek. Peter told Tim, "You look like you are afraid to build a clubhouse down by that old silly little creek." Then Paul said, "He always looks like that when he's excited." Then Peter said, "I never paid that look any attention until now, I just thought that look on his face was just plain stupid, like a country pumpkin ready for the picking. With that fire-red hair and those freckles all over his face, those teeth, he could rent himself out as corn pliers, and if country had another name, it would be Tim." Then Tim came back with his own words of pain and said, "At least I know what I am." Then he started to sing, "Am I black or white, or maybe I'm just a mutt." Then they all started to laugh. Paul told Tim, "Maybe he should be a singer," and they laughed some more. Then Tim asked, "Hey, you guys, are you guys for real about the clubhouse." "Yes," Paul said. "Then don't you guys think we should be making some plans. About supplies." Then Peter said, "You're right, builder Tim." Tim said, "You always have something smart to say, you fish-eyed city slicker." Paul said, "You boys don't get started again, because you both know you are like brothers." Peter said, "You're right, since we moved here from New York, both you guys are like my brothers. We just live in different houses." Tim said, "I am glad you love me, Peter. Now do you want to kiss, I have been practicing." Peter said, "Get away from me, you little sissy boy," and started to laugh. Tim started to chase him, laughing with his arm stretched out, saying, "Just a little bit, baby." Paul said, "Tim, I hope you were just playing about the kiss. You worry me sometimes, you know. Cut it out, you guys. Tim, you know you're not gay. But like I just said, sometimes you make me wonder. Now let's get to planning. It's getting late, now you and Peter will be in charge of the nails and hammers. Tim, you will be in charge of the wood." Peter and Tim said, "What are you in charge of?" "I am the boss." Then he started to laugh and said, "I was only joking, I will draw up the plans for the clubhouse." Tim said, "That's okay with me, besides, you won't find anything around your house. Your father doesn't work." Paul said, "My father has the best job. He works for the Lord, he save people from themselves and from the devil and today that's a big job." Tim said, "I am sorry, Paul, didn't mean to get your panties in a bunch." Peter said, "That's enough of that. Paul's dad does what he does, and that's that. Now we will meet here tomorrow after school." They all said okay, and they left. Still walking out arguing about Paul's father's job that's not a real job, Peter said to Tim, "And Paul's father drives a new car, and his mother has one too. Just maybe that preaching job pays real good. But yet Paul is right, his dad does have a real job, preaching is not easy. Especially to knuckleheads like you. We have a plan then. We will meet here tomorrow after school." Soon they had reached the curb; they all said good night.

And the next day after school, they met at the same place. Peter asked Tim, "Are you ready to go in the dark scary woods." Paul said to Tim, "He's only trying to scare you, Tim, so don't let him." Tim said, "That punk is only fooling himself if he think those little woods will scare me. I was raised in the woods." Peter said, "That explains it, that's why you have no class," and started laughing. Paul said, "You walked right into that one, Tim," and started to laugh. Tim said, "Are we going to go or stay here and listen to that silly little guy. That multicolor guy, he don't even know if he's black or white, and he is picking on me." Paul said, "We better be going, before you and Peter get into a war of insults." So finally they made it into the woods. There they saw it, salters creek. It was a very quiet place. The little creek looked like it was made of glass, how the reflection of the sun danced off the water, with a large old oak tree hanging over the water of glass. With patches of tall grass around the creek, surrounded by perfect dark green carpet of grass surrounding the little creek, as if someone had just cut it, with large rocks scattered through the low grass. The rocks where almost as big as a house, and at one corner of the creek, there was a pile of little rocks leading into the water; it was a lovely sight to behold. Also there was a tree with large leaves with skinny limbs overhanging on the water. With a big patch of green grass leading into the water, you could see the grass under the water; it was a lovely sight to see. Tim said, "That was the most inviting part of the whole creek." Peter said, "I will agree with you, Tim, and that's a pretty rare thing for me to agree with you, Tim." Tim said, "Let's put the clubhouse right here." Peter said, "Once more I agree." But Paul said, "No, this spot just seems too perfect, it's the wrong spot, I tell you. There's more here than meets the eye." Tim said, "What makes you a prophet and a know-it-all." "I am not trying to be a prophet or to know it all," Paul said. "It just don't feel right to me. It scares me a little, and I am not ashamed to say that. That's all right to say to you guys." Then Peter said, "Paul, we have to respect you for that, we will find another spot." They walked over to that large old oak tree and said to Paul, "How does this spot feel. This oak tree seems like it goes on forever, look, you can't even see the top of the tree, Paul." Then Tim said, "Yea, the limbs go right into the clouds. Maybe they go all the way to heaven." Paul said, "This feels more peaceful and more warmer." Peter said, "Well then, I guess this will do. Do you all agree?" Everybody said yes. Tim said, "Let us look around for a while." They all said yea. Peter walked over to the edge of the water and looked in; there was a big group of dark green grass. That led down into the water with little rocks at the bottom. The water was so clear, then Peter looked up in the sky at the clouds and then looked back in the water's edge and started back walking, looking up at the clouds and back in the water. Paul and Tim were wondering what he was doing looking up at the clouds and then back in the water. Then Peter stopped and picked up a rock and placed it on the ground and then turned to Paul and said, "I think this will do for me. I have found my spot. Now, Paul, show us the spot for the clubhouse. And let us do the layout for the clubhouse." Paul walked back over to the middle of the tree and looked up and said, "This is the spot, come see, Tim." Tim said, "This could work, now, Peter, tell us what where you doing with all that walking around and looking up in the sky." Peter answered, "When I lived in New York, I always wanted to go fishing, and I was looking for that perfect spot to fish. My dad promised me that he would take me fishing, but he never got the chance." Tim then said, "I understand that was the first time you have ever told us anything about your father, Peter." Peter said, "That will be the last time too." Paul said, "Come on, you guys, and pick up some little rocks and mark out the corners and the doors and step of the distance. So we will know how much wood to bring." Tim said, "That's a good idea, Paul." So each of them picked up stones, and Paul did the layout, then he asked them, "Do you all agree on everything that we have done?" Peter and Tim said yea, then Paul said, "Okay, guys, we are now done with everything. We know exactly how much wood and other supplies we will need. It's getting late, you guys, and we better be going, okay." Tim and Peter headed for the path to the road. Paul was behind them looking back at the future spot of the clubhouse. They walked out of the woods singing and laughing. Tim said, "I can't wait until tomorrow, after school, I will have all the things we need." Then Paul said, "Remember, you can't let your folks know anything about this, Tim, or you, Peter." Tim answered, "We will remember that, Paul." Then Peter looked at Paul and said, "I see that stupid look on his face." Then Peter said, "I forgot he looks like that all the time." When Paul looked up, they were at the street. Tim was the first one to say good night, then Paul said, "Wait one minute, before you all go, let me tell you guys this, we will meet by the old oak tree. Now we all better be going home, I will see you all tomorrow." And with that, they all said good night and left for their houses.

That next even they all met at the old oak tree just as they had agreed. Tim had gathered together a lot of old plywood. It was enough to get started, and then Peter came with hammers and nails. Paul had a drawing of the clubhouse and showed it to Tim and Peter. Tim said, "It looks great. All we have to do is make it just like the drawing." "It will be great," Peter said. "I see that stupid look coming on Tim's face." Then Paul said, "You're right, Tim is getting excited. Let's get started, you guys." Tim dragged over the plywood, and Peter brought over the nails and hammers, then they started to nail the plywood together. They got the ends of the plywood nailed together just enough to make it stand up on its own. Then Tim said, "Let's take a break and look around for a while. Paul said, "That is a good idea." Then Peter said, "I want to look at my fishing spot." Then they all walked over to the area where Peter had marked for his fishing spot. Then they heard something splash in the water; it was a loud noise like a giant fish. Then Peter said, "It must have been a fish the size of you, Paul." Then Paul answered them, "There can't be a fish that big. I wonder what it could have been." Then Tim said, "Did you guys ask what could that loud noise have been, well, I guess I will tell you boys." With a smile on his face and a wink at Paul, Tim said, "Down here, Peter, we have a lot of strange things here, you wouldn't understand, coming from New York. Peter, you better pay close attention to me and what I have to say about these woods. Then Paul started to laugh. Tim looked at Paul and winked his eye again. Paul dropped his head, and Tim went on talking; Peter was paying close attention for the first time to Tim. Tim had Peter's attention;

he was hooked on every word, and Tim had not said anything to say what it was. Tim said, "Maybe it was a gator, they can eat a whole man in one bite. And can run real fast, or maybe it could have been a water snake. They can get real big as big as men, and they have a deadly bite." Then Peter put his hand to his face and covered it. Paul looked at Tim to stop joking around, but Tim kept on, then Tim said, "It was a water turkey for sure, that's what it is. They make a big splash like that, when they are getting ready to feed. They eat meat, you know." Then Peter said, "Oh my god, what in the world is that. It must be awful to see." Paul turned his back and started to walk away; he could not hold the laughter in. It was coming out; he walked away and turned away so that Peter could not see him laugh, and he thought to himself, *Tim is heading for a big beat down from Peter when he finds out that Tim has been playing with him. Whoever heard of a water turkey? Boy, Tim is really going to get it real bad. When Peter finds out that there's no such animal as a water turkey.*

Then Paul looked up and saw the biggest squirrel he had ever seen. Then he called Tim and Peter to come over, and they came running and said, "What's the problem, Paul?" then he said, "Look up in the old oak tree." They did as he said, then they saw that squirrel. Tim said, "That is the biggest squirrel I have ever seen." Then Peter said, "They are never that big in New York." Then Tim said, "Yea, the big city of lights and a place for fools, that's big city New York." Then Paul said, "Peter, I think there's something that Tim wants to tell you." Then Peter said, "What are you talking about, Paul?" Then Tim said, "Well, he is talking about what I told you about the things that might have been in the creek. So, Peter, don't tell anybody about the water turkey." Peter said, "Okay, Tim. I won't tell anyone 'cause I don't want to look like a fool, I know that there's no such thing as a water turkey. You had me going awhile until I saw that squirrel and that smile on Paul's face before he walked off and saw that squirrel. That was a pretty good joke, Tim." Then Paul said, "You're not mad." Peter said, "No, because some of the things he said just might be in the water. So he help me to decide not to fish in the water, but I am still going to fish." Tim said, "How you are going to do that?" Peter said, "You will see I am still going to fish all summer." Paul said, "Hey, you guys, it's getting late. We should be trying to make it out of here, before it gets too dark, but before we go, let's see how many more pieces of plywood we need for tomorrow." They all agreed and went over and checked. Tim said, "Just about five more pieces should do it, but I can't bring that much by myself." Peter said, "I will help you out, Tim, my little wilderness man, okay." Tim said, "After school, we will go to my dad's shop to get the plywood we need. We will use my wagon, is that a deal?" Peter said, "That's good enough for me, little wild man, you are not stealing, are you, Tim, from your dad's shop, I don't want to go to jail with you, knucklehead. Then Paul said, "Then let's get out of here." "What are you afraid of, Paul?" Tim said. Paul said, "I am afraid of that water turkey that might be in the water." He started to laugh and said, "Okay, guys, let's go." They all walked out to the curb, and there they all said their good nights. Tim said to the guys as he walked away, "I don't think I will sleep tonight, because I am so excited about the clubhouse." Then Tim said, "It will be almost done tomorrow, and school is almost over, boy, things are really getting good now." Peter said, "I can tell you are excited by that stupid look on your face, Tim." Then Paul said, "You guys don't get started, we have to go before we get in trouble." So they left for their houses, already dreaming of tomorrow, each one with their own idea of the clubhouse and the summer they would enjoy together; they finally said good night.

That next day, Peter met Tim like they had agreed on. They loaded the wagon with the plywood, then they headed for the woods; they soon arrived at the clubhouse. There they saw Paul nailing up some plywood that he had brought, two pieces. Tim was amazed; he asked Paul how did he get the plywood to the clubhouse. Paul said, "It was easy, you think you're the only one who has a wagon." Tim started to laugh and said, "Yep." Then they laughed, then they heard something coming through the bushes. Tim jumped behind Paul. Peter laughed and said, "What's wrong, Daniel boom." Then Tim said, "Don't you hear that." Peter said, "Yes, it's only the wind blowing through the bush." Tim said, "That's no wind, it's probably a bear." Peter's eyes got big as a quarter and jumped behind Paul too and said, "What are we going to do? I heard that you should climb a tree." Then Tim said, "Don't be stupid, Peter, bears can climb trees too." Again Peter said, "What are we going to do?" Tim started to laugh and said, "Don't wet your pants, Peter. Paul and I will protect you, baby boy." Then the noise stopped. "See," Peter said, "just as I said, the wind," and laughed. Then Paul said, "Now let's get to work." Tim and Peter started to unload the wagon. Paul started to hum as he dragged the plywood over to the clubhouse, then Tim started to whistle, and Peter just looked and shook his head in amazement. Then he said, "You guys are nuts, or crazy." "Why," Tim said, "are you afraid? You said it was only the wind, Peter." Then Peter said, "Oh yea. I forgot that it was just the wind." Then Tim said, "You're just a little chickenshit with a big mouth, Peter." Peter said, "Those are fighting words." Just like always, Paul stepped in and said, "Cut it out, you guys, come on, we have enough wood to get this done." "You're right," Peter said. "Tim, I am sorry." As always, Tim had to have the last word and started it all over by saying "I knew you love me. That's why you're always fighting with me. Now we can kiss and make up. Peter replied by saying, "Tim, you want to keep it going, but I am not going to play your sick little game, but I do think you're gay." Then they all laughed and placed the last sheet of plywood on the clubhouse. "Finished," Tim said. "Not quite there, still a little more to do, yea, but not a lot. You know, you guys, this is the first clubhouse I have ever built, can you believe that?" Paul said, "Let's stand back and take a good look at her," then they did. Peter said, "Oh, she's beautiful." Then out of nowhere came a sharp sound like wild pigs from the bushes. Peter again jumped behind Paul. Tim grabbed a hammer. Then they could see the limb on the tree shaking. Then they heard a voice. Peter said, "Pigs can't talk, at least the ones I've seen can't." Then they heard it again; this time it was a roar like a lion. Then Tim said, "You in the woods, you can't scare us anymore, come out." Then they heard laughter and the bushes moving as if someone was moving through. Tim gripped his hammer more tightly. Peter ran over and picked up a long stick and drew it back like he was getting ready to swing at a baseball. Paul just stood there with a smile on his face. After a while, there was another voice; this time it said, "You in the camp. I am coming in, are you ready, you bad boys, who built this clubhouse here in my woods without me." Paul and Tim looked at each other, wondering who it could be. No one knew about the clubhouse but them. Then they looked at Peter; he shook his head as to say he didn't tell anyone. They were stunned. Tim still held the hammer back, and Peter still had the long stick ready to swing, and they both said, "Nobody is going to take our clubhouse from us, I mean no damn body. Peter said, "That's my boy. I am with you all the way"; just then a small figure appeared through the bushes. It was a little kid; Paul said, "He looks like you, Tim, with freckles all over his face and with red hair." Then Peter said, "Not another one. Now we will have two country pumpkins." Then Paul asked him a question, "What did you mean by saying in your woods and why did we build a clubhouse without you, we don't even know who you are." The little boy only laughed and said, "These woods are mine, you see. I claimed them, it's all my hunting ground." Peter started to laugh. Then the little boy looked at Peter with a strange look, and Peter dropped his head. Then Paul said, "What is your name?" The little boy stood back and said, "They call me Big Ben." Then Tim started to laugh and said, "They should call you Little Ben," and kept on laughing. Then Big Ben said, "I get that a lot," and started to laugh. Then Paul asked him where did he come from. Big Ben said, "From my mother." Peter and Tim started laughing. Peter said to Paul, "Yep, we got a smart one here." Then Peter looked at Big Ben and said, "That's real funny ha, ha" and walked away. Big Ben said, "I am sorry, Peter, I was only joking, the way that you and Tim play around and Paul." Then they all said at the same time, "How do you know our names?" Then Ben Big said, "I have been watching you guys for days." But Paul didn't believe that. He felt that there was more to Big Ben than what he was saying, but he did not let Peter and Tim know that. Then Big Ben asked, "So are you guys going to let me join?" Tim said, "That wasn't a good way to ask by trying to scare us." "Yea, you're right, I was only trying to scare you guys off so that I could have the clubhouse to myself," Big Ben said. "I am sorry for that, if you guys let me join, I will show you a lot of things about these here woods, you see, I know every inch of these dag darn woods." Then Peter said, "If we let you join, you will have to stop talking like that." Big Ben answered him, "I will surely try awful powerfully hard, Mr. Peter." Peter just laughed and said, "Tim, I think you have just found your long lost little brother," and they all started to laugh, and they laughed hard and long. After the laughter had stopped, Big Ben said, "So am I in, boys, or out." They all looked at Paul. Paul did not want him to join, so he said, "You have to be twelve years old to join." Peter and Tim looked at each other. *The little guy was so short he could not have been as old as they were*, Paul thought to himself. Then Big Ben put his hand in his pocket of his overalls and pulled out a picture. It looked like he just had made it and handed it to Paul and said, "Here you go, boss man." Then Paul said, "Yep, he's twelve all right, according to this ID. Okay, but you have to bring something for the clubhouse." Big Ben said, "Wait just a moment," and went back the way he came through the woods and came back with a picnic basket full of their favorite snacks. Even with Big Ben bringing the picnic basket, Paul really didn't want Big Ben to join, but he was feeling the pressure from the guys to make up his mind. But he was confused because everything that he came up with to keep him from joining Big Ben had already planned for that, just like the picnic basket he got from the woods, how easy it was for him. It was as if he already knew. When Paul told him that he had to bring something for the clubhouse, just like magic, he went behind the bushes and pulled out the basket. That had Paul very mindful of him. Again Paul thought to himself, *How strange it was that he would have that picnic basket and everything else. It seem like Big Ben had the answer for everything.* When he brought the basket from the woods, Tim and Peter were acting like a pack of hungry dogs. They were just stuffing their faces with sweet treats. Tim came up for air from eating out of the basket of goodies to ask Paul, "Are you going to let him in?" Paul said, "It is not all up to me, we need to vote on it." Tim said, "He would be a good person to be in charge of the snacks." Paul said, "It seems like that's all you and Peter think about is sweet treats." Tim laughed, and then Peter said, "What else is there. I think we should let him join, Paul." Tim said, "Me too, now that makes two against one." Paul dropped his head and said, "Okay, if that's the way you guys want it. All it took was a couple of sweet cakes to make you guys forget that Big Ben has been watching us for days and trying to scare us off. He even knew our names before we even told him, and no one told him." Peter said, "Just like you said, he had been watching us for days, he had to hear us use our names, Paul." Peter said, "Paul, I think you're just mad about the fact that he scared you and that he was watching you." Paul said, "Maybe you're right, but I still think that there is something strange about Big Ben." But he pushed his feeling aside and said, "Welcome, Big Ben, to our clubhouse. I hope you prove to be a good friend to us all." With that, Big Ben walked over and shook Paul's hand and said, "I offer you my hand in friendship, boss, and I will do my best to win you over, and don't wonder too much about those little things that's on your mind. Everything is the way it should be, Paul. We will have many journeys together, and the journey has already started, my friends. Don't be afraid." He then turned and walked over to Peter and Tim and said, "I must be going now. It's getting late, and I have a long way to go." Paul said, "Where do you live, Big Ben?" Big Ben didn't answer right away. Paul saw that and started to wonder more about him. Then he answered, as if he didn't know what to say, "Just beyond the woods." Tim said, "Do you want us to walk you home?" Big Ben answered them, "If you guys walk me home, then that will mean that you will have to walk back through the woods in the dark. That would not be fair." Then Tim and Peter looked at Paul and said, "You see, Paul, he's all right." Then Paul said, "Big Ben is right about one thing, it is getting late. We should put away our tools and tighten up the plywood." "All right," Peter and Tim said. Big Ben asked to help too, so they started putting things away. Then Big Ben said to them, "Tomorrow I want to show you guys how to enjoy what is here in these woods. But you guys first need to learn a few things. Then you will see why I enjoy this place. There's something here for everybody, you can get lost in all this stillness here." Tim said, "I don't want stillness, I want to be adventurous and explore." Big Ben laughed and said, "The best adventures come from being still first, to see what is worth exploring." Peter said, "See, stupid, I told you." They all laughed, even Paul. Soon they had everything ready, and they gathered under the giant old oak tree where the clubhouse was and stood back and looked at one another, complimenting one another on how wonderful the clubhouse looked. Then Paul said, "It is time to go." Peter asked Big Ben, "Are you sure you will be all right?" It seemed to Paul right then that Peter had taken a shine to Big Ben. That seemed strange to Paul. *Because Peter never got close to anyone*, Paul thought to himself. But nevertheless, Paul shook it off and headed for the path with Peter and Tim, looking back at Big Ben. Big Ben went the other way. Then Tim started singing an old song. It was a catchy little song as they started through the path. Peter started to hum the song as Tim sang that old song. Paul started to walk faster. He was thinking to himself that he had to keep an eye on Big Ben. *There's something about him that is not right. I know it*, he thought to himself. Tim and Peter had stopped singing and were watching Paul. Tim and Peter were behind him talking and laughing. Then Peter said, "Paul, you're jealous of Big Ben, Paul. He seems smarter than you." Then Paul stopped and turned back toward them. Tim and Peter started to run because they knew that would make Paul angry. Paul was tall for his age and on the heavy side. And he was only twelve years old. When Peter and Tim got far enough away from Paul, they stopped running; they felt that they had put enough space between themselves and Paul. So they started saying, "Paul is jealous, that's why he didn't want Big Ben to join," over and over again. "Paul is jealous. Paul won't be the boss anymore." They started to dance around just having a good old time laughing and pointing at Paul, not paying any attention to Paul. Paul was steadily moving closer and closer to them when they stopped dancing and singing. They looked up, and Paul was right on them. He grabbed Tim. Peter ran off and stopped and yelled back at Tim, "Run, Tim, break away from that little sissy boy. That's right, you're jealous of our new boss. And you won't have anyone to boss around, stupid Paul." Then Paul squished Tim a little harder. Tim yelled back at Peter, "Will you stop saying those things, you're not helping me. What are you trying to do, make him kill me?" Paul turned him loose and started laughing and said, "Tim, you're real funny." Soon they all were laughing. Peter and Tim said, "We were just joking. Don't take things so hard, Paul. You are the boss man." Paul said, "I don't want to be the leader. I just want to be one of the guys, that's all I want, to enjoy this summer. We have better be making faster steps, boys." They heard a noise in the bushes. Peter said, "Maybe it's Big Ben," and laughed. Paul said, "That's not very funny, Peter." Soon they were at the curb, and they said good night to one another.

That next day after school, Peter, Tim, and Paul met at the clubhouse. Big Ben had not got there. They heard the bushes ruffling; there appeared Big Ben with a picnic basket full of goodies. Paul could see Peter's and Tim's mouths watering for the sweet treats that Big Ben had brought. Big Ben walked into the camp. He greeted everyone and walked over to a stump and sat on it. He picked up a stick and started drawing on the ground. Paul said, "Hey, you guys, we should finish the clubhouse, all right." They all said, "Okay, it wasn't that much left to do." Tim said, "I will finish the top because I am the lightest, okay." Peter took over the walls with the nails. Big Ben got up from the log and said, "What will you guys have me do?" Everyone stopped and looked at Paul. Paul said to Big Ben, "You can help out wherever you want to." Big Ben looked at them all and said, "I thank you all again for letting me join, when we finish with the clubhouse, I want to play a new game. It's an old game, but new to you guys. You all will find it very useful one day soon." After a while, they were finished. Big Ben took them to the edge of the limbs of the oak tree, just where the sun stopped and the shade began on the old oak tree, then Big Ben said, "Lie on your backs and close your eyes." Then Tim said, "You're not going to kill us, are you." They all laughed, but Paul wasn't so sure; he didn't fully trust Big Ben, and Tim also had his doubts about Big Ben. Paul knew that now by what Tim had said. But they all did as he said and lay half in the shade and half under the sun on their backs. Tim asked Big Ben, "Why are we laying like this?" Then Big Ben said, "Because man lives in half in light and the other in darkness." Paul knew exactly what he was saying because he had heard his father say that to a lot of people, his father being a minister. Tim said, "I don't understand that." Paul and Big Ben said, "Be quiet." Big Ben said, "Be still and listen to all the noises you hear. Then put a name to the sounds and the one who names the most will win." Big Ben said, "Tim, you can't make any noise, you have to be quiet and still. Now let's start." Tim kept on making crazy little sounds. Finally he gave up after no one paid him any attention. Soon they started to hear all the sounds in the woods. Peter said, "I hear a frog." Mr. Noisemaker Tim said, "That doesn't count because you can hear them all the time." Big Ben said, "Peace be unto you, Tim." Paul heard what Big Ben had said to Tim. It made him wonder even more. *It was the words he used*, he thought to himself. *The way he talks, no one talks like that anymore.* But he pushed it aside and tried to listen for the sounds. Tim said, "I hear something that sound like a pig." But no one paid him any attention. They all thought he was just playing around. Peter said, "I hear birds." Then Big Ben said, "Can you name them, Peter." Peter answered, "No. I can't be sure, but I have seen a lot of blue jays around here." Big Ben said, "Try and picture the birds in your head sitting on a limb, singing. Do you see them, Peter." Peter didn't say anything for a minute. Then he said, "Yes," and started to smile. Tim wasn't making any more noise. He was just giggling at Peter. Peter seemed so proud of himself that he could see the birds in his mind. It seemed as if he was standing under the limb watching them. Tim heard a turkey sound. Big Ben asked him to do the same as Peter. Soon he too was full of smiles. Big Ben heard a strange sound he said to the guys in a real low voice, "Do you guys hear that. Listen. They listened, but they did not hear the same sound. Paul heard something; he said, "Hey, you guys, I hear water dripping. Like a waterfall." Big Ben started to laugh and said, "I thought you guys would never hear it. This is one of the things I wanted to show you guys. This can be your guide in finding your way back here. If you ever get lost in the woods, just be real quiet and listen for the dripping water, you can find your way back to the clubhouse, it's not far from here." Tim said, "Why didn't you just tell us or just show us." Big Ben said, "You wouldn't have learned what you have already learned. You would be still blind to the woods, and there are animals here that you don't know. If you can't picture the animal in your mind after you have heard the sound, you will have respect for the animal because you can not see the animal in you mind and you will know to respect the animal and fear of the animal." Peter laughed, and Tim started to laugh too and said to Big Ben, "You are very smart. I think that you are the smartest of us all. How do you know all these things, Big Ben?" He just smiled. Paul said, "Yes, tell us," in a strong voice. Again he smiled. Then he said, "The same way every boy learns from his father. The same as you, Paul. My father taught me the woods before he died, and your father is teaching you of God and to see not only with the naked eye, but the eye of God, with a godly eye. That makes you smarter than I." Paul then said, "Yes, I guess you're right, I am smart. Tim was listening very carefully to the words he spoke. He started to think to himself about the things his father taught him. His father didn't teach him those things that Big Ben was talking about, and his father is one of the best woodsmen in all the state. He could not think that there was someone else smarter than his dad. *That was a hard thing to believe. It must be something else,* he thought to himself. But he did not say anything to Big Ben. He just looked at Paul and winked his eye and laughed. After a while, they all were laughing, and they didn't really know why. Peter said, "Can you show us the waterfall now." Big Ben said, "I was waiting for that." Big Ben said, "Paul, can you lead us to the waterfall by the sound." Tim got all excited about it. Tim said, "Adventure at last. Now that's what I have been talking about all the time." But Paul was hesitant; he didn't want to. There was so much doubt in his mind about Big Ben until Paul felt he could not trust Big Ben. He didn't know why, but he didn't. Peter said, "What's wrong, Paul, are you afraid of the unknown." Paul said, "There is only one thing I am afraid of, and that is Tim's mom's cooking. Let's do this. They got up and started. Big Ben said, "Paul, let your ears be your eyes, see not with your eyes to what is around you. Instead listen for what is far but near." Somehow Paul knew what he meant and did as he said. Peter said, "If he does not look with his eyes, then how will he find it." Tim said to Peter, "The blind people do it all the time, stupid." Peter laughed and said, "You're right, Tim, I forgot that," and he laughed out loud again. Big Ben said, "One more thing you guys," as they walked toward the waterfall. "Even in life, it is good to see with your ears. For sometimes they can warn you of trouble before you can see it." As they walked, they came by a patch of tall grass. A large flock of birds flew from the grass. They scared Tim; he screamed. Peter asked him did he shit his pants. They all laughed as they made their way through the tall grass. The grass looked like bales of hay all brown, dead. The area was heavily shaded. That made it kind of dark in spots. Tim said, "It's getting kind of spooky." Big Ben said, "Tim, don't see with your eyes, remember, only with the ears. Remember the sound of the waterfall. How wonderful it must be. If you don't listen for that sound, you will miss something wonderful that only a few have laid eyes upon her." So Tim focused on the sound of the waterfall, and before he realized it, he was not afraid anymore. He could see the waterfall in his mind and began to smile. Then they came to a real green area. Big Ben said, "We are close." They walked a little further, and they saw a wonderful sight. Paul had done it. He had led them to a wonderful waterfall. They saw water coming out of an old dead tree. The limbs were about four feet off the ground; there were three limbs. The trunk seemed to keep going up to the sky. The old tree looked like it was made of stone. But it was wood, as the water fell from the limbs of the old tree. It looked like it was crying, with green and white moss hanging from the limbs. At the base of the tree, there was a strong gust of water running out of it, like a river to the ocean. The roots were all out the ground. There were little ferns growing all around the roots of the old stonelike tree. Water was coming right out of the roots; it seemed like there was a water pump underground. The water was falling against a pile of small rocks; there was green fungus all over the little marblelike rocks. You could see the little fish swimming in the creek as the water fell into the creek from the limbs of the tree. It wasn't a lot of water falling; it was like little tears rolling down a child's cheek. It seemed as if the water was falling in slow motion from a slow rain. In the background, you could hear the frogs and birds and the crickets. The noise wasn't a loud noise but a very soft sound. It was a relaxing sound. It was very strange how everything worked together to make that beautiful, relaxing sound. There was moss hanging from the other trees, like an old man's beard. The grass was so green and thick. It looked like a soft carpet. Peter said, "This place is so amazing and so wonderful. I wish I had my camera, this is something you should share with someone special. The whole world should know of this wonderful sight." Big Ben said, "There are many people who know of this place. My father brought me here long ago. For all that know of this place none will ever speak of it, nor will they show it to anyone." Tim said, "Why, Big Ben." Big Ben answered him, "You know, in your heart of hearts, if the world knew of this place, it would be no more. Man would destroy the innocence of this wonderful place. You all know this to be true. So you see, guys, you cannot tell anyone of this place. This is for your eyes only." Peter said, "We can't tell anyone, Big Ben." Then Paul said, "Big Ben just told you why because of man. And one more thing, Peter, you know we are not supposed to be out here." Peter said, "You're right." Then Big Ben said, "I have a surprise for you, Peter. Do you remember what you learned at the clubhouse? How to picture things in your mind. So you can take a picture of this place. So you can see it, Peter, whenever you want, that's the best picture of all, the one that is in your mind, you don't need a camera. You have already taken the picture. This picture you have took, no one can steal it, and you can't lose it. So file this place in your mind and heart. For this is a true treasure to be kept. Now you can visit this place whenever you want to see it, or when you are feeling sad." "We had better be getting back. You know tomorrow is the last day of school," Paul said. They all said, "Okay," as they were taking their last look at the old tree of water. Tim had started to wonder more about Big Ben. *The things he says and the way he can make you feel,* he thought to himself. Paul was right; there is more to Big Ben than what meets the eye. He wanted to talk to Paul alone about Big Ben. They all started back to the clubhouse. It didn't take long. It seemed like they got back quicker than it took to go. Then they were back at the clubhouse. There, Tim asked Big Ben where did he go to school. "I have never seen you at our school. It is the only one in the neighborhood." Then they all stopped and looked at Big Ben, waiting for a answer. Paul thought to himself, *We have him now*. Big Ben said, "I don't go to public school." Then Peter said, "Do you go to private school? You must be rich, Big Ben." Big Ben laughed and said, "Nothing like that," with his head down. "My grandmother teaches me at home." Then Paul said, "I should have known Big Ben would have an answer." Then Peter said, "You mean homeschool. It's a lot of kids in New York that have homeschooling." Tim said, "That explains why we never saw you at our school." Paul said, "You guys, we better be breaking camp." Then Big Ben said, "I will show you guys something else tomorrow, after school." Peter reminded Big Ben not to forget the snacks, and they all left.

That next day, they all met back at the clubhouse, excited, wondering what Big Ben was going to show them and what would they learn today. They thought to themselves. Then they heard something coming through the bushes; it was Big Ben, with that big picnic basket. They thought he had something special because this was the last day of school. When Big Ben got inside, he put the basket inside the clubhouse. Then he greeted everyone and went over to sit on his favorite log, as he always did, and picked up his stick and started drawing on the ground like he always did. He wasn't excited that there was no more school. It was summer all day and all the fun one could handle. Tim and Peter went over to where he was sitting and said, "What are you going to show us today." Big Ben laughed and said, "It is not what I am going to show you all. But what we are going to show each other. Let's go to our spot where the sun and shade meet and watch the parade in the sky." Tim said, "What parade." Big Ben answered him, "The clouds. They can be anything you can imagine. Just look up in the sky. Let your mind go. Once you do that, the sky comes alive before your eyes." They all got up and started to the edge of the shade. But Paul was slow in getting up. Tim ask him, "Are you coming, Paul." Paul said, "Yea, wait for me." Then Big Ben stop and said something strange, "This will be good for you guys because man never take's the time to look up in the sky they only look straight ahead and they miss one of God's gift. Then Paul said. "I am ready." So they went over and laid on their backs and looked up in the sky. Peter said, "I don't see anything but clouds." Big Ben said, "Are you sure, look again." Then Peter said, "Yep. I don't see a thing."

Then Big Ben said, "I see a elephant." "Where," Peter said. Tim said, "He's not talking about a real elephant, you nut. He's talking about the shape of the clouds, you nut," answered Tim back. Peter said, "I know that." Tim said to Peter, "Why did you say you didn't see anything then." "I was just playing," Peter said. Tim answered, "Yeah right," and started to laugh. Paul said, "Don't start, you guys. Just lay here and look in the sky and see what you can see, maybe you nuts will learn something. This is a game, and whoever sees the most shape wins. And that person can name the next adventure, all right," Big Ben said. They all said, "Yea." Then Paul said, "Get ready, set, go." Tim saw an angel, a pretty cotton angel. Then Paul saw a horse. Then he said, "It's changing to a unicorn." Then Paul said, "That makes two for me," and looked back to the sky again. Then Paul said, "I see a cloud that looks likes Peter's head. It is changing now, it looks like Tim's head. That's four points for me," and started to laugh. They all laughed hard and long and started pointing out clouds that looked like one another's head. "It's almost time to go," Paul said. Big Ben said he wanted to stay and do some more looking around for tomorrow, because we will be here all day tomorrow. Peter said, "We have to eat the snack before we go, right." Then Tim said, "Let me at them." Paul said, "Wait, you pigs, save some for me." They all laughed as they ate the sweet cakes and drank the sodas that Big Ben had brought. As they finished the last of the snacks, Tim ask Big Ben was he going to be all right if they left him there alone. Then Big Ben said, "I was born alone, I wasn't born with a bodyguard." They started to laugh. Paul started picking up things and putting them away. Tim and Peter where finishing up the last bit of crumbs in the basket. Paul said, "Everything is all put away." Peter said, "Tomorrow I will bring my fishing rod to fish. I think I will fish the whole day away." They soon left.

That next morning they met there at the clubhouse. Big Ben had not gotten there yet. But they knew he would show up with a big basket of goodies for everyone. Peter had brought his rod as he said he would. Then Peter said, "I am going fishing until Big Ben gets here with our breakfast." He walked over to the spot he had already had picked out when they first came there to lay out the clubhouse." Then Peter threw out his rod, not in the water but right at the edge of the water. Tim said, "Hey, nut, you are supposed to throw your hook in the water." Peter said, "You fish the way you want, and I will fish the way I want." Then Peter picked up a piece of straw from the ground, then put it in his mouth and laid on his back and said, "Now this is a good spot, I ought to catch one from there," and pushed his hat over his head and started humming. Tim said, "Paul, look at that city nut. He doesn't have enough sense to throw his pole in the water. That little nut. You have to throw your hook in the water to catch a fish." Paul said, "Tim, that's Peter's pole, and he can fish any way he wants. Even if that means fishing like a little scary girl." Tim said, "You're right, Paul, he can fish like a girl, because he is afraid to put his pole in the water. Why are you afraid, Peter. Are you scared that you might catch a water turkey." Then Peter said, "Let me tell you a secret, there is no such thing, Tim, but there's no telling what's inside Salter's Creek. Tim answered, "Whatever, man, or should I say, you little sissy boy. If that makes you happy, then go for it, Peter," and then walked over to Paul, who had walked over to where Tim was standing watching Peter fish. Then he said to Tim, "I wonder where Big Ben is. He should have been here by now. Tim said, "Don't worry so much about Big Ben, he can take care of himself." Then Tim said, "I am going to climb this tree all the way to the top." Paul said, "You're not because you are scared to go that high." Tim said, "Not only will I go to the top, but I will climb it naked. But if I go all the way to the top, you will have to give me your part of the snack from the basket that Big Ben is bringing." Paul said, "It's a bet." "Then let's ask Peter does he want to bet too," Tim said. "I can eat all the snacks myself." Peter said to Tim, "Please don't take off your clothes. It is too early in the morning to see such a sickening sight like that. It will upset my stomach," and then they all laughed and laughed. Tim said, "It's time to blast off," and started to take off his pants and underwear. Peter said, "Oh my god, Tim, you just blinded me with your snow-white ass, the reflection from your ass is too bright." He pushed his hat over his eyes. Peter kept on saying, "I am blind," and kept on laughing. Paul was laughing so hard he tripped over a stick, and that made it funnier. They laughed for a long time making jokes at Tim's snow-white ass. Peter started calling him little Miss snow ass. Tim decided not to climb the tree after all. Those jokes made him think about something else instead. Tim said he was going to give his ass some sun. They all laughed again as he lay on his stomach with his ass pointed at the sun. Peter told him he had better be careful and not to get too much sun. "You don't want to get a sunburn on your bun." Tim did not pay Peter any attention. "Okay," Peter said, "you will be sorry, if you stay too long in the sun. Your bun is going to be blacker than Paul's face." Tim said, "I will be a soul brother," and started to laugh. Peter told him, "You won't ever be a soul brother, but your ass will be sore if you stay too long in the sun." Paul started to laugh. Then Paul said, "We have been here for couple of hours, and for sure Big Ben should have been here by now." Tim answered Paul, "I don't think anything has happened to Big Ben, maybe he's running late." Then Paul said, "I hope you're right." Peter said, "Tim, your butt is turning pink, I think you should be getting out of the sun, Mr. soul brother." Tim answered him back with a smart answer, "Mind your own damn beanies." "Okay," Peter said, "but you will be real sorry soon." Tim said, "Only couple more minutes laying here and the color will be just right." Paul was quiet; he wasn't saying too much about Tim and Peter. He was thinking of Big Ben. What could have happened? Even though Tim was so sure that nothing had happened to Big Ben. Tim got up; he walked over to Paul and whispered in his ear, "Paul, I don't want that knucklehead to hear us, but Peter was right, my ass feel like it's on fire." Paul started to laugh, but he didn't; he whispered back into Tim's ear, "I guess you are a soul brother now. Your ass is going to be blue, not black," and smiled. He could hardly keep the laughter in. Paul told Tim to put on his pants, but don't put on his underwear. Then Peter said, "What are you girls whispering about, Miss hot cheeks, or should I say Miss pink cheeks. Paul fell to the ground in laughter; he laughed so hard until tears were coming from his eyes. They laughed for hours; even Tim had to laugh at himself. When they finally stopped laughing, Tim said to Paul, "What am I going to do. I can't tell my mother I was tanning my ass. My dad will kill me, he already thinks I am too soft and act strange, he says." Peter told Tim, "Your father is a smart man." Tim said to Paul and Peter, "Come on, you guys, what am I going to do." Peter said, "Okay, Tim, I will tell you, take some butter and honey and rub it all over your buns." Tim said to Peter, "What will that do." Peter said to Tim, "You will make honey bun on your buns. They taste great, you little sweet thing," and started to laugh again. Paul told Peter to give him a break. Paul said, "I will tell you what to do. Ask your sister for help." Tim thought for a moment and said, "There goes all my savings for sure." "Why," Peter said. "Because she is going to blackmail me for sure," Tim said to Peter. Then Peter said, "Tim, you have a lot of smart people in your family, what in the hell happened to you." Tim told Peter, "I got all the good looks and this hot body," and started to laugh. Then Tim said, "I guess in my case I will have to ask my sister for help, what else can I do." By that time, Peter picked up his rod and started winding it in, as if he had caught a fish. Tim said to Peter, "You know, you don't have a fish on your pole." Peter answered Tim back, "Damn right, not now, I missed him. Damn, he got away, and he was a big one too." Tim said, "You're crazy, Peter." "No," Peter said. "I am just a nut. Because I never threw my hook in the water," and started to laugh. "I know there's no fish on my hook. Tim, let me tell you a secrit if I were to catch a fish, I could not take it home so you say what's the use in fishing, well let me tell you this country boy I owe it to myself theirs another reason but that one is for you." Then Tim said, "What ever man I know what you just said is all a pack of lies, but what ever float your boat buddy and they all laughed. Tim laughed and cried at the same time from his sweet buns, as Peter had said; they were burnt and hurting. Paul said, "Well, you guys, Big Ben has not come yet. I guess we should be going home for the day." "You're right," Peter said. "I'm hungry, and Miss sticky buns here needs to take care of his problem as soon as he can. So let's pick up and put away our stuff for tomorrow. You guys, tomorrow I am going to bring some snacks just in case Big Ben does not come." Paul said, "Peter, that's a good idea." Paul said, "I will bring something too." Tim said, "You guys, you know Big Ben will be here tomorrow for sure." So they picked up and headed down the trail for the day. "The day was cut short because Tim did a stupid thing," Peter said to Paul, "and I am hungry too." Tim said, "That's not true, bighead frog-eyed Peter, you were hungry, that's the reason, you said, okay, let's go, Peter. Not because of me." "Whatever, man, call it what you want, sweet buns," and started laughing. Then Peter said, "Who in their right mind would strip naked and try to tan their ass and get a sunburn on it." Paul said, "I will tell you who, Tim. Tim is the only guy in the world who can get his ass burn for real." And they all laughed as they went down the trail.

That next morning, they met at the camp. Peter was with his rod and ready for a day of pretend fishing and a bag of snacks. Paul brought a bag of snacks and his thoughts about Big Ben. Tim wasn't there yet. Peter said, "I can't wait until Tim gets here. I bet his butt is sore." Paul said, "You will soon get your chance to find out, Mr. inspector of butts, Peter. Here he comes now." Peter had already started laughing as soon as he saw Tim. Paul started laughing too. Just by saying, "Here come sticky buns," that's all it took, and they were laughing just like it had just happened. Tim made his way into the camp, and he had a bag of snacks too. Tim said to Peter and Paul, "I was thinking about what you guys said, Peter and Paul, and you guys are right. There's no need in starving waiting on Big Ben, hell, you guys, he might not even come today. I wish I knew where he stayed. I would go by his house to make sure he's all right." Tim went on to say to Paul, "Thank you again for telling me to talk to my sister. She help me real good, and it feels so much better. It only cost me everything I had save up.

But I will get her back, and also she agreed to keep her mouth close. Something else I learn, Paul, it's not what people think of you, it's what you think of yourself that matters. And I did something stupid, I tried to be more like you guys. But I guess I am just a snow bunny." Peter laughed and said, "Yea. You are truly one ignorant country boy, Tim. If you wanted to be more like us, why did you tan your ass. Why couldn't you just tan you front side, your face, and stuff like that." Tim said, "Now who's the stupid one, you know I could never let my dad see me with a tan. It was for you guys because you guys are my friends. No one else would ever know, I thought. I wanted to be like Paul and you, even though you don't know what you are, black or white, Peter." Then Peter said, "Tim, that was a stupid thing to do. You were just plain stupid to do that. To stay out in that sun that long." Tim said, "You right, Peter. I guess am a stupid old country boy." Then Paul said, "Peter, you are a fine one to talk, Peter. You are just as stupid as Tim. Sorry, Tim, I didn't mean it in a bad way, Tim." Then Paul told Peter, "You fish with a rod that you won't even threw in the water and pretend to fish when the water is right there. Now who's stupid." Peter dropped his head and walked off. Then Tim said, "What about Big Ben, do you think he's coming today." "I don't know," Peter said. "I hope he didn't try to swim in that creek. If he did, maybe he's at the bottom of the creek." Paul and Tim dropped their heads. Tim said, "What are we going to do, we can't tell our folks because we are not supposed to be here. If we do tell, we will be in big trouble. We will lose our clubhouse." Then Peter said, "We don't know for sure he is at the bottom of the creek." Then he thought to himself, *If it was him at the bottom of the creek, he would want someone to tell his mother, so she would not worry so much.* Then he said to Paul, "Maybe we should tell someone." Paul had the calming voice, the voice of reason. He said, "We just don't know for sure. So let's just wait for a while." They all wanted to cry. For the first time, there was no laughter heard in the air, only stillness and a cold feeling of not knowing what was going to happen next. They started wishing that they had never found this place, or built this damn clubhouse. Tim could not hold the tears; he started to cry and said, "Poor Big Ben done went and got yourself drowned," and continued to cry and cry. There were no smiling faces to be seen from anyone of them. No joking around, only tears were in the air; the sound of stillness surrounded the clubhouse. The clubhouse was filled with a feeling of tears of sadness, for their new found friend was gone, they thought. Then Paul said, "Remember, guys, Big Ben said that he was going to look around. I don't think Big Ben was that stupid to go into the creek. He seemed too smart for that." "Maybe he's not at the bottom of the creek. Maybe he went to the waterfall," Tim said. "Maybe he left a clue or something at the waterfall and maybe he want us to track him," Peter said. "Can you lead us back to the waterfall, Paul." Paul didn't answer him right away. Then he said, "I am not sure." Tim said, "Why don't we do what we did with Big Ben. Let's go back to that same spot and lay on our backs and close our eyes." So they went to where the sun and shade meet. Then Tim said, "Just like it is in life, half in the truth and half in the evil." Peter said, "Big Ben may not be here, but his words are." They all laughed. "That is something Big Ben would say," said Tim. Then they laid on their backs and closed their eyes. It was quiet, total stillness. Tim was not making noises with his mouth, like the last time. Peter wasn't joking around at Tim either. This time it was different; they knew they had to see with their ears, like Big Ben had taught them. So they laid there motionless with their ears open and eyes closed. Then they started to hear the sounds of mockingbirds chirping on that old early cool summer morning and an owl perched on a limb making owl hoot sounds. They could hear the frogs croaking near the creek. It was so still, they could hear the leaves blowing in the early summer morning; it was a breezy morning and the wind blowing through the tall green grass. They had finally reached that place that Big Ben had tried to take them. They had become one with nature, a part of the woods, feeling gentle changes of the woods. The wind blew so smooth against their warm bodies like a hand massage. Then Tim opened his eyes and looked at Paul; he was smiling. He seemed like he was at peace. Tim knew he was on his way to the waterfall in his mind. Then he looked over at Peter; he was also smiling with his mouth open. Then Tim closed his eyes, and he was there at the waterfall where the limbs of the tree seemed to cry, with the water falling so ever softly; finally he could see the wonder of the waterfall without being there, and he knew how to get there. It was so beautiful. Then he remembered what Big Ben had told Peter about the camera, that he did not need a camera. That he had already taken the best picture in his mind. It would always be there whenever you need it, and like all good memories it will become a part of you; it won't fade or rust or break apart with age. *Yes,* Tim said to himself, *this is the best picture you could ever take.* He knew the other guys were seeing the same thing. He knew now that he could see this anytime he wanted to. *Big Ben was right, the best adventure does start by being still and quiet,* he also thought to himself. Then he realized that he could see all the animals. He could put a face to the sound that the animals made. Now even the unknown sounds didn't scare him anymore. Tim knew the other guys felt the same way; his mind was at peace and at ease. Then something strange happened; they all got up at the same time and looked at one another and started toward the waterfall without a word spoken between them. They walked with a smile and their heads held high as they walked through the path, without a care of what was going to happen along the way. It was like they were in a trance; it didn't matter. They had found something special inside themselves; it felt like magic. Even when Tim got to the spot where the birds had scared him, they flew out again the same way, but this time they didn't scare Tim. He only put his hand to his ears for a moment; he didn't realize that they were so noisy. They kept on walking, getting closer and closer to their goal. The sound of the waterfall was getting stronger and louder. They knew they were close, and they were not afraid. If they found Big Ben, that would be good, but if they didn't, then that would be good too. Because in trying to find Big Ben they had found peace of mind and for that moment that felt good. Finally they reached the waterfall. Peter remembered something about Big Ben. Peter said, "Big Ben wouldn't touch anything here because this place is special." Tim said, "You're right, he wouldn't move a single stone here or break one limb from a tree." Paul made his opinion heard by saying, "You know what, you guys . . . I think what happen was meant to happen. Look at what we have learn. We could not find this place on our own, no one could remember the way, but in our minds we did. We had total recall of the waterfall and how to get here, we would not have learn that if it hadn't been for Big Ben. Look at this special gift we have found, this special place in our minds. This is a good thing. For sure this is something we would have never did if Big Ben hadn't gotten himself lost. Well, boys, we better be heading back." Tim said, "Since we are already here, let's look around, I mean, we are not looking for Big Ben, because we know he's not here, and we are not looking for clues for Big Ben, but to look at the beauty of the waterfall and all the wonders she gives." Peter said, "He didn't need to look around because he could see everything in his mind, from the first time with Big Ben. You know, Big Ben was right, the best picture is the one you take with your mind." Paul said, "Yea, that is a pretty smart little guy. I don't understand how can a kid be that wise, not smart, but wise." Peter started to laugh. Tim turned to him and said, "What are you laughing about, Peter." Peter said, "Something someone used to say to me, that's all. Let's go, you guys." They started back to the clubhouse. Tim said, "When we get back, we should have lunch." "Did your mother make the snacks?" Paul asked Tim as they walked back to the clubhouse. "What are you trying to say, Paul," Tim said. Paul said, "Tim, you know your mother can't cook." Peter said, "Your mother can't boil water." "That's a mean thing to say," Tim said. But Peter kept on he came back with more Peter ask Tim, "How can you guys eat that food, your mom cooks." "My mom cooks it with love," Tim said. "And let me tell you guys something about love. My mom does not have to try and cook, but she does and she tries real hard to. When she is in the kitchen, she is always humming a little song as she tries to prepare our food. She seems so happy. She is so alive, and she's always reading cooking books to learn more, she knows she's not the best. She could easily go out and buy frozen dinner. But she tries to make it homemade. My mom tries for us because she loves us. Now I ask you, what could be better than trying to cook out of love. Even when you know it's going to taste bad, but we still eat it with love. When mom served the food, we eat it out of love. But I must confess. I do eat it real fast so I don't taste it. Just in the mouth and down the throat to the stomach. All it takes is four chews then swallow. Then water and that's the end. Like I said, it's easy because I love my mother very much, you guys. You guys should be ashamed of yourselves anyway." Then they dropped their heads and looked like they were going to cry. Peter and Paul felt bad about the things they had said about Tim's mom's cooking. Tim knew that he had made them ashamed of themselves. After making them feel bad, Tim said, "Hey, you guys, my mom didn't make the sandwiches that I brought. You're right, Paul and Peter, my mom can't cook, but you should never put a person down for trying." Paul said, "You're right, Tim, and I am sorry, Tim, I never thought about it the way you explain it. That's a lot of trouble to go through, just to cook food for you and your family. To take the chance that the everyone you are trying so hard for might laugh about your food. When you already know it taste bad. That take nerves. That can't be anything but love."

Paul and Peter told Tim that they would eat Tim's food first. Peter said, "When we finish eating, I am going to go fishing." Tim looked at Paul and started to laugh. Paul said, "All right, Peter, but this time don't let the big one get away," and grabbed his stomach and laughed. Because they knew his fishing was all make-believe fishing. Paul and Tim laughed for a while off that one. Tim said, "One day, Peter, you're going to catch a fish, and it is going to scare the living shit out of you." After the snack, Peter went over to his fishing spot and threw out his reel at the edge of the creek and laid on his back, pushed his hat over his eyes. Then Peter yelled out, "I ought to catch a big one in this spot," and laughed. Paul and Tim laughed along with him as they walked over to the big log where Big Ben always sat; each one picked up a stick from the ground and started to play tic-tac-toe. Tim asked Paul, "I wonder what really happen to Big Ben. I know he's not dead." Paul asked Tim, "How do you know he's not drowned in the creek?" Tim said, "He's too smart for that. You know that too, Paul. It's just a feeling right here, that's how I know he's all right." Tim put his hand to his heart and rubbed his chest. That seemed to have made Paul admit that he too had the same feeling. They looked at each other and nodded their heads as if they were speaking to each other without saying a word. They gave each other a big smile. Then Peter said, "What are you girls doing over there." Tim yelled out, "Never you mind, egghead. You just keep your eye on your pole. You might catch that big one any minute," and laughed. Then Peter said, "I already know what you girls are talking about anyway." Tim said to Peter, "All right, egghead, tell us then." Then Peter said, "You guys were talking about Big Ben. He's all right, he's somewhere playing Daniel Bune in the woods." Tim said, "How do you know that." Peter said, "I had that feeling ever since we left the waterfall, that he is all right. And that feeling gave me this peace about Big Ben, not to worry." Then Tim looked at Paul and said, "You know, that old bonehead over there has made me realize that we shouldn't worry about Big Ben." Paul thought to himself that was strange how they all got that peace about Big Ben, about the same time. Being the son of a preacher, he had always heard of miracles, but had never seen one until now, he thought. Then a big smile came over his face. Then Tim said, "I win. Tic-tac-toe, you want to play another game." "No," Paul said, "I think we should get some wood for a fire and for cooking." "All right," Tim said. Peter said, "We will never cook out here, stupid." Tim said, "We won't be frying chicken, stupid," but Peter said, "We can roast hot dogs and marshmallows. So they spent the rest of the day gathering dried wood and making fun of Peter fishing. "Maybe you should change bait, what are you fishing for, Peter, bass or brims," Tim said and started laughing. That went on until it was time to go. At the end of the day, they put away their things, feeling just a little sad that Big Ben had not showed up. So they headed for the path to go home.

The next day came; they all met back at the clubhouse except Tim. Peter said to Paul, "I hope Tim is not going to try and play Daniel Bune too, like Big Ben." Just then they heard someone running through the path. They knew that it wasn't Big Ben because he came from the other side. Peter said, "That has to be my country pumpkin." Tim yelled out,

"Hey, you guys." Before they could answer, he yelled out again, "Hey, you guys." Paul said, "What's wrong, Tim, are you all right." By that time, Tim had made it inside the camp, saying, "Yea, I am all right." Tim bent over, out of breath from running to the clubhouse, putting his hand to his knees, saying, "I ran all the way here, when I heard it." As he tried to catch his breath, Peter said, "Come on, man, spit it out." Tim said, "I am trying to, just give me a second." Peter was getting upset. Peter said, "You country hick, you race in here dying to tell us something, and now you're out of breath, boy, you country folks are really strange." Paul was getting inpatient too and said, "Breathe, Tim. Now, Tim, take your time and please tell us." Tim slowly began to tell them the news. "Big Ben is missing." Peter said, "No shit, Sherlock, we already know that. You must have been drinking some of your papa's moonshine again. Next time, why don't you share it." Tim said, "No, stupid, I heard it over the radio. There's a missing kid alert out. His name is Benjamin T. Powell, and his family is one of the richest in all of Carolina. His family dates back to the founding fathers of Carolina." Then Paul said, "That's why he was able to bring those good old snacks and why he knew so much about the outdoors. He probably has a private tutor that taught him that stuff." "He taught us," Peter said. "He didn't have to teach us any of those things, but he did." A still coldness filled the air. It was a powerful feeling of sadness in the camp again. Even the trees didn't make that joyful noise of the wind blowing through their branches. The leaves were not turning over in the wind. The birds were not making that magical music that filled the air with song. It was truly a sad time. It was like a stillness of a cold winter's night. Peter said, "Maybe he's been kidnapped." "Kidnapped," Tim said and burst into tears. "Poor, poor Big Ben done went and got his self kidnapped," and he started to cry even more. Peter put his hand to his heart and took a deep breath, as if he was trying to keep from crying. Paul was not paying the drama queen's any atention any mind. Instead, he was looking out across the creek, the side where the waterfall was. Then he said, "You little drama queens, look over there. What in the hell is that coming toward us. It looks like a big round log with something on it." Tim cried out, "I don't know, you guys. But I am going to get the hell out of here." Peter said, "What's wrong, Tim, are you afraid. Tim said, "No, I'm not afraid, but someone has to stay alive to tell what happen to you fool's, and that will be me. Tim took off like a bullet fired from a gun running. Paul yelled out, "Wait, Tim. I think it's Big Ben." By that time, Tim was at the mouth of the path. Paul thought to himself, *Tim can really haul ass when he's scared.* Tim stopped, but he did not come back. Paul then said to Peter, "Let's move closer, Peter." Peter said, "What do you mean move closer. I don't what to see a dead body, no sir." And he started running to where Tim was standing. Paul moved closer and turned and looked back for Peter. As Peter was running to where Tim was standing, Peter yelled out to Paul, "You can move as close as you want to, but I won't be with you. I might be behind you, over there with Tim." So Paul moved closer to the creek. Paul looked back at Peter and said, "Are you coming back." Peter answered him and said, "I might, I am still thinking about it." Paul called them both little girls and moved even closer. Then he yelled over to where Tim and Peter were standing and asked them what did Big Ben have on. Tim yelled back, "A striped shirt and some overalls, with white sneakers. Paul said, "The clothes looked to be the same." Peter moved closer to Tim, saying, "I don't want to see a dead body." As the log floated closer to Paul, he could see for sure it was Big Ben. He yelled back at Tim and Peter, "It's Big Ben all right." Paul moved closer to the water's edge and reached out for Big Ben and started pulling him in. He yelled over at Tim and Peter for help, but they were too busy crying. Tim's eyes were red as fire from the tears. He kept on saying, "Poor Big Ben, he done went and got himself dead," and burst into tears. It was as if his eyes were like the waterfall with tears flowing like a river. And Peter sounded like a broken record just saying, "I don't want to see a dead body," over and over again. While Tim and Peter were having one of their many emotional breakdowns, Paul was struggling by himself to get Big Ben out of the water. He finally got him out of the creek and said, "He's breathing." Then Paul yelled over to the drama queens Tim and Peter, "He's alive." But they didn't hear him. So Paul screamed out again, "He is alive, you guys, help me." Tim, realizing what Paul was saying, started running back over to him. Peter started running back also to help drag him over by the clubhouse. Tim said, "We have to go for help." Peter said, "I will go, I can run the fastest than all you guys." "Okay," Tim said. Paul realized that they could not bring anyone out to the clubhouse to help because they would be in deep shit. Paul said, "Stop, you guys, we can't do that." Tim said, "Paul, are you crazy, we have to get some help." Paul said, "I know we have to get help, but we don't want to get in trouble too, you guys. Have you all forgotten that we are not to be anywhere near this creek and for damn sure not to build this clubhouse here. We can take him to the strip mall and place him in the back and then go for help. Do you all agree." They all said yes, and they took an oath not to ever say anything about this to anyone; they all said yea. So they carried Big Ben's body behind the little strip mall.

It didn't take long to get there; it seemed like they were flying in the air. They were running so fast. They laid him on the ground behind the little strip mall. Then Tim said, "What about fingerprints, I don't want to go to jail." Peter said, "Stupid, nobody is going to be checking for fingerprints, stupid. Now go in the mall, Tim, and yell for help. Then say there's a boy laying in the back of the building not moving and run back outside. We will meet you over behind those bushes over there, you got it, stupid." Tim said, "All right," and ran inside and started yelling just as Peter had told him. He got caught up in the lie and said the boy was covered in blood and ran out. People started to run behind him. He led them to the back of the building. The people ran over to Big Ben. He waited for a minute until all the people were busy and then headed over to where Paul and Peter were waiting. Tim said, "We can see everything from here, this is a good spot." Paul said, "Now let's just wait and see what happens next." They saw Big Ben sit up and start laughing and smiling. One man asked Big Ben, "Are you all right?" Big Ben shook his head up and down as to say yes and kept on smiling. One lady pulled out her phone to call the police. Big Ben screamed out, "I am fine, all right." By that time, the police was pulling up. Tim said, "Oh shit, man, I hope they don't check for fingerprints." Peter said, "Don't be stupid, Tim." Then the police picked up Big Ben and put him in the backseat of the police car and pulled off. The small group of people left and went back inside the mall. Peter, Paul, and Tim came from behind the bushes and walked over to where Big Ben was lying. Paul said, "Did you see how fast Big Ben got up, you guys." "Do you think he was fooling around," Peter said. "Maybe, and maybe it was just time for him to wake up." Tim said, "For sure he was completely out of it. I don't think he was playing around." Then one of the men that was behind the building with Big Ben saw Tim and started yelling, "There's the boy who found that kid," and started moving closer to Tim, then the man saw Peter and Paul, saying, "What did you kids do to that other boy. I think I should call the cops, boys." Tim, Peter, and Paul took off running; they ran through the woods back to the clubhouse. Peter said, "I wonder what's going to happen to Big Ben." "Maybe the cops are going to take him to jail," Tim said. "You are a total jackass," Peter said to Tim. "They are going to take him to the hospital, you are so silly, Tim, he's not going to jail." Paul said, "They are just going to take him to the hospital like Peter said and then home. I know his grandmother will be glad to see him. He is the only one left. Her son and daughter-in-law are dead. I wonder why he didn't tell us that and that he was rich and that he lived with his grandmother." Paul started to look back at the creek and said, "What happened to the log that he floated over on." Tim said, "I can't wait until he comes back. I am so glad we did what we did for him, I feel proud." Peter also said, "I feel proud too. We did a good thing, you guys, I have never saved anyone's life before, it feels good. Paul said, "Yes, you guys, we did do something good today." But Paul couldn't help but think to himself that there were so many strange things that had happened today, including the one with Big Ben. And the way he showed back up. That strange log that brought him to the edge of the water. And now it's nowhere to be seen. But Paul said nothing to Peter or Tim; he kept it to himself. Because he knew how Tim and Peter would act. After thinking to himself, Paul said, "Guys, I have had enough excitement for today. I guess we should be going, so let's get all our things together and go." They all said, "Okay." So they left for the day.

That next day, everyone got there early; it was a cool early summer morning with a heavy dew. As the early sunlight hit the blade of the grass, it shine from the dew all though the meadow. The fog was slowly being eaten up by the strong early morning sun. Tim was so excited about the thought of Big Ben might be coming to the clubhouse. Peter also was excited; it was as if you could feel the excitement from Peter and Tim in the early morning air. Paul was just the opposite. He seemed to be deep in thought, as if he was blind to Tim and Peter's foolishness. He kept looking across the creek as if he was looking for something. Then Tim asked Paul, "What are you looking for? What's out there?" Paul said, "I don't know, Tim. But it has something to do with that funny log. I don't think that was a log. Did you see the log that Big Ben floated up on." Tim said, "Now, Paul, I didn't pay it any attention with all the excitement going on, and, Paul, don't go and make a big deal out of a silly old log. So what if it looked liked it had legs. That could have been limbs on the bottom of the log. That's nothing, Paul, don't get all work up." Paul said, "I thought you said you didn't see anything." Tim dropped his head and said, "I might have seen something, I just didn't want to get you started thinking too much about something that could be explain so easily, anyway I didn't mean to say anything about legs on the log." "Did you see legs on the log, Tim." Tim said, "No, Paul, I didn't mean to say legs, they just looked funny, anyway I told you those were not legs, only broken limbs on that old log." "Maybe you're right, Tim," Paul said. Then he walked over to where Big Ben sat on the big old stump and picked up a stick and started drawing on the ground. You could tell Paul seemed to be waiting for Big Ben to come too. Then Peter walked over to where he was sitting and stood there, not saying anything, just looking at Paul. Paul asked him, "What do you want, Peter?" He said nothing, just stood there. Then Paul raised his stick in the air and said, "I am going to knock some sense back into you, Peter." Then Peter said, "I know what you are thinking about, Paul, and I am starting to feel the same way about Big Ben. There's something about what happen, it was very strange, wasn't it, Paul." Paul didn't say anything. He nodded his head, he thought maybe Peter was only trying to find out what he was thinking about Big Ben. Paul thought Peter was just trying to get something to laugh about. So Paul kept his mouth closed, because he knew that's all Tim and Peter needed, a reason to make jokes at him and laugh, and if Paul gave them the smallest chance they would act like a pack of wild dogs to meat, laughing and making jokes at him. Just then they heard a noise coming from the bushes. Tim yelled out, "Could that be Big Ben." Then a voice answered back, "You in the camp. Permission to come in." Everyone yelled out at the same time, "Come on ahead." Tim started to dance around, saying, "Here comes Big Ben." Then Peter said, "We will soon know everything, Paul. I can't wait to ask him about his money and his folks. I bet he gets like a million dollars to spend on anything. He can get anything he wants whenever he wants it." Paul said, "I have something to ask him too." As Big Ben got closer to the clubhouse, the excitement grew. It was all the questions they wanted to ask Big Ben, as Big Ben was making his way into the camp and to the stump where he always sat. Peter asked Tim, "What are you going to ask, Big Ben?" Tim said, "I don't know. I guess, first I will ask him where has he been and if he's all right." Peter looked at him and laughed and said, "You country pumpkin, after all the lies he told us, that's all you're going to say." Tim looked at Paul and said, "What's wrong with that. I am going to ask more than that. But first I will ask Big Ben that." Paul looked at Tim and said, "That's a good question to ask," and dropped his head, feeling ashamed of himself for what he had planned for Big Ben. I guess you could say that day, Tim was the biggest man of all of them. Peter yelled out, "Where in the hell are you, Big Ben, are you coming or what. Are you lost," and started laughing. But that time nobody laughed with him; instead Paul called out to Big Ben and said, "We are all here, my friend, come on in," feeling a shame of himself for what he plain for Big Ben. Big Ben started to laugh and said, "That's good. I have something to tell you guys, and you won't ever believe me, not in a hundred years." Tim said, "Hurry on in, Big Ben." Peter said to Paul, "You know he going to make up something. So we don't ride him about the lies. You know that is what he's going to do." Paul said, "Maybe." Finally Big Ben made it to the clubhouse and to the log and sat down, with his head down, waiting for the question, with a smile on his face. As if he already knew the question and had already an answer for them and knew just what to say. When Big Ben sat on the stump, it was quiet in the clubhouse. All you could hear was the sound of the birds and the wind blowing through the trees. Then Big Ben raised his head and said, "Come on, you guys, what's wrong." Nobody said anything. After all that talk, they all were silent. Then Tim said to Big Ben, "What does it feels like to be rich." Big Ben didn't answer him. Then Peter said, "How much money do you get a week." Tim asked him another question, "Do you go to a private school. What type of clothes do you wear at your school, I bet they wear those fancy clothes, I bet." "What's wrong, Big Ben, you can't think of any more lies to tell," Peter said it with hurt in his voice. It was hard for anyone to get close to Peter, but Big Ben had gotten though to Peter. Tim said, "You are one lucky guy, Big Ben, why don't you tell us how does it feel to be rich. Big Ben raised his head and said, "You are already rich, and if you don't know, I can't tell you. Because I don't know either." Peter said, "What do you mean. The radio said you where the richest kid in all of Carolina, Big Ben." Big Ben raised his head and said, "Still you are richer than I." Tim said, "We only get five dollars a week for allowances, and that's not a lot." Peter said, "I have had these same shoes for two years or more." Tim said, "Yea, I have had the same T-shirt for at least that long, and I have been trying to get my dad to buy me a new bike all year long." Peter said, "I can't remember the last time I got something new. So how can we be richer than you, Big Ben." Big Ben raised his head and said, "You have what I will never have. You have a mother and a father. Some of you even have brothers and sister. A mother to bake you cookies and to do special things with you. Someone to love you and when you are hurt or lonely. When you are hungry someone to feed you and to kiss the hurt away, when you are hurt. Just to hear those magic words *I love you, son.* Those words alone is worth more money than anyone can have. I will never hear those words from my mother or father because they are gone from me forever. Now, you guys, tell me how does it feel to have a family, what does that feel like. To belong to someone." After Big Ben had finished saying those painful facts, it was quiet; there wasn't a sound to be heard, not even the birds. The birds seemed to stop chirping; again the wind wasn't blowing that cheerful sound. It was a strange feeling. A feeling of sadness and shame. They all thought of those things that Big Ben had said, and they all realized how thoughtless they were of the things they had. That made it more lonely and shameful. Then they thought how much Big Ben must hurt on the inside and not show it. And Big Ben could have anything in this world he wanted and more. The boys realized that there is more to life than having lots of money and being able to buy whatever you want. Paul was thinking to himself, *I never thought that, you can have the world and still be sad.* They all were thinking the same thing even though no one was saying anything. They all knew how much Big Ben must be hurting on the inside, and they all realized that in fact they were richer than Big Ben. Tim started to cry, and Paul just dropped his head in shame. Peter looked off toward the creek and started moving from side to side, putting his hand to his ears, as if the words that Big Ben spoke were hurting him, more than Paul and Tim. They didn't know that Peter could understand what Big Ben was saying more than them. But they could tell the words that Big Ben had spoken was like a knife cutting at him, at Peter. Paul had started to cry too. Then Paul said, pushing away the tears, "I am sorry, Big Ben, we didn't mean any harm, we just wanted to know. We never meet a rich kid before, and we have never had one for a friend. All we ever thought of was how wonderful it must to be rich. But thanks to you, Big Ben, now we know, we have all the most important thing in life we need for now." Tim said, "Yea, now I don't feel so bad about those shoes. I have had them for two years, and they're about worn-out. But they are great, and I don't want a new pair. And if my dad buys me some of those knockoff brand shoes, I will wear them proudly, my shoes don't have to be name brand, and I will tell my dad *thank you*, like I never told him before. I am sorry, Big Ben, and thank you for making us realize that money and clothes and fine cars and other things like that mean nothing. It's not what goes on the body or what other people think of the body, it's what the body needs to live and that is love and family. That's all that really matters, right, Paul." Paul said, "Right and, Big Ben, we are going to give your body what it needs." Big Ben said, "What do you mean." Paul said, "We will be your family. Our mother will be your mother too and the same with our father. Everyone, form a circle and hold hand. Lord, bless our new member of our family. Lord, this is my new brother." And Tim said the same and Peter said the same. Then Peter said, "Something is not right," and reached in his hand in his pocket and pulled out his knife and cut his hand, and a little stream of blood started to roll off his hand, and he passed the little knife to Tim, and Tim did the same and passed the knife to Paul, and Paul did the same. And Big Ben did the same. Then Paul said, "Let the blood flow through our bodies and join us together as brothers, we will be blood brothers forever." They did a little dance. The dance of happiness, and once again there was laughter in the little clubhouse beneath the giant old oak tree. Paul thought to himself once again, *Big Ben had taught them important lessons in life, and to make him their brother was a good thing to do for him.* But little did Paul know this was only the beginning of what was to come. They never saw a bigger smile on Big Ben's face than that day. He seemed as if he had won the world's biggest prize. Then Big Ben said something that made them feel so proud. Big Ben said, "I came here alone, without a friend and tired of being alone, not knowing what brothers was and what a family was, I will leave here with three new brothers who have adopted me as one of their own. Who are willing to share what little they have with me at no charge. And willing to share their mothers' love with a stranger, that could only happen out of love, and will love me as they would their own brother. For that I am truly blessed. Thank you all." With those words, they all felt a little taller and a whole lot richer. Then Tim said, "This is what it feels like to be rich," and they all laughed and said, "Yea, Tim, you're right. But this feeling is much better. No one can steal it or take it away. Only we can lose it ourselves by not appreciating it, and even then, it's not lost. And by taking it for granted." Tim said, "Gee, it's a good feeling," and they danced around for hours just laughing and playing tag. Tim asked Big Ben what did he had to tell them. Big Ben said, "Come over here and sit with me, and I will tell you, Tim." Tim went over and sat down beside Big Ben, but Big Ben didn't say anything; he had started acting strange. When Tim asked him what was it that he had to tell them, Big Ben seemed upset. Tim didn't understand after all that they had just shared. Tim thought maybe he was thinking of his parents again. Then Big Ben got up and started to dance around and seemed to be happy. Paul was still thinking of Big Ben. *You never know what a person is carrying around inside themselves*, Paul thought to himself. Paul had remembered that Big Ben had said that he had something to tell them. Paul wanted to ask like Tim had tried to, just a little while ago when they were sitting on the log. But Paul decided not to. They had started back having a good time laughing and running around and acting a fool Paul didn't want to spoil it by asking what it was that Big Ben had to tell them. Then the dancing stopped and the singing stopped. Tim and Big Ben and Paul walked back over to the log and left Peter standing by the creek. Then Big Ben started to tell them where he had been all that time. Big Ben started to tell them about this amazing cave he had found when he stayed behind that day. Inside the cave was a giant turtle by name of Reno and other animals, a catfish and a snake, all giant animals. They stood in front of these doors. Then Peter heard what Big Ben was saying and walked over to the log where they were sitting and said, "Big Ben, you have do better than that. Nobody believes that. Not even Tim and he will believe anything, right, Tim." Tim laughed and said, "You're right." Big Ben then said, "I can prove it. It's the truth, in the cave you can see the future. Or whatever you want to see." Then Peter put his hand to Big Ben's forehead and said, "Paul, he doesn't have a fever, so he must be crazy." They all laughed, then Big Ben said, "Tim, your mother will cook the best meal you have ever eaten tonight. And you will overeat and get a stomachache, and you, Paul, will break your dad's vase and will be on punishment." Then Paul said, "Now I know you're crazy because I will stay the hell away from that vase like I have always done. I have always stayed away from that old bottle. And I will do the same." Then Big Ben turned to Peter, who had this scared look on his face. When Big Ben looked at Peter, he dropped his head, as if he was waiting for Big Ben to reveal this big secret about him. Then Big Ben said, "And you, Peter, will have a good night, and this will be peaceful night." Then Peter started to laugh; he seemed relieved and said, "I hope you're right, Big Ben. It would be nice to have a peaceful night." Then Big Ben said, "Tonight, Peter, you will sleep like a baby." And with that, Peter started to smile, and that smile slowly turned into a loud laughter, and then Peter said, "That's good enough for me"—and turned—"I am going fishing. I don't want to hear any more of those lies and tall tales." Peter seemed very upset as if he wanted to believe it, but felt it was all a lie. Paul thought to himself, *Maybe Peter is hiding something*. But nevertheless, as always, Paul pushed it aside and said, "Well, tomorrow will tell the truth about Big Ben and his vision of the future. And about Tim's mom. Because everyone knows that Tim's mom cannot cook and that is hard to believe and to cook the perfect meal." Then they all laughed, even Tim. Paul said, "Tim, I know your mother tries real hard, and she does it out of love for you guys. But the perfect meal, that's hard to believe. I hope you understand, Tim." Tim said, "Yea, I understand. That is pretty hard to swallow, and I can swallow almost anything," and started laughing. "I sure hope so, I'm hungry. Maybe tonight it won't be one, two, swallow, then juice to wash it down. Then pray to keep it down." Peter was quiet the whole time; he didn't take the chance to make a joke about Tim's mother's cooking. Tim asked Peter, "Are you all right over there." Peter didn't say anything. Then Big Ben said something strange about Peter. He said, "Just like me, he must find his own peace within himself, before it's too late." They all looked at Big Ben wondering what did he mean by that.

But it was getting late, and Tim was in a hurry. It was as if he had a special gift waiting at his house. Tim was in a hurry, so they put away all their things and said their good nights and headed down the path.

The next morning came; they all met at the clubhouse, but Paul was late. Peter and Tim walked over to where Big Ben was sitting on the log drawing on the ground with a stick. Then Tim said, "How did you know, Big Ben. Tell me." Then Big Ben said, "I have already told you guys how. When Paul gets here, I will take you all to the cave so you guys can see for yourselves, but, Tim, you must not be afraid." Peter said, "Tim, don't believe it. So your mother got lucky and cooked a good meal. My god, son, she was well overdue. The only reason why you overeat is that you were hungry. By your own words, Tim, that is fact. That's what you said, Tim. Before you left, you silly little egg head." Then Tim said, "Peter, why are you so angry, Peter." Peter answered, "I am tired of these country folks. I want to go back to New York, far away from all this craziness." Then Peter walked away and said, "I am going fishing." Tim said, "Look who's calling who crazy. Peter, you don't even know how to fish. You never throw your fishing line in the water, you silly little dumpling head. Then Peter said, "You fish your way, and I will fish my way, you little country pumpkin." Just then they heard a loud noise coming through the path that led in and out of the woods. It was moving real fast, and they could hear a voice, but could not make it out. As it got closer, Tim said, "That's Paul and what is that he is saying." Peter said, "He is saying Big Ben jinxed him, what Big Ben said. Of all the crazy things to say." Then Peter started to laugh. "Looks like you going to get your butt kick, Mr. prophet Big Ben," and he started singing, "There's going to be a party here, I mean there's fixing to be some country dancing." Then Peter said, "Let me find a good seat to watch Big Ben get his butt kick." Tim said, "Don't worry, Big Ben. I won't let Paul hurt you." Peter said, "Hot damn, this is getting better and better. Two ass kicking for the price of one." Just then Paul came running in, saying, "You jinx me, Big Ben," and punched him in the arm and grabbed him. Tim came up behind Paul and pushed him in the back hard. Then Paul turned with his fist to hit Tim. Tim yelled, "Paul, please don't hit me, don't do it to me, my friend." Paul stopped, and Tim said, "Paul, you know Big Ben didn't jinx you. The question we need to be asking ourselves is how did he know." Paul stopped and dropped his fist and started to ease up a little. Tim realized that he was getting through to Paul. Then Tim said, "Just think about it, Paul. Please, that's what important." "Tim, I have pass that old table where that old vase sat so many times, and I did the same thing I always do. I put my hand on it, and bam, it fell. Nothing ever happen like that before. I just don't understand," Paul said, shaking his head. Then Peter yelled out from across the way, "Maybe Big Ben is a witch." Tim yelled back at Peter and said, "Stupid, boys can't be a witch, so shut up, stupid, and keep on fishing. And remember, one day you are going to catch a fish, and it is going to scare the living shit out of you, Peter." Then Peter said, "I don't think so, I never put my hook in the water," and laughed. Then Big Ben called them over to where he was sitting and asked Tim and Peter a question, "What do you guys know about this creek?" Tim said, "Not that much, only what I have heard. About the missing kids." "What happen to the kids?" Big Ben asked. "Nobody knows," Tim said. Then Big Ben said, "Look at the water, it's like glass, so clear but you can't see the bottom, but yet it's so clear and inviting. How long has this creek been here?" Tim said, "Maybe as long as I can remember. I guess as long as I have been born. And that is twelve years." Then Paul said, "My dad says it was here when he was a boy." Then Big Ben said, "And it never goes dry." "No," Paul said, "my dad says it's a underground spring that keeps it full." Then from across the way, they heard Peter say, "I have never heard such backwards answers before in my life. I will tell you the answer to those kids, they all are runaways, nothing more or nothing less. To answer the question about this little creek, look at it. It's surrounded by all these trees that shade it and keep the sun from evaporating the water, and it's down in this valley. You little backward hillbillies can't make this little place into some kind of mystical place. Big Ben with his giant turtle and fishes and snakes, boy, you guys are really something else." He started laughing. Then Big Ben said, "Peter, nobody is trying to make no more out of this than it really is. What it is what it is. It is time, come, I will show you." He stood up. Come on, you guys, I am going to let you see for yourself, but don't be afraid." Big Ben started toward the waterfall. Peter followed behind them, repeating what he had told them. Then Tim said, "Wait for a minute," and turned to Peter. "If you really believe what you just said, why don't you throw your pole in the water and fish like a real man." Then Big Ben said, "Yea, why don't you, Peter." Paul said, "Because he really knows that there is more to this place than what it seem. He's scared to fish in this pond, isn't that the truth, Peter." But Peter didn't say anything; he stayed quiet the rest of the way. Soon they reached the spot. Big Ben said, "Look in the water." They all stopped and looked in the water. All they saw was pretty crystal-blue water. Peter said, "See, I told you guys, Big Ben is full of shit, there's nothing here." Then Big Ben said, "You have to wait for a while," then they saw like stairs appear leading down into the creek. They were covered with mildew, all white and green. Then Big Ben said, "What did I tell you guys," with a big smile on his face. Paul, Tim, and Peter just looked at one another in amazement. Then Tim said, "You went down there in all that water. Weren't you scared." "No," Big Ben said." "It was a chance to explore." Tim said, "Oh, I understand that being a man like you, I too like to explore." Then Peter started to laugh and said, "Tim, the only thing you have ever explore is your way to the bathroom, with the lights off." They all laughed, then Paul said, "Well, guys, it's been fun, but you know I won't be going with you all down there in all that water." They all turned and said, "Why, Paul." Then Paul answered them, "I am black, and black people have a old saying when it comes to things like this. And it is if it's not messing with you, don't bother with it. That's a black thing, you know." Then Peter said, "That's another way of saying I am a chicken. My mother is black, and she has never told me of any old saying like that." Then Paul said, "That's because she is from New York, and only us Southern people know about it." Then Tim said, "Stop stalling, are you guys going or not." There was a moment of silence and stillness in the air, and there was a chill in the midst of it all. It was the fear that everyone felt, that paralyzing fear. Big Ben was the only one not afraid; he stood there with a big smile on his face. But somehow Big Ben knew what to do; he started singing and making jokes, saying, "Who's afraid of this big old bear," and making bear noises and rolling around in the tall brown grass. He even started eating some of the grass, saying, "Bears eat it, and I am a big old, ugly old, dirty, stinky old bear who's not afraid of anything." Before you knew it, they were all laughing at Big Ben, and the fear had left them. Then Big Ben said, "Now, who is going to come with this old bear." Down these here steps they all got quiet. Then Tim said, "I will go with that old bear," and started laughing. Then Paul said, "I will go too with brother bear. But I still believe in that old saying if it not's bothering me, I won't bother it. But I will go with brother bear too." Then they all looked at Peter. Peter dropped his head and said, "I want to, but I can't swim." Then Tim said, "You don't have to swim. All you need to do is walk down these steps and hold your breath." Peter said, "I guess I can do that." Then Big Ben said, "That's right, Peter, that's about all to it. We will put you in the middle. If you can't hold your breath, just give us a push, and we will let you go back to the top and back up to the bank." Peter finally said, "All right." So they were ready; they started down the stairs slowly, hand in hand, singing, "Who's afraid of this here old bear." They got deeper in the water. The water started to come up to their waist. They kept on going, slowly singing. Soon the water was almost to the nose. Big Ben told them, "Get ready to hold your breath." Then it happened; the water swallowed them up. Peter came back up. He couldn't hold his breath. Then they opened their eyes. They were in some type of cave. Tim started to look around; he saw a turtle. He cried out to Paul. Paul looked and said, "That is the biggest turtle I have ever seen." Then Big Ben walked over to the turtle; he said, "Hello, Reno." Reno answered him, "Hello, Big Ben. How are you doing." Big Ben said, "Fine, and I have brought them. The ones who are suppose to be here with us, Reno." Paul was looking at Reno; he walked around him, just looking. Reno just laughed, then Tim saw this giant catfish. He was standing on his tail. The catfish was standing in front of this door. The more Tim looked around, the more he saw. There was a giant snake half in a coil with his head straight up in the air; he too stood in front of a door. Then Tim saw this giant old eel that was standing on his tail. He too stood by a door; he saw the name Present on it. There were other animals in the cave; they all had their eyes closed, including the snake and eel and the catfish. Each one of them stood in front of these doors with names on them. The catfish stood by the door with the name of Past. The snake stood by the door that had no name on it. The eel stood by the door that had the name Present on it. Reno, the turtle, stood by the door that had the name of Future. Paul said to Reno, "I have seen you before." Reno laughed and said, "You will be one to watch," and laughed some more. Then Reno stopped and said, "Yes, my young friend, you have seen me before." Then Paul said, "Reno, you were the log that Big Ben was floating on." Then Tim said, "You're right, Paul." Then Reno said to Big Ben, "Where to this time. One day in the future or more, Big Ben, or would like to go in the past." Then Tim said, "That's how you knew all that stuff, Big Ben." Big Ben answered him, "You're right, Tim. With Reno's help, I saw you guys at the camp. I saw the way you all miss me and worried about me." Then Tim said, "I want to see too." Paul said, "I want to come along and see too." Reno said, "You all shall see, but first thing's first. You must hear the rules first. Once a man looks into the sun and tries to look back again, he will never see the same again. Keep this with you as you travel through time. Now here are the rules. You must not take what you have seen from this cave and try and change your future or your family's future. You must put yourself last and your family last also, you must be as a lonely wanderer with no ties. Because what you may see might be good or bad. For if you break this rule, you will never be allowed to come here again, and you will never know your family again." Then Tim whispered to Paul,

"Maybe that's what happen to all those missing kids we heard about." Reno turned and look at them and said, "What missing kids. Everything and everybody is in its proper place and time. Now, my friends, take my words to your hearts and remember this. In some cases, wanting is sometimes easier to bear than to having what you wanted. Now go and watch." They walked over to the door that had Future on it, and they went inside and saw this big wall of water; it looked like a large TV screen made of water. Then the room got dim, and the giant wall of glass of water lit up, and they began to see people and things happen. Tim said, "It will feel funny to watch ourselves." Then Paul said, "I see my dad, he buying me something." Tim said, "It looks like a new Game Boy." Then Paul smiled. Tim saw his sister steal a kiss from a boy. Tim started to smile; he said, "I got you now," and started to laugh out aloud. It was then that they saw evil raise his ugly head of pain. They saw Peter get an awful beating. It seemed like there was so much rage and anger in Peter's father every time he hit Peter. You could see rage in the way he hit Peter, but Peter didn't cry. It got real quiet in the little room after watching that beating. Nobody knew what to say. Paul and Tim both had got beatings before but this was different. Tim and Paul felt the pain for Peter beating. The little room was feel with sadness and tears, tears that had to stay on the inside, for none of them wanted to spoil the excitement of seeing the future but still it was gone that feeling of happiness was now set on the side, they all where thinking it, but it was if nobody new what to say but they all felt the same but did not know how to say it they new if you act up with your parents you would get a beating and you would pay the price. If you acted up with your parents, then you would pay the price. They both felt that there was more to this whipping than they saw; it was more like tortures. Then a spanking, but at the time they accepted it. Big Ben got angry and said that guy should be put in jail for what he did to Peter. Tim said, "He only beat his son, maybe Peter did something to earn that beating. We all get whip every now and then. Sometimes badder than others." Then Tim said to Paul, "Big Ben doesn't understand because he doesn't have a mom or dad, just a grandma." Big Ben said to Paul and Tim, "Maybe you're right, but I did not see Peter do anything to get a whipping like that." Then Tim said, "Come to think of it, I didn't see anything either." Paul said, "You guys didn't hear his father tell him that he was going to beat him when his father walked into the room. Remember that?" Then they both said, "Yes, we remember hearing that but that still doesn't justify that whipping." Big Ben said, "I did not hear his father say why." Then Paul said, "I heard his dad say it was for Peter interfering in grown people business. You guys really weren't paying too much attention." Tim and Paul had already started having their doubts about the beating, but sense they both got beating, it was hard to understand that kind of abuse a father could have for his son but they were beginning to see that may be Big Ben was right but they kept it to themselve's and they did not say any thing to Big Ben. They just kept on watching the screen. Then Reno came into the room and said, "It is time to go, boys. You have seen more than enough for today. We have let you guys find this place so that you might understand," and then he walked away. Then he stopped again and said, "Many have stood in those same spots and with that same look. They all thought to themselves what was going on. Wonder not, my young friend, of my words and what I am saying, you will soon know your reason for being here. Now go, for tomorrow you will learn the answer to the proverb that I spoke to you early." Then Tim said, "You mean about the sun." Reno laughed and said, "Yes, my young friend, this will be one of the many life lessons you will discover in your journey to manhood. To live a life lesson is to understand it. Now go, my young friends, it is time to leave. Now you have seen the future and know what is going to happen for the next couple of days. When you return to the clubhouse on the second day, you will discover what my words in the proverb mean because you will have lived it." Reno said his good-byes, and the guys got on their way to the stairs back up. Big Ben said to the guys, "We better not say anything about that awful beating Peter took by the hands of his father. So if Peter ask us what did we see, we should say we saw nothing about him." Paul and Tim said yes, for they knew that was the best thing to do. They made it to the stairs; they could hear the water rushing over their heads, the same way the water was running when they went down into the cave; it did not make any sense. After about the third or fourth step, they held their breath and stepped up to the top of the water to the bank to the clubhouse They made their way to where Peter was waiting; he was jumping all around, asking, "What did you guys see? Was it just as Big Ben said? And did you see me—what happen to you guys? You have to tell me now, or I will explode into little question marks." Then they all laughed, and then there was silence; no one said anything for a minute. They looked at one another and then said, "It was everything Big Ben said it was and more." Peter said, "That's not telling me much. I want to know what you guys saw, now let me hear it." Then Tim said, "What time is it, Peter." "It is almost four PM." Paul said, "That can't be right. We were only gone for a short time, about a hour or more." Then Big Ben said, "The time is different there. I will ask Reno to explain it to you guys." Peter said, "I want to go the next time, you guys." Tim said, "First, Peter, you got to hold your breath, tonight practice and in the morning you will be ready." Paul said, "It's getting late, and we must put away our things. We will hang the leftover food up in the tree and hope the raccoon don't get it." Tim said, "We haven't seen any raccoons." Then Big Ben said, "There is always a first time." They finished putting away the supplies. Peter was still asking them to tell him what they saw while they were down in the cave. Tim and Big Ben told him, "It would be better tomorrow when you see it for yourself tomorrow." He laughed and said, "You're right, it would be better," and then got in a hurry to go. Peter wanted to go so he could start to practice his breathing. Tim and Paul finished putting away the tools. Soon they were done. They all said good night. Paul and Tim and Peter asked Big Ben was he going to be all right walking through the woods alone; he answer them by saying, "These woods here are my friend. The same way you guys are." Then Big Ben said good night and started humming a song and went through the path. Paul and Tim and Peter went the other way humming the same song. They soon reached the curb, and they went home. They all lived in the same neighborhood.

That next morning, Peter was the first one at the clubhouse; he sat on the log that Big Ben sat on, drawing in the sand with a stick. Then he raised his head; he heard a noise. It was Tim and Paul. Peter yelled out to them, "Come on, you sleepyheads." They came into the camp area to where Peter was sitting. Paul said, "Peter, how long have you been here. Did you sleep here." "No," Peter answered "I have only been here a hour maybe, I practiced most of the night holding my breath, and I am ready, you guys. Will you guys give me a test." Tim said, "We will when Big Ben gets here." Then Paul said, "He's coming now. I hear him humming that old song he's always humming." Tim said, "Yea, I hear him too." Big Ben was at the edge of the clubhouse. Peter couldn't wait; he ran and met Big Ben, saying, "I am ready now. I can do it, come on, you guys, watch this." Big Ben said yea and walked past him to where Tim and Paul was. He greeted them as he always did and asked them, "Do you guys think Peter is ready." Tim said, "I don't know, but that fool is still holding his breath, look at him, he is changing colors." "What a nut," Tim and Paul said. "How long has Peter been holding his breath." Big Ben said, "I don't know, he told me to watch this. That been at least five minutes or more. "Look, Paul," Tim said, "does he look purple to you." Then they all yelled at the same time, "Breathe, you nut." Then they ran over to him and picked him up from the ground. Tim said, "Peter, you win first place in the stupid race, you peanut head." Paul said, "What were you trying to do, kill yourself. Now, Peter, you can never call Tim stupid again or call him honey buns again because that was truly the most stupidest thing I have ever seen." Big Ben said to them, "Don't be so hard, Peter was only trying to show you guys he's ready." They all said, "One thing for sure, he really can hold his breath a long time." Tim said, "I think he's ready," then Big Ben looked at Paul. Paul said, "Yea, he ready." Peter said, "Thanks, you guys, I told you I would be ready, let's go." They all started for the stairs in the water; as they walked, Paul said, "I want to ask Reno a question. About something that happen to my father and mother and me. It really has been bothering me." Big Ben said, "Reno is the person to ask, he knows everything." Tim said, "Yea, but it will take you days to understand it, he talks in riddles." Big Ben said, "That because you could not handle the straight truth." Paul said, "I don't care, I need to know this." Soon they were there. Peter looked into the water and said, "I don't see the steps." Tim said, "You have to wait for a while." They did, and the stairs appeared. Then they put Peter in the middle and went down the steps. When the water was almost over their heads, they closed their eyes and opened them inside the cave. Peter was amazed; he walked over to Reno and looked and said, "You are a turtle, and you're the biggest one I have ever seen." Then he looked at the catfish. "That is the biggest fish ever," Peter said. "Look at that awesome-looking snake." Reno was laughing the whole time. Peter was looking around Reno who was watching Peter real close, as if he already knew him. Then Reno said to them, "Know that everyone is here and everything is in its proper place. Let the journey begin," and started laughing and put his big hand on Peter's shoulder and said, "The one has come." Then Big Ben said, "Reno, Paul has a problem, he wants to talk to you about it." Then Reno said, "Let us sit and talk." They went in this room; it had a round table with twelve stonelike chairs inside. Off to the side was a long bench with other stonelike chairs. Reno walked them over to the area where the benches were. Tim asked Reno, "Why didn't we sit at the round table?" Reno said, "In life, there are times for serious planning and deep meditation, and this is not the time. This is a time of fun and learning, so we should be in a relaxing place. Sit, my friends, and ask me what you will, I cannot lie. In your world, when one man lies, another man will pay for that lie. Here in this world, you will always hear the truth, even when you expect a lie. Although it may be in a parable. Because you might not be ready for the truth, for many ask for the truth, but when it is upon them, they do not believe it or want it." Then

Reno went on and asked Paul to tell his story. Paul asked Reno, "Is it possible for a person to hate you and don't even know you." Reno said, "I will answer that when you tell me the rest of the story." Paul said, "My father and I and my mom were on a drive like we always do when this big rusty old truck pull up on the side of us. There was a kid in the old truck about my age. I look over and wave at the boy, and the kid said to me, 'What are you looking at, you red-eyed nigger,' and spit at me. Then his father gave the boy a high five with his hand, and they drove away. My dad didn't say anything, he only said we have to pray for them. My mom gave me a hug. If I were my dad, I would have chase down that old truck and beat the heck out of them for disrespecting us like that." Paul got angry all over again. Then Reno said to him, "Now I will answer you, but you will find little comfort in the truth. My young friend, so you are upset with your father. What your father did was right in that case. Those where only words, Paul, but they were words of hate, for they can hurt the most. The sting of the words will last longer than the words themselves. Paul, you can't let the sting of the words drive you to hate the one that said the words. For it is better to let the sting of the words of hate fade away without scratching the sting, and then the sting will stop. This is not an easy thing to do. For the words did not hurt the body. It hurt the heart, and the sting of the words will poison the heart and will destroy what is good in the heart if you scratch the sting. Your father did not let the sting of the words enter his heart, for he knew what it would do to the heart. Your father knew he had to pray for them, for they are blind in hate and full of rage for anything different from themselves. But you think your father should have chased them down and caught them and beat the heck out of them. What would happen to your father if he did that, Paul. Do you think he would go to jail or maybe get himself killed or hurt, or something could have happened to you or your mother. Your father is well disciplined. For he didn't react from the sting of the words of hate. For he knows that hate only brings more hate. And can cause a lot of problems. Remember these words, Paul, for every rock that is cast at the body, know this, it will not kill the body, it will only make the body stronger. For the one that threw the rock will have it returned to him twice. For he shall find his own reward for that act of violence. Paul, if you let the rock poison the heart, it will kill the body. And if you do that, the one that catches the rock will win. But, my friend, let not that makes you hold anger toward anyone. So, Paul, you must pray for them that wishes you harm. You must let it go, my friend, and in the future, when hate comes at you, then you will know how to handle it. Now take these words with you also when there are more people like your father. There will be less of those with the words of hate, and they will be put to shame." Paul said, "Reno, I don't understand all that. But I do understand that I must forgive the boy and his father, and now I understand that my father did the right thing. But, Reno, I don't know how to forgive. What do I do, Reno." Reno said, "You have already started by admitting your fault and putting your anger aside and opening your heart to understanding." Then Paul said, "I have done that, Reno." Reno said, "Yes, but yet there is still one thing left you must do, Paul." Paul said, "What is that, Reno." Reno said, "You must tell your father you understand and that you forgive them that hate you." Paul said, "That won't be easy because my father and I don't talk that much." Reno said, "When you go home and you say good evening to your dad, don't stop talking, just keep on talking, no matter what, and you will discover that you will have started the conversation and then say what you need to say when you feel comfortable. The words will come if you let them." Paul said, "All right, Reno, I will try it." Then Reno said, "Remember, whenever you speak to your father, don't stop talking until you have said what there is to be said." Then Tim said, "Reno, I don't have a problem, but I feel the need to say I am sorry to Paul." Reno said, "Tim, you feel responsible because you're white, but I say to you, every man must stand for himself. Yes, it's true that we all are responsible for each other. But each man must be weighed alone. So his sins are his own and not yours. You must pray to Tim for his soul, and you, Tim, must not take on his weight." Tim said, "Reno, I don't understand what you are saying. But I do get it a little, Reno." Then Reno said, "It is better that you understand a little than none at all. Now, my friends, there's much work to do." Then Reno leaned over to Paul and Tim and said in a low voice, "Big Ben has Peter's attention." Big Ben walked Peter over to the round tables. Then Reno said to Paul and Tim, "Now that the three are here, the journey can begin and, my young friends, you all will find out that your fates are entangled. For this is your fate. Now you must go to the cave of the future, and I will not tell you what day it is that you will see or how far in the future you will see. Now be ready for what you will see." Then Reno called to Big Ben and Peter, "Come, we are ready to go over to the cave of the future."

As they walked by all the other animals, they opened their eyes and tears were falling from their faces. For the journey had begun. On the way to the cave, Reno told them that they would not know the time or the year of the things that they will see. Then Reno said, "The time is not that close to you and not that far from you," and Reno would not tell them what they were looking for; he only said, "The things that is common to you is not the thing common to God. Watch and enjoy, for that thing is what will determine your fate." Then Peter said, "What was in that orange juice Reno drunk this morning. He must have had a shot of liquor in it because I don't understand a damn thing he said, and I don't think Reno really understand what he said. So how can Reno expect us to understand. We are only twelve years old." Reno heard what Peter said and answered him, "Even a newborn baby can tell his mother when it is hungry and can also let her know when he is full and when they are sick, and when the mother says be quiet and cry no more, the baby stops, are you not older than that newborn." Tim laughed and said, "No, he's a baby in the brain," and they all laughed. Then Reno said to Paul and Tim, "What you guys will see will be different from the others. For what you guys will see is part of the whole of your futures. Only the three will see it, and that is you, Paul, and you, Tim, and Big Ben. Peter will not be allowed to see all of his future, because his future is the journey. Peter will see what he proceeds his future to be. For this is the way it must be. You cannot reveal to him what you will see. For we have suffered for this to be this way. It must be fulfilled, so ask no questions. So you must act as if I didn't tell you this. For it has already been written that you must suffer this for the reward is great." So they went on in the cave of the future; they all gathered around the wall of glass waiting for the screen to light up. Tim was watching Peter real close, trying to see what was going to happen to Peter. Then he reached out and grabbed Peter's hand and rubbed it over the round stone, and the big wall lit up like a big movie screen, but the screen was blank, like a blank sheet of paper. Then Reno came back into the room and called for Peter to come with him; there was something he must see. Peter didn't want to go with Reno. Peter told Reno that he wanted to stay with Paul and Tim and Big Ben, that he wanted to see the same thing they would see. Reno said, "You will see the same thing as your friends. So have no worry of that, do you also want to see what your friends saw on their last trip. For now you must catch up to your friends so that you will be up to them." Somehow Paul and Tim knew that Reno was removing Peter from the room. Finally Peter left the room with Reno. Peter had a scared look on his face, but he was smiling and laughing. Peter even made a joke with his favorite enemy Tim as Reno and Peter left the room. The moment they left, the screen lit up. They started watching themselves playing baseball in the road. Tim said, "I

see you, Paul, you look a little bigger, Paul. I don't see Peter and you, Big
Ben." Then the game ended. The screen jumped to the clubhouse; they
saw Big Ben swimming in the creek. Peter was in the giant old oak tree
swinging from a rope. Paul and Tim were sitting on the log talking real
close; they couldn't hear what they were saying. There was laughter all
around in the air; it was a joyful day full of laughter. They could see it was
a fun-filled day, then the screen jumped again. Then they saw the awful act
of evil, the thing that no child or man should ever see. A thing full of rage
and destruction, then they saw Peter in his house playing in his room. They
saw him looking toward the door, then they saw him throw down his toys
and run out the door into his mother's room and jump on his stepdad's
back. His stepdad threw him off his back and said, "So you want to be a
man today. It is time to teach you a lesson you will never forget. This time
you will mind your own business when I finish with you." Then he raised
his hand, and the belt appeared in his hand. He pushed Peter to the bed
and started to hit him; the sound of the belt landing against the skin of
Peter's back was almost unbearable to hear. With every strike, a blister
would appear, then the belt would land again and burst the blister, and
blood would gush out. But Peter didn't make a sound; that seemed to make
his stepdad more angry. He started to hit Peter with more force and rage
over and over again. The sound of the belt growing louder and louder was
almost unbearable to hear, but Peter didn't make a sound. Peter's stepdad
kept hitting Peter, trying to make him scream. Then his stepdad said,
Scream, you little piece of dirt, scream." Then he hit him again. Tim put
his hands over his eyes. Tim started to cry; Paul started to cry too. Big Ben
put his hand to his ears and started to sing and hum. The little room was
full of tears and sadness, and cold air filled the room. A damp feeling was
in the little room. The more they watched it, the sadder they all got. Then
the mood changed to hatred toward Peter's stepdad. Tim started to curse at
Peter's stepdad; he said, "You need to meet my dad, you dirty piece of dirt,
he would kick your sorry ass. You little bully who picks on little kids." Big
Ben was punching the air, saying, "I kill you, I will somehow, you no-good
piece of dirt, I put a curse on you for hurting my brother." Paul did nothing,
nor did he say anything; he only held his head down. He was trying to hold
it in and trying to be strong, like Reno had said. It was then when they
thought it could not get any worse for their brother it happened. Peter's
stepdad reversed the belt and started to hit him with the buckle. His stepdad
was out of his mind. Tim started saying, "Cry, Peter, cry, go ahead and cry,
please scream, you stupid little fool," and Tim fell to his knees in tears. Big

Ben was saying the same thing, crying. Tim and Big Ben, with tears in their eyes, kept saying, "Please cry, Peter, please, my brother, cry." They knew if he cried his stepdad would stop. But it looked like Peter was not going to cry. Paul dropped his head in tears again. The tears had starting falling from their faces like a water from a waterfall. Then Paul lost it just as Tim and Big Ben; he heard the words of Reno in his head saying watch this closely, but he couldn't hold it any longer. He started shaking his head, and he put his hands together, like he was going to pray, and that is what Paul did. He said, "Lord, make me strong, not for myself, but for Peter and Tim and Big Ben. Lord, this is more than I can bear," and started to scream out in a loud voice for Peter, saying, "No more, sir. No more, please, sir, no more." Rage was felt in the little room; it started to feel hot and steamy. The anger was so strong in the room, you could cut it with a knife, and you could see it on the faces of the boys. Then the screen went blank; they could hear Reno coming back to the room. They all looked at one another wondering was Peter with him. Tim started saying, "What are we going to do," and started to cry. Paul told him to "shut the fuck up." Big Ben turned and looked at Paul. Paul was not one to use those kinds of words. Paul was still full of rage. Then Reno came into the room; they all looked at him. Reno started to laugh and said, "I can see you boys have discovered some important emotions. That is good, you will need them to help your friend." Paul said, "Reno, how could you laugh about this, have you no compassion." Then Reno said to Paul, "You guys watched this with your heart for that place is one of parts of the body that store's love and it is that love that has blinded you for you guys should have watch it with your eyes, for the heart has blinded you to some key things. That you will also need to save your friend. I had already gave you guys a warning. But yet the words did not find home." Then they all asked Reno where was Peter. Reno answered them, "Peter is in a safe place. He has been watching the past in a private place." Tim asked Reno, "Why did we have to see that, Reno. Reno, we are only kids, you know. That was too much for us, Reno." Paul told Reno that Tim was right and that he should feel real bad for that. Big Ben said nothing; he just stood there with a strange look on his face, just smiling, not saying a word, like he was enjoying the whole thing with Reno. Tim turned and looked at Big Ben and said, "What do you think, Big Ben." Big Ben started to smile more and said, "Paul and Tim, at what age does a boy become a man. Yes, it was a hard thing to watch, but we did it, and if that will save Peter, then I guess it was all right. I think we were stronger than we realized. That makes us men. We have become men today, we stood straight and tall. It was a hard thing to do, but we watch it. I wanted to kill Peter's stepdad for what he did to Peter, but I didn't, you guys." Then Reno said, "My friends, we would not put this upon you if guys were not ready. And if you guys were not ready, we would not have let you find this place. You stand in the same place of your fathers." Tim asked, "Reno, was my father here in this same spot that I am standing in now?" Reno answered Tim, "Not only was your father here. Paul's and Peter's fathers stood where they're standing too, and their fathers before them and their fathers before them. We have raised many generations to get to you guys. For you guys have a job to do. I cannot tell you now. But in time it all will be revealed to you. For Peter's and your fates are mixed together, and that must be broken. For if you guys do not save your friend, all the generations will be for nothing. So, my friends, we must move with haste, my friends, you must make yourselves ready. For you must see one more thing, now come with me. For you, Tim, ask me no question. Only come." So they got themselves ready and went over to the cave of the past. They passed by the old catfish; he stood up taller and shook his big head side to side, as if he was saying no. Then he lowered his head, and the boys stepped aside, and they went in. Once in, they saw the same kind of screen. All at once the screen lit up; there they saw Peter playing in his room. But it did not look like Peter. This was a little kid who looked about five or six years old. Then a man came in the room; it was the boy's father. He told the little kid he had to go to work and that he would be back later. The little boy told the man that he didn't want him to go; he started to cry. The man called the boy's mother in the room; she said, "Peter, what's wrong, baby." Peter said, "Don't let him go, Mom, he needs to stay here with us." Peter's mom said, "Daddy has to go to work, he will be back soon, honey." Peter said, "He will never be back," and started to cry. His dad tried to give him a kiss, but Peter ran to his mother, and his father said, "I will see you later, son, and left." Peter stayed close to his mom; everywhere she went, Peter was right there. She tried to get him to go in his room, but he wouldn't; he stayed right by her side. They watched him for a while just hanging on to his mom, crying. Then the phone rang. Peter started to cry more and ran around the room with his hand to his head. His mom answered the phone; she listened for what seemed like a minute or two. Then she dropped the phone and ran over to Peter, but Peter ran away; she yelled out for Peter to come. But he did not; instead he ran to their bedroom and grabbed his father's picture. Peter held it to his heart. His mom came into the room and grabbed him and said, "Baby, we have to go. Daddy . . . Daddy has been in an accident, so we have to go." It was then that Tim and Paul looked at each other, and they said to Reno, "Peter knew it all the time. How did he know, Reno." Reno did not answer them. He only said, "Watch and see what makes Peter special just like you guys are special too." Then they looked back at the screen; they saw Peter and his mom leave and get in the car. Once they were in the car, Peter stopped crying and told his mom, "I told Dad not to go to work." Peter's mom said, "Yes, baby, you did." Then Peter said, "Dad is not at the doctor's." His mom said, "He at the hospital." Peter said, "No, Mom, he is not there either." His mom said, "What do you mean, Peter." Peter didn't say anything; his mom got upset with him. She started yelling at little Peter, saying, "It's not true, Peter, don't say things like that, baby, Daddy will be there waiting for us. You will see." Then they reached the hospital. They went up to the desk and asked for Peter's dad. The lady behind the desk told them to wait, then a doctor came and told her that her husband was dead; she grabbed Peter and started to cry. But Peter did not cry; he had a strange look on his face, like he was looking at something else, then the screen went blank. Reno said, "Now I will answer your question now, Tim. You asked me how did young Peter know his father was already dead. He could feel the light go out in his father's life. His father transcended this world. Each of you have a special gift. Some of your gifts may be the gift to feel when something is not right, and one may have the gift of love, that no matter what can happen they can still bring a little love in your life. And some gifts may be the gift of giving, and some may see with the third eye what is not visible to the natural eye." Then Tim said, "What talents do we have, Reno." Reno said, "When the time comes, everyone shall realize his or her true talents, and then their eyes shall be open. They shall never see the same again." Paul asked, "When will that time come?" Reno answered, "For no man alive can say what will the next hour will bring. So how can I tell you when will your eyes will be open to your talents. Perhaps they are already open, and you cannot see it." Tim said, "What do you mean? You know the answer to everything, and you can tell us." Then Reno said, "If I told you now, I would not be doing you a good deed and would be robbing you of your adventure, Tim." Tim smiled and said, "Yes, that is good because I am waiting for a good adventure." Then Paul said, "Reno, tell us about young Peter and what happen to him and his mother." Reno answered, "There is nothing else to say or to see. You already know that his father died in the car accident and his mother stayed in New York for a while, but just couldn't get over the death of Peter's dad. His mother had given up everything for his dad, her family turned their back on her when she married outside of her race. They have never even met Peter. So you see, all she had was her husband and Peter. She felt all alone, with no one to share her grief with, 'cause there was no one but little Peter. So she moved here to north Carolina to start over with her and Peter, with no memories or nothing to remind her of her husband, so she thought. Now remember this what you have seen and heard here. There will come a time when all of this will matter and you will understand why some people can put up with anything. They can take a lot of abuse because they are afraid of being alone. For all of the good gift's that your God has given man, fear is not one of them. For in your world man has excepted fear, but fear is a tool of the wicked. Take this I say and burn it in your hearts for in time fear will show herself to you guys and you shall know her for your self's. Remember this, my young friend, and remember this also, when there's a hole in a bucket, it can never be filled with water until you first fix the hole. There's a leak in Peter's and his mom's life. She tried to fix it, but she didn't know she only patched the hole with clay. When it mixes with the water in the bucket, it melted, and the hole is back again. So as it is in life, man will always search for the quick fix and easy answer, and in doing this, they are deceiving themselves. In the end of it all, they will find themselves naked to the whole world. You must not be like them that search for what is far and forget to look for what is near. Now, my young friends, we must be on our way back to the cave of the future."

It was then that Paul realized that Big Ben was not with them. Then Tim asked Reno, "What happen to Big Ben, and why didn't he stay and watch with us and learn like we did?" Then Tim turn to Paul and said, "You were right, Paul, there is something strange about Big Ben, it's very odd that he just come and goes and nobody ever sees him or how he always does the right thing." Then Reno started laughing, and he laughed hard and long. Tim and Paul looked at each other, wondering what they had said that was so funny. Then Reno put his hand to his knees and said, "Yet you have eyes, but you see not, and you have ears and you hear not." Then Tim said, "Reno, why must you talk in riddles." Then Reno said, "This, my young friends, is not a riddle. Just as it is in your world, man is blind to the truth because it is so simple. So man thinks there must be something else, so man closes his eyes to what is right before him and go in search for a lie. He can accept the lie because he has searched for it and labored over it and made it more acceptable, now he can accept it now. Then Paul said,

"Reno, I am tired of this, it makes no sense at all." Tim said, "Yes, Paul, you're right, let us go." Then Reno started to laugh again, shaking his head and holding his stomach; he laughed and laughed. Then Tim said, "Paul, let's find Peter and leave this madhouse." Then Reno said, "My young friend, for I am sorry. But it has been a lifetime since I have been among men. Now let me tell you what you have forgotten, my friends. Do you not remember that Big Ben was here for three days before he showed you guys. What do you think he was doing all that time." Then Tim laughed and said, "I forgot that, Reno, he must have seen these things before. That makes a lot of sense, and the answer was right there all the time." Then Reno said, "Let that be a lesson to you, Tim," and Tim started laughing, but Paul was not laughing; he still felt that there was still something about Big Ben that was not right. Then Reno said, "My little wise man Paul, be at ease, for your thoughts and what you feel soon all will be answered to you. So don't let that steal your joy. Now back to young Peter, you see at the age of six years old how Peter became aware of his gift. But he soon lost it. He stopped feeling, he shut down, Peter's gift came too early for him, and there was no one there to help his gift grow. Peter couldn't understand the pain of the gift. So in his young mind, he decided not to care or feel. So now you say to yourself, he was just a baby. So how can a baby shut down his feeling, you must remember, you guys are not like other kids." Tim said to Reno, "That's why he doesn't cry when his stepfather beats him. Peter is able to shut down his feeling, and he does not feel anything, pain are love." "That's right, Tim," Reno said, "but soon he won't be able to control it. He will be lost in darkness. The heart must have a way to release the pain, or the heart will burst and die." Paul asked Reno, "What can we do to help him?" Reno said to them, "The day of help grows near. Now we must be going, but now I must ask you guys this. What you have seen here and what you have learned of young Peter, can you walk with this burden? Will you be able to look at Peter without pitying him or treating him any differently? This is a heavy burden to ask of you, but I know you guys can start your inner star and draw the strength from it. Let love be the match and the desire to help your brother be the fuel. Once you light your inner star, start to shine and warm and satisfy your heart and mind, it will give you all the strength you will need, and you can draw from it when you get weak. Now, my young friends, we must hurry, for Big Ben and Peter wait for us." As they walked out, Tim said to Paul, "Did you see how big Peter's head was. He makes me think of Dumbo the elephant, big head and big ears." Tim started to laugh, so did Paul, even Reno laughed. Then Reno said, "Guys, we are here." Tim said to Paul, "I can hear Dumbo," and they went inside the cave laughing. Peter asked them, "What are you girls laughing about?" Tim said, "Nothing, we just saw something funny." Peter said, "Tim, I saw your sister kissing a boy, and I have a plan how you can get your sister back for the money she charge you to help you with your little sunburn problem." Paul and Tim and Peter started laughing. Big Ben asked them, "What are you guys talking about?" Big Ben was laughing too and really didn't know why he was laughing. Then Reno said, "It is time for you guys to go, my young friends, in your time it is about five thirty. It will be dark soon, so you must be going." Then Paul said, "How can that be possible, it seems like we have only been down here for about a hour or so." Then Reno said, "My time and your time is like the day and night." Reno started to walk them to the opening to where they came in. They all said good night. Then Reno said, "The next time you guys come, you will not take any trip. Instead we will talk, and you will be able to ask me anything, and I will answer you." Then he started laughing. "Now, my young friends, you must hurry, for the night knows no one and the night has more enemies than the day, for the things that seek to harm you has the cover of night." They all laughed as they made their way back to the top to the clubhouse. Once they got to the clubhouse, Tim saw that old raccoon leaving the clubhouse dragging a bag. He took off running after the raccoon, but he couldn't catch that old raccoon. Tim started cursing that old raccoon, "That damn old raccoon has stolen his last free meal. Tomorrow, I am going to bring Daniel. Daniel is the best old damn hunting dog in all of Carolina." Peter started laughing and said, "Tim, when that old hound dog move, it's like he is moving in slow motion. That is the biggest shit eater in all of Carolina. That old raccoon is going to kick Daniel's ass to the next county." Tim said, "Peter, you don't know what you are talking about, you're just jealous, that's all." Then Paul said, "We must be getting things together, it will be dark soon." "Right," Big Ben said. And they started picking up the things that old raccoon had scattered all around the clubhouse. Then Big Ben said, "You're one hundred percent right, Peter. If Tim bring his dog, I think that old raccoon will kill his dog, but that is Tim's right after all. It's his dog right. Anyway, maybe that old hound dog of Tim's just might chase that old raccoon away from here." Peter said, "It makes no different to me, but you guys have never looked at Tim's dog like I have. I just don't want to have to help carry that old stinky dog out of here when Mr. raccoon finished with him." Paul said, "Peter, then you tell Tim to let it go and don't bring his dog, that's all you can do." Then Big Ben said, "Guys, I will see you all tomorrow, we have pick up everything, so I am going to walk with Tim. Good night." Then Tim and Big Ben left for home with Peter. Peter was still trying to talk Tim out of bringing his dog as they walked out to the curb to their house.

That next morning, Paul and Peter got to the clubhouse at the same time. They sat on the log under the big old oak tree. Peter said to Paul, "I hope Tim doesn't bring his old dog out here, that raccoon is too smart for that old dog." "Yea," Paul said as they sat on the log. "Peter, that is a smart raccoon. I thought about what you said yesterday about Tim's dog, and if he brings him this morning, we will have to help him. I hope Big Ben comes before Tim, we need to let him know too. So he will know to help with that old dog if Tim bring him." Then they heard what sounded like Big Ben and the sound of a dog, and not just a dog. But they knew it was Tim's hound dog when they heard old Daniel's long bark and heard Tim yelling, "He's on the trail, Big Ben." Then Paul looked at Peter, and they both got up at the same time and started toward the noise. There they were, Tim and his dog and Big Ben with a hunting outfit on. Tim had his face painted with makeup. Peter just fell to the ground; in tears of laughter, he said, "Tim, you are the most ugliest girl I have ever seen. That old raccoon will not want to date you no matter how much makeup you put on. Boy, you are ugly and, Big Ben, what are you suppose to be, a warlock with that funny-looking hat on with that long walking cane." Peter starting laughing, and he laughed. Then Paul said, "Peter, Big Ben can't be a warlock, that hat is too pointy, he must be a witch, and a ugly one at that." Then Peter put his hand to his side and said, "You're right, Paul, he must be a witch if he thinks he going to catch that old raccoon, with that old stinky hound dog. Then he's going to need all the help he can get. Then I guess it would be good if he was a witch. So Big Ben can make a magic potion to trap that slick old raccoon," and started back laughing. Then they all laughed for a while. Then Tim said, "Do you guys want to come along for the hunt, but you will need some of my sister war paint to put on your faces, to keep that old raccoon from picking up your scent. They both looked at each other, remembering what they had talk about earlier. Then Peter said, "I will." Tim said, "Just rub some of these leaves on your clothes." Paul said, "I will do the same, I think that will do." Then Peter said, "Your sister is going to kill you, Tim." Tim said, "She won't ever miss this little bit of war paint she wears. I didn't steal a whole lot, just a little bit, anyway I added some baby powder in and mix it up. It is at the same level before I took out this little bit, she will never know the different. Are you guys ready." Paul said, "We wouldn't miss this hunt for the world." Then Peter said, "Hey, you guys, we should pray first." Tim asked why. Then Peter said, "For old Daniel, he going to need all the help he can get. Look at him, he looks like he wants to go to sleep." Tim said, "Leave my dog alone, Peter." "All right, you guys," Big Ben said, "let's get started. Turn old Daniel lose, Tim." Tim reached down and unclipped his collar; old Daniel started barking and howling and sniffing around, and then he took off. With the guys close behind him, just like a bullet fired out of a gun, old Daniel was running hard. Then he stopped and started barking right by this big old pecan tree. They all looked up, and there was that old raccoon just sitting there, not moving, just looking down at old Daniel barking and running around, jumping up at the tree. Peter said, "Look at old Daniel go, he looks like a real hunting dog." Tim said, "I told you guys." Then Big Ben said, "How will we get that old raccoon down." Peter said, "We can throw rocks and sticks and knock him out the tree, and Daniel can get him. Tim, are you sure that old Daniel can handle that raccoon, he seem real tricky." Then Paul said, "Well, you guys, I have gathered these rocks and sticks, let's start throwing." They all said okay. Tim threw a rock, then they all started throwing after Tim threw the first one. Then that old raccoon fell to the ground. They all ran back. As soon as the raccoon hit the ground, old Daniel was on top of him. Tim was yelling, "Get him, boy, that's right, bite him." Peter said, "Old Daniel looks pretty good. He is handling himself better than I thought." Then the raccoon somehow got on top of Daniel's back and clamped down hard on old Daniel. Daniel let out a loud noise and started trying to shake Mr. raccoon off. He shook hard and then fell to the ground and started to roll on his back. Then the raccoon turned loose and started to run. Daniel was right behind him. Peter said to Paul, "I bet old Daniel was a good fighter when he was younger." Then Paul said, "Remember, don't get caught up in this, Peter. We both know why we are here." Peter said, "Yeah, you're right, we don't want Tim to do something stupid." Old Daniel seemed to be doing okay; he might just kill that old raccoon after all. Then Tim yelled out, "Where is that old raccoon running to." Big Ben said, "To the water, he going to the creek, don't let him take Daniel in the water." Then Peter screamed, "Why, Big Ben." Big Ben screamed back, "That's an old raccoon, he's full of tricks. They can swim better than a dog. He will try and get on Daniel back and try and drown him." Tim started screaming at old Daniel to come back, but he didn't stop. Old Daniel kept running after that damn old raccoon. Then they were at the water's edges. The raccoon jumped in, with Daniel right behind. Then Peter remembered what Paul had said about watching Tim. So he wouldn't do something stupid. So he ran as fast as he could to catch Tim. Paul was right behind him. It seemed like they had remembered at the same time. Finally Peter caught up to Tim and grabbed him. Tim turned and said, "Let me go, you little punk. I have to save my dog, my dad is going to kill me if anything happen to old Daniel. I took him without permission. So let me go." Then Paul came and said to Peter, "Boy, you sure can run real fast. Maybe you should think about playing football." Tim was still trying to break free. Peter and Paul had him held up pretty good. Then out of nowhere Big Ben came flying past them, saying, "I know what to do, you guys," and dove in the creek after Daniel and the raccoon. Peter yelled out, "Big Ben, don't do it." By that time, Big Ben was swimming out to the middle of the creek to where Daniel and the raccoon were fighting. The raccoon had made it on Daniel's back and biting and crawling toward Daniel's head. Peter said, "Yep, old Daniel is a goner for sure." Then Paul said, "Maybe not. There goes the second half of the nuts. What in the Sam Hill is that fool trying to do." Big Ben reached out his hand and tried to knock the raccoon off Daniel's back, and then the raccoon jumped off and started swimming back to the edge of the bank. Tim yelled out at that raccoon, "I am going to kill you," and started trying to break free from Peter and Paul. When Big Ben had hold of old Daniel, Paul and Peter let Tim go; he ran over and started throwing rocks at the raccoon as the raccoon swam away. Big Ben was bringing old Daniel to the bank. Tim waded out to meet Big Ben with the dog; you could see old Daniel was tired. He was barely breathing. Tim picked him up and said, "Don't die, please don't die, Daniel," and fell to the ground and started crying. Then Big Ben came over and said, "He will be all right, all he needs is rest." Then Peter said, "Shit, man, old Daniel just drunk a whole lot of water, his stomach must be about to burst." Then Tim burst into tears and ran off. Peter called for Paul to come over, and Big Ben was already there. They started talking. Peter said, "Tim is real lucky that old Daniel will be okay. You know, Tim took him without permission. He needs to be taught a lesson before he does something else and we are not around." Then Big Ben said, "Leave it to me. You guys just play along, we will give him a good lesson." Then Big Ben screamed out, "Oh my god, old Daniel is not breathing." Then Peter said, "Tim, he's not breathing." Tim started to run back over, but Paul ran and met him before he could reach them. Paul said, "Tim, what is your dad going to do." Tim answered him, "I don't know, but this I do know, he is going to be so mad at me. If I only would have ask my dad, if I could take old Daniel for a walk. I know he would have said yes." Then he started crying. He cried so hard and looked so sad until Peter asked Big Ben to let old Daniel up from the ground. Old Daniel had got his wind back and was looking better than he ever did. But Big Ben said, "Tim still needs a little more pain." Then Peter said, "That's okay, but now it's hurting me to watch him. Why should I suffer for his mistake." Then Paul walked over. Tim was still crying in the same area. Paul said, "He has had enough, let's tell him his dog is all right." But Big Ben said, "No, he still needs a little more." Peter said, "I don't want to watch him anymore. Look at him, he's on his knees." Paul said, "I don't want to watch this anymore either too, Peter." Big Ben said, "Now we have all suffer for our part in this, it has hurt me just as much as it did, you guys, because we all could have stopped Tim before this. But we let him kept on going, we forgot the actions of a friend will affect those who are close to them as much as themselves or even more than himself. It will impact those that surround him and love him A good friend would be strong enough to stop him or tell his friend now he is wrong, even if it means you might lose him as a friend." Paul said, "You're right, I don't know what we could have done." Peter said, "I for one should have never rode him so hard about his dog. I put him in a situation that he had to prove that his dog was the best old hunting dog. I am sorry for that." "Now then," Big Ben said, "we all have learn something. Even I knew it was a bad idea, but I just went along with it instead of speaking up." Peter said, "Let's call Tim and tell him that his dog is fine." Then Big Ben said, "Okay, we all have suffer enough from this. Now we know to speak up when we see someone doing wrong and to do something about it. Even if it means we will be unpopular." Peter said, "You're right, now let's tell Tim." Then they all yelled out, "Tim." Tim turned and looked toward them, with tears in his eyes, and he fell to the ground on his knees and dropped his head, knowing that what had happened to old Daniel was all his fault. Then he raised his head again, and there he saw old Daniel standing between Peter and Big Ben. Tim jumped up to his feet and ran to old Daniel with a smile from ear to ear, crying and laughing; he was running so fast until he tripped and fell face-first in the dirt. Old Daniel broke free from Big Ben and Peter and ran to Tim. Then he started licking him in the face. Tim grabbed him and hugged him and said, "I love you, old Daniel, and I am sorry for bringing you out here, you are too old, boy, to be chasing raccoons. You should be laying under that old tree taking it easy."

Then Big Ben said, "Hey, you guys, we should be getting ready to go. I think we should walk old Daniel around for a little while to make sure he's all right." Then Peter said, "What if we run into that old raccoon again." Paul said, "That old raccoon is long gone by now. Old Daniel ran him off real good." Tim started smiling; that made him feel good to know that old Daniel did run that old raccoon off. Peter dropped his head. Paul and Big Ben knew he wanted to say something smart, but he didn't. Tim said, "Thank you" to Peter. Peter said, "Why are you saying thank you, Tim." Tim said, "You know why, that's for not saying something smart." Peter said, "Today you have suffer enough, but tomorrow is another day." Paul said, "I think old Daniel is going to be all right, you guys. We better be going." Tim stopped in his tracks, and old Daniel sat down. Paul said, "Tim, what's wrong." Tim said, "I don't know what happen today, but I am glad you guys were here today, thank you for your help. I will see you all tomorrow and, Peter, I will be ready for all of your smart jokes." Then he pulled for old Daniel to come. But he didn't; instead old Daniel walked over to each one and gave them a lick and a big old bark as to say thank you too and then followed Tim out of the woods. Paul and Peter said good night to Big Ben, and they left humming a little song, skipping through the path, feeling good about themselves. Big Ben was also humming as he went through the path.

That next day they all met back up at the clubhouse. Tim was all full of smiles, like he had a secret that only he knew. Paul asked him, "Why are you smiling so?" Peter said, "He's waiting for me to say something about his dog and yesterday." Big Ben said, "Peter, why don't you say something to take that silly smile off his face." Tim said, "It's not that, I told my dad what happen yesterday." They all got quiet. Paul said, "Tell us what happen, Tim." Tim said, "At first my dad was angry with me, but I just kept on talking, and the more I talk, the easier it got. When I finished telling him what happen and that I had learn a good lesson and that it would never happen again, that I would always ask for anything else I wanted to borrow, then my dad said these words to me. 'I no longer have a little boy for a son, now I have a man for a son.' My dad also said, 'What you just told me I know it was not easy for you, Tim, to tell me, son, and you could have gotten away with it. But you chose to tell the truth, and for that I am thankful and proud. Now for your punishment, you will take old Daniel for a walk for the next three months.'" Then Peter said, "You got off too easy. You should have gotten a old-fashioned beating. Your dad should have put the belt to your butt. That would have taught you a lesson." Then Big Ben said, "Hey, you guys, today is the day Reno said to come and that we could ask him anything." Peter said, "Yea, it is." But Paul and Tim were thinking of Peter's remark about the way Tim's father should have beat him, and they remembered what Reno said about Peter's actions and the way he was being raised in his house with the beating are a way of life for him. They knew that he was wrong in the way he was thinking. Paul and Tim wanted to go down in the cave and talk to Reno more and tell him that they could see what he was talking about Peter's behavior. But they didn't want Peter to be with them when they talked to Reno. Then Big Ben said, "Are you guys ready." They all said yes; they all got up and started for the entry of the cave. Then Paul reached for Tim and whispered to him, "When the time is right, we need to get Peter out of the way, so one of us can ask Reno about Peter, all right." Tim said, "Yea, I will be ready when the time show itself." They hadn't forgotten that awful beating Peter was going to get soon. They reached the underwater steps that led down to the cave; they went down together. There they saw Reno in the same spot they left him in on their last visit. He greeted them with a smile and a hug and said to each of them, "I am glad you came, you guys are late. Come and let us visit for a while." He led them past the door of the future. Paul hit Tim on the shoulder as they passed the door of future, and they both shook their heads as in agreement that they did not want to go in there. Then they passed the door with no name on it, and Tim said, "Reno, where are you taking us." Reno said, "To the room of the round tables." Tim said, "We have been there before, but you have never taken us this way before." Reno burst out into laughter and said, "Tim, once again you saw through me. So go ahead and ask me. That is why I brought you this way for the question you all have been wanting to ask me since your first trip here and you saw the door with no name." Tim said, "Yea, the rest of them have names, but that one does not, and it has been troubling me a little. I would like to know what the room does and what is inside, and I know you guys want to know as bad as me." Then Peter said to Tim, "Okay, stupid, go ahead and ask Reno, we all would like to know and ask him why does the snake guard the other door." Then Reno said, "One question at a time," and chuckled as he made his way to the room of the round tables. Then they reached the room. Reno told them to sit wherever they wanted to but sit together. Then Tim said, "All right, Reno. What is in the room." Reno said, "What is inside is what is inside every man and woman that does evil against another. And the name of this room can only have one name, and that is the hall of shame. That is an easy-enough name for you guys. Because you could not pronounce the real name. All right, ask me another." He had a great big smile on his face. Paul, Tim, and Peter seemed like they were in shock. They sat there with this blank look on their faces. Then Peter said out loud, "What in the Sam Hill did he say, hell, I can answer question like that. All you got to do is answer them with another question or better yet just say something stupid." Then the table began to shake, and the floor trembled. Then there was a loud chuckle that had turned into what was the loudest laughter you could ever imagine. You could hear the echo all through the cave. Reno was stomping his feet and hitting his large hand against the table. Tim said to Peter, "Shit, man, maybe you should be a comedian," and that seemed to make it worse. Before long, they all were laughing; the cave seemed to be full of warmth and happiness. Then Reno stopped as soon as he started; and Paul, Tim, Peter, and Big Ben were still laughing. Then Reno said, "Those words were more funnier than I had expected. I told you all to ask me whatever, you will, and that on this day, I would tell you straight the answer. And that is what I have down." He started to smile. Then Tim started to smile and said, "Yes, you did." All of the guys started to laugh because they knew that Tim was about to ask one of his out-of-this-world questions. Then Tim said, "Reno, will I find love, and how will I know it when I find it. How will I know it, and can love make you do things that you don't want to do, and tell me of my wife, will she be pretty, will she be fat or skinny." Reno laughed and said, "You asked a hard question, my young friend. I will tell you this first, Tim, think of the most strongest thing you can think of." Tim said, "A train." Paul said, "Superman." Then Reno said, "Now, boys, multiply that by one hundred, and that's how strong love is." Tim said, "That is strong stuff, nothing to play around with." Reno laughed and said, "Yes, my young friends, it is. But people play with love every day. It is the strongest weapon there is, but yet the most misused one of all. Now, Tim, what a man searches for, that is what he will find. But be now warned, there are many types of love, but only one true love. You guys can call it fool's love. Listen to this story. A young prince is sent out on a journey by the elders of his village to bring back a special pony. The young prince asks the elders how will he know the special pony, what color will it be, or will it be big or small. Will it be female or male. Then the elders said to the young prince, 'What your eyes see and your heart feels and the mind says yes to and all three parts of the body are comforted and the soul is at peace, that is what will be special to you, and that will be the special pony, your first pony. Maybe it will shine like gold and as warm as the campfire on a cold night.' Then the elders said a little prayer and they told the young prince to listen closely to the words. 'May God open your eyes to what comes freely and cost little and let not your eyes be blinded by what is perfect to you.' Then the elders left the young prince. Then the young prince left the village in search of a special pony. He came upon a herd of young pony grazing in the meadow on an early summer morning. The morning dew was still in the air. There in the herd he saw the one that he thought would be his. A jet-black pony, so black until the pony looked blue. When she walked, the morning sun made the coat shine like black gold. Then he knew he had to have that pony, he did not look at another, for he was smitten by the young stallion. He took off with a rope in hand, casting the rope upon the pony's neck, each time the pony would shake it off. He went at it for days. Then he realized that all the ponies would run when he started casting his rope, but one did not run, he realized that when he was chasing the stallion, there was one pony chasing him, but he did not pay that any attention, he only said, 'Crazy old horse, who would think you're special,' and kept after the stallion, casting the rope again and again. On the last cast, the other pony ran up from behind, and the rope fell upon her neck. She didn't fight to get away, instead she walked up to him. Again the young prince took the rope from the horse's neck and said, 'You stupid old horse, get away,' and picked up a rock and chased the horse away and started back on his journey of casting the rope for the stallion, this went on for weeks. The weeks turned into months, the months turned into years. On the third year, the prince returned to the village with nothing, the elders of the village called to the young prince and said, 'Did you not find that what is special to you. Out of all the ponies in the meadow, you could not find one.' The prince answered them and said, "What was special in my eyes I could not have it. I tried to catch a young stallion but failed. The elders of the village said, 'Your father, the king, will not like your failure, for the slave boy went out and brought back a very special pony who is as gentle as a newborn baby, never has anyone ever seen such a thing and is beautiful and so peaceful animal and was only gone a short while. The whole village knows that is the most special pony they have ever seen. The pony is not afraid of nothing, why, your father himself came to see the slave boy's special pony.' The young prince said, 'There is no such pony alive that is like you say, and if there was, I would have caught the pony myself.' Then the young prince said, 'Take me to the slave boy's pony so that I may see the pony.' The elders took him, and there he saw the same pony that he had chased away. The young prince felt ashamed, for he knew he had his special pony and chased the pony away because he was blinded by the other pony, then he remembered the prayer the elders had prayed for him, 'What comes freely and costs little there is where you find what is special to you,' and he dropped his head in shame." Tim said, "I understand that, Reno." Then Reno said, "Tell me, what do you understand?" Tim said, "Sometimes in the pursuit of love, love will sometimes pursue you. So one should be ready when love comes, and sometimes love will not come in the way you want it and not to make any big expectation about love. And don't be blind to the way love looks or comes." Reno laughed out loud and put his hand to his head and said, "May the star shine bright tonight, Tim. Tim, you truly understood," and he laughed until tears fell from his eyes. "Thank you, my young friend, you have pleased my heart." Then Paul said, "That was a good story, and I learn a lot, and I am thankful for Tim too. He always asks the right question at the right time. But, Reno, I want to get back to where we left off with the doors in the cave and the other stuff, you never got a chance to finish answering the question we were talking about earlier." Reno said, "Yes, Paul," then Paul said, "Now tell us straight. Tim won't interrupt us anymore, will you, Tim." Paul shook his fist at Tim as he said that to Reno. Then Paul said, "Now tell us the purpose of the hall of shame and what is in the room." Then he smiled, then Tim said, "That's right, Paul, put it to him straight." Then they all laughed. Reno said, "My young friends, sometimes in life it is good to be blind to the truth when you expect the answer to be more than it is. Remember this before your ears hear the straight of it. The truth is always the simplest answer and is always the thing you don't want to hear. For in your mind you have already decided that what is in the room must be very important and must be a great secret. Now your mind has blinded your ears and eyes to what is the truth. Now get ready for the straight of it. Let me first tell you what's inside, what's inside is what's inside of every man and every woman and you and Tim, Paul. You do not understand, and I have given it to you straight, but yet let me go further. The hall of shame is for all the things we want to do. But we know that the things are wrong for us to do and know that it is wrong in the eyes of your God. But yet we do them anyway. Remember what I told you when a man lies, another man will pay for that lie. That belongs in the room, you have heard of someone's attack and beating with rage and hatred in his heart for his fellow man. That also belongs in the room and the words of hatred, Paul, you know the words that sting. They too belong in that room. When the time comes, every man or woman before they meet their Lord must be weighed in that room for their acts of evil. For when a good man finds that he has done evil against another, he will find that his reward is regret. It will eat away at the soul of the man. And know this about regret, it is known by many names, but they all mean the same thing, that who I have just said rules that room and lives there, let not regret be a part of your life, for he is the one in the room. Do not let him in. Always think before you act, and regret will know you not, my young friend, for all the things that are evil, regret is the worst because he can live inside of a man, and no one will ever know, slowly eating away at the soul and making a slave of the one he is in. Now let me tell you this, my young friends, regret is a thing a man can live with, but it is a hard thing to bear. It will destroy you in time. For this room is justice for them, and Venges will come for those that use this room. Let not yourselves be caught up in this room. For you shall feel the wrath. As I have told you twice now, my young friends, do you understand." They looked at one another in amazement, for they were lost in the words that Reno had said. Then Paul said, "Reno, I don't really understand what you said, and I know Peter and Tim don't understand, maybe Big Ben understand, but I am not sure about that." Then Peter said, "Speak for yourself, Paul." Reno said, "My words have not fallen on deaf ears, only one that is almost in the door of the hall of shame can understand it." Then Tim and Paul looked at each other; they knew what Reno was saying to them. Then Peter said, "The hall of shame is for the people that do evil to others and they know that it is wrong, but sometimes they can't help themselves. Right, Reno." Reno looked at Paul and said, "You're right, Peter." Then Tim looked at Paul and said, "Peter, do you want to do some looking around." Big Ben heard what Tim asked Peter and said, "Yeah, let's do it, there's a lot of things I have yet to show you guys." They all got up, Big Ben and Peter and Tim. They all headed for the little door. Then Peter stopped and said, "Are you coming, Paul." Paul said, "Go ahead, I am going to talk to Reno for a while." Peter said, "Good luck, Paul, talking to Reno is like talking to someone who doesn't speak English." Then Peter and Tim and Big Ben all laughed as they walked out the room. Paul thought to himself how strange it was how everyone seemed to know what was going on. Paul knew that Tim knew the plan to get Peter out of the way so one of them could ask Reno the questions about Peter, but that brought up another question, how did Big Ben know. Or was it just an accident that Big Ben was a part of it. Then Paul said to himself, *Maybe there's something strange about the way Big Ben just seem to know what*

was going on, or maybe there was something around here Big Ben really wanted
to show them, as the guys left out of the room. Tim said, "Paul, are you sure
about not coming." Paul looked at Tim with a big smile and said, "No, but
thanks for asking, Tim, I will stay here with Reno," and Tim looked back
and nodded his head. Paul knew what that nod meant as soon as they left
the room.

Paul asked Reno, "You have to tell us what is going to happen to Peter."
Reno laughed and said, "You and Tim should be very happy with yourselves,
you have gotten Peter out of the way. That was a good plan, I can see the
love you have for your friend, and it is that love that will save you and Tim
and Peter. For all of your lives are connected, his tomorrow will determine
your fate." Then Paul said, "Reno, I don't understand. You must tell me in
plain talk, what you mean." Then Reno said, "Paul, I can tell you about the
stars in the sky. I can tell you what you ate yesterday. I can even tell you
your favorite color. But I cannot tell you what the future will be. I will tell
you this, my friend, in the coming days you will begin to understand those
words which I have spoken to you. For you will hear these words, and the
action of one can affect many." Then Paul said, "I have already learn that,
with Tim's dog." Then Reno said, "You have learned only half of a whole,"
and started to laugh. "Yes, that was funny to watch Tim really learn
something." Then he changed the subject and said, "To learn more, you
must watch more in the cave of the future. But you must leave your heart
at the door, for this is for you and Tim's eyes only. Big Ben will take care of
Peter. So, Paul, you and Tim will come to the cave of the future." Then
Paul said to Reno, "I guess you have given me enough reason to help Peter
and myself. I guess it's like you said, it is up to us. We must do it for Peter
and ourselves." Then Paul heard Big Ben and the guys. He looked at Reno,
remembering the words he had spoken. Paul heard the words of Reno
ringing in his head, "leave your heart at the door." Then Peter came running
in and said, "Paul, you will never guess what we saw." Then Tim walked
over and tapped Paul on the shoulder and said in a low voice, "Paul, did
you have a good talk with Reno." Tim had a smile on his face. Paul looked
at him and dropped his head. Tim knew what that meant. Then Peter said,
"Go ahead and try and guess what we saw, Paul." Paul said, "A naked lady."
They all laughed. Peter said, "No, stupid, it was a pool full of all kind of
fishes, there were all different colors. Some were multicolor, when they all
swam together, it looked like a rainbow in the water. It was so beautiful, it
gave me this calming feeling, man, I felt like I was just born, and to think

I never thought that there could be anything so wonderful to look at and could make you feel so calm and warm on the inside. I only have one regret, that I could not share it with my mom." Big Ben said, "Why not, we can find some paper and get some crayons and a pencil, and you can make a picture for your mom while it is fresh in your head. She does not have to know where it came from." Peter got excited and said, "Man, why are we still here, let's get going." Tim said, "Yea, go for it, man," with a big smile. He really wanted to talk to Paul; he looked at Paul, but Paul had this strange look on his face, like he was puzzled about something. Tim said, "Did you hear that, Paul, Peter and Big Ben are going to draw some pictures of what Peter has seen," and winked his eye. Paul said, "Yeah, that's good, go ahead." Then Reno said, "My young friends, go ahead, call me when you're ready." Big Ben and Peter went out of the little room in search of crayons and papers. Tim thought to himself, *Where in the world would they find those things down here.* That had Tim wondering. But it didn't matter. Peter was out of the room, and he could talk to Paul. Then the room got real quiet after the guys left. The only ones there were Paul and Tim. Reno had left the room behind the crayon hunters. It was as if they were left alone by a plan. Then Tim said to Paul, "What's wrong. I know you didn't get a straight answer from Reno, so what's wrong." Then Paul began to tell Tim the things that Reno had told him. Paul said, "Reno had told me that Big Ben would take care of Peter, and he did. "But how did Big Ben know what to do about Peter? How could Big Ben know that, Tim, to keep Peter busy so we could talk. I know Reno said that Big Ben had already seen all this, in the cave of the future, when he was missing that time. But, Tim, it just does not feel right to me. There's more to Big Ben than what Reno has said. Look, Tim, there's no one here but you and I. This was already plan, before you and I made our plan, so that one or both of us could ask Reno about Peter." Then Tim said, "I never thought about that, Paul, it sure is strange like you said, Paul." Then Paul said, "Tim, I am going to tell you something else, and don't think that I am jealous or crazy, but I don't think Big Ben is like us. I don't even believe he's a real boy like us. Come on, think about it. We don't know that much about him, we have never been to his house, or we have never seen his grandmother, and look how smart he is. No kid can know all those things." Then Tim started to smile and said, "Paul, I had that feeling ever since he had told us about the woods, my dad taught me about the woods, and my dad is the best teacher on the wilderness there is, and everybody all over this county says the same thing about my dad. But Big Ben seem to know more about the woods than my dad, and that is impossible. That is when I started to wonder about Big Ben." For Tim to say those words about his dad, he had to truly begin to wonder about Big Ben too. Then Tim said, "Maybe, Paul, we were left alone not to talk about Peter, but Big Ben. Reno said that all of our futures are tied together." Paul started to laugh and said, "Tim, you are smarter than you look." Then Tim said, "Paul, what are we going to do about it." Then Paul said, "Nothing yet, Tim, we will do some more research on Big Ben when we get back. We will go to the police station and check that report about missing kids. Now let's call Reno, he will want to take us to the cave of the future, if Reno does take us there, you must remember, Tim, you must leave your heart at the door, because we cannot act the same way as last time, we have to watch and learn to know what to do to help Peter, we must be strong." Then they both called for Reno. Reno came into the room with a smile and said, "You guys are beginning to see with a third eye, that is a good thing. Come, my young friends, we must sit awhile and talk. I know there are some things that we must talk about, Paul and Tim, now you can ask me again what's on your mind." Tim said, "Tell us about Big Ben, Reno." Reno answered, "What do you mean?" Paul said, "He means the way he acts and the things he says and how he always knows what to do and what's going on. Big Ben is too smart to be a kid." Then Reno said, "What is too smart. I think you guys are giving him too much credit, and you forget that he was here for three days and saw many things." Then Paul said, "Reno, you and I know there is more to Big Ben than that." Tim said, "Maybe you're right, Reno. But I think we are asking the wrong question, I will ask you this straight, Reno. Is Big Ben a real boy like us?" Then Reno said, "I will tell you this, and we will not talk about this anymore. Tim, what do you see when you look at Big Ben." Tim said, "I see a boy like me, but that does not mean he is a boy like us." Then Reno said, "To find out more, just keep looking, but remember what you have learned this far and you will have started to find your answer." Then Paul said, "What is so important about Peter, why must we watch all these things." Then Reno said, "Peter is a part of you guys, to help him is to help yourselves. This is the only way for you guys to save your own selves and to save mankind from the world. You three will play a big part in the changes in your world in the future. For we have waited for hundreds of years for this day to come, and we have raised many generations to get to you guys, and the wait has not been in vain for you, Tim, and you, Paul, and Peter, even Big Ben had made me reach out hard to make the answer as simple as I can." Then Paul started to laugh and said, "If the answers you give us are easy, then I really would hate to hear the hard answer." Then Reno fell to his knees in laughter and started pointing at Paul, shaking his head. Tim started laughing too; he didn't understand why he was laughing. It was just so funny to see Reno on his knees like that. Then Paul said, "Reno, that is not very nice to laugh right in my face like that. That is not a good thing." Then Reno said, holding his stomach, "It is not you, Paul, it is what you said, if I were to tell you the hard answer, you would understand it better, because it is in plain talk, not a parable, for you guys are not yet ready for plain talk or straight talk, Tim, for the answer you guys seek are for you to learn them, for there's a reason and a purpose for all of this, and when the time is right you will understand it all. It is time for you guys to come to the cave of the future." "But, Reno," Tim said, "what about my question." Reno said, "Tim, the hour grows late, and there is still plenty to see and learn, your question is safe with me, and the answer is to so worry not, my young friend." After all the things Reno had said to Tim, that made Tim a little scared. Then Reno said, "When the time comes, you will understand all that I have taught you. Now let me tell you guys, what you are going to see in the cave of the future, it will not be nice, nor will it be pretty. For today you shall see how strong Peter is for real. You guys might be thinking you're not ready, but if you were not ready, I would not allow you to see this, if for any reason you cannot bear what you will see and cannot carry this burden, I will send you to the room of forgetfulness, but if you should go, you will lose what you have learned and the chance to save your friend and yourselves. So I will leave you for a minute so that you can talk among yourselves." Then Tim said, "Wait, Reno, you don't have to leave, I am ready." Then Paul said, "So am I, Reno," then they both said, "Let's do this." Then they were on their way to the cave of future to see how strong Peter really was. As they were walking to the cave, out of the blue, Tim asked Reno a silly question. Tim said, "Reno, how long will I live." Reno looked at him as if he was puzzled. Paul looked at Tim. They could not believe the expression on Reno's face. Then Reno said, "Why do you ask me this, Tim, is it because you think Peter is going to die. If that is the reason, I cannot answer that. But if you want to know for yourself, then I will tell you." Then Tim said, "No, it's not for Peter. Reno, anyone that has the chance that I have to see the future and learn the many secrets of life would want to know that and much more." Then Reno laughed and said, "You're right, Tim." Then Tim said, "Is Peter destined to die, Reno." Reno said, "Come back in the room and sit down, there is still more to understand, we do not have the time for you to learn all there is to know, and even if you did hear all there is to hear and learn all there is to learn, it would do you little good because it would only be words, and the words that you would hear would made no sense to you because to truly understand the words it must be words that you have lived, and that is a life lesson. The best lesson in life are the ones you lived. But, my young friend, I will give you this, one day we all must leave this world and go to the next one. But first you must understand the living first, before you can understand death. For life is a gift, not a promise. So like all gifts, you should be thankful for life and live it in the way God intended you to live it, for if any man should give you a gift of this magnitude, you would thank him every time you see him or when you think of the gift. So I ask you, my young friends, why is it that man does not give thanks for the gift that their God has given them and live his life as God intended him to live it. Keep these words close to your heart, for life is but a little while. Only a blinking of an eye." Tim said, "I have never thought of those things before, Reno." Then Reno said, "That is why you, Tim, and all the men in your world do not understand death because they cannot understand the living, so, Tim, that is why I can't fully tell you about death. Tim, you must not be like the rest of the world and take life for granted, for men do every day." Tim said, "Reno, you're right, even I do it. At night when I go to bed and get ready for sleep, I never think about, I might not wake up, and when I wake up in the morning, I know that I will be awaken by my alarm clock, and I always say thanks to the alarm clock that I woke up this morning on time, and I can go to school, or go out and play, or whatever I had plan for the day." Then Reno said, "It's not your alarm clock that wakes you up in morning. For sleep is the closest you can get to death without dying, my young friend. So you should say thanks to your Lord for waking you up, not to the alarm clock. All those that go to sleep tonight, not all will wake up. So count yourselves among the lucky ones for you woke up, with the help of your Lord." Paul was standing there looking at Tim and Reno with a smile on his face. Then Paul said, "Reno, you have told Tim a lot, but you have not answer his question. The words you spoke, I have heard them all my life, Reno." Reno said, "Yes, Paul, for those words to you were only words that have little meaning to you, but yet you have heard them, and yes, they enter your ears, but they did not get to your heart, the part that matters the most and for that is a shame." Paul dropped his head, feeling silly. Then Reno said, "But you are a child with childlike thoughts. It would be worse if you were a grown man. But although you are a child, you have much wisdom, more than some grown men. Although your eyes and ears and mind have not fully opened up to the truth, but in time it will, and when it does, you guys will be men among men." Then Tim said, "Paul, Reno did answer the question for the first time I listen. Reno said that someday we all must die, for life is not a promise, it is a gift." Then Paul said, "Tim, you really surprise me, you caught what I missed." Tim said, "Thanks, Paul, that mean a lot coming from you." Then Tim asked one more question; it seemed like he was on a roll. Tim asked Reno, "How will you know the truth when you hear it, Reno." Then Reno said, "Some people say the truth cannot be hidden. But yet you see the truth hidden all the time." Tim said, "Sometimes, it's hard to see the truth, or when you see it how do you know it is the truth." Then Reno let out a loud laugh, shaking his large head side to side and said, "By your own words, Tim, you have answered your own question. You see, my little funny friend, I know you don't understand the words I have spoken, but in time you will understand that the truth is always there. Soon, my young friend, in your lifetime the truth will vanish and will be hard to see, and to know it will be even harder, but you guys will have a way of knowing the truth. But it will be there and will not be far, for the good book tells you the answer, and I have given you a way to know it and feel the truth. The truth is the key to all things good and bad. The truth is like many lights in a row, but the truth will shine the brightest of all the lights, but yet you will still have to look. For the light that you seek will shine the brightest and the longest of all the lights. Now, Tim, you want to know how can you know the truth. Now, Tim, after all that I have told you and all that you have learned, you still will ask me that." Tim said, "Yep," and started laughing. Then Paul said, "Reno, I think Tim was only kidding around, he must know what you mean I know I do," then Reno said, "Then tell your young friend, better yet tell me, maybe he will be listening." Then Paul said, "The truth will always find its way home, and you will know the truth when it feels all the parts of the body, the mind, the heart, and the soul." Then Reno grabbed Paul and said, "My teachings have not been in vain, for you have given me the best gift a son can give his father, and I am not your father, but you have made me just as proud as a father." Then he looked at Tim and said, "Thank you too, Tim. If you weren't playing around like you did, pretending not to understand, I would not have known that my words had fallen on fertile soil. Now, Tim, don't feel bad or think that I am not proud of you, for I am. For you are the tool in which I can hear and see my words, and I am just as proud of you, thank you, my young friend. Know, my young friends, we must be on our way to the room of the future so that you can see how strong Peter is. You must prepare yourselves and leave your hearts at the door for your emotions will not help your friend. For this will not be the end, you guys will come to me once more, and then you will see the end." Then Reno started walking toward the room of the future. Tim looked at Paul and shook his head and dropped his head and began to follow Paul and Reno to the cave of the future. Tim tapped Paul on the shoulder and said, "I don't want to see any murders, Paul." Paul told him to stop it and he better not cry. They kept on walking. Reno did not turn his head to look back to see what was going on with Tim and Paul. Tim started making moaning sounds. Paul shook his fist at Tim. Tim said, "One day, Paul, you won't be able to bully me around, you piece of dirt," then Reno said, "We are here." Then Tim started sniffling like he was crying; he had made up his mind that he was not going in because he thought that Peter's stepdad was going to kill him. Then Reno said, "Come, let us go in." Paul grabbed Tim and pushed him in front of him. Paul kept pushing Tim in the back calling him names, but Tim did not go in. Reno was already in the cave waiting for Tim and Paul to come in. Reno called for them to come inside; once again Paul tried to push Tim inside. Then Tim put his hands out on each side and braced himself and started crying and saying, "I don't want to see a dead body," and started shaking all over. Paul pushed him again, then Tim turned and let go a wild punch and knocked Paul back on his butt. Paul said, "Tim, why did you hit me." Tim did not say anything; he just stood there with his fist up in the air, ready to fight like a real boxer, then a voice came from the cave. It was Reno; he called to Paul and said, "Try no more, Paul, for fear has him. Fear is a bad thing, it can take lives as well as save lives." Then Reno came toward Tim and said, "Will you raise your hand at me, old friend." Then he reached out his hand and taught him in the chest, and Tim fell to the ground. Then Paul ran up to Tim, and Reno also came, and together they carried Tim over to a spot in the cave. Then Tim came through and said, "Reno, where am I and what happen." Then Paul said, "You knocked me on my butt, you little piece of dirt," then Tim said, "I am sorry, I didn't mean to hurt you. I don't know what happen." Paul said, "It will take more than you to hurt me." Then Tim said Reno, "I am hurt and disappointed that I did not make it in the cave of the future, I did not realize that I was that scared. Reno, I thought you guys knew everything and you all would not put us in any danger, but yet you all did, and if you knew that I would do the things I did, then that was just wrong." Reno said, "Tim, you're right, I did know this would happen, but in life you must learn you and Paul must face your fears. And, Paul, you guys have come a long way, may this be one of the last things you guys must overcome before you can see the ending. Now let me tell you this, for both of you guys have the same thing in common, and that is fear even though Paul did not show his as openly as you, Tim. Think of it, Tim, why did Paul push you in front, to go in first." Then Tim said, "He was afraid too, Reno." Reno said, "Yes, Tim. Paul was afraid, go ahead and speak the truth, Paul." Then Paul scream out, "Yes, you're right, Reno, are you happy now. That's right, Tim, big old black Paul is afraid," and started to cry. Tim walked over and grabbed his hand and said, "I forgive you, Paul, for pushing me and calling me names, when you were just as scared as I was." Paul said, "Thanks, Tim, but I don't deserve your forgiveness. I tried to hide my fear by pushing you in front and trying to get a free ride off of your weakness. So no one would know my fear." Then Reno said, "For men do that all the time, Paul, in your world live off the weakness of the weak, and yet you boys have forgotten our talk earlier about death. I am not saying that Peter is going to die. We all must receive our reward. That is what death is, and death is one of many steps in the stairway to heaven. It is the reward for living. If you never live, you will never die. So you must live your life to the fullest, not with gold or silver but with the things that God will give you. Which is good health and the promise of tomorrow. You need not drink from that worldly cup, that bittersweet nectar that the world will offer you. For it will make you drunk as the rest of the unhappy people that believe that they need the gold and silver to be happy, and let not fear come to you for fear is not from God and is not a good thing, fear can keep you from living your life and reaching your true gold in life. Now I ask you, Paul, and you, Tim, what place does fear have in your young lives. Now take this time to think of these things that I have told you. For Big Ben and Peter shall soon be upon us. Now I must go, but I will return shortly." Then Tim said something that stopped Reno in his tracks. Tim said, "Reno, after hearing the things you have said, I have realized that we were never accepted to go in the cave of the future, this was just a lesson, a learning lesson." Then Reno started to laugh and said, "You see right through us, Tim, for you are becoming aware," and kept on laughing as he walked away. Paul said to Tim, "That was pretty smart of you, how you realized that. I never thought of that, Tim." "Tim said, "Yes, but I didn't tell Reno the real reason why I figure that out." Then Paul said, "And what was that." Then Tim laughed like Reno and said, "It was love and trust, I know those were the things Reno taught us in the beginning. I know Reno would never put us in any danger, because he cares about us. He needs for us to finish the journey to save

Peter and ourselves, he told us that, and he said that they had raised many generations to get to us. So thinking of all those things made me realize that we were not accepted to go in the cave, Paul." Then Paul said, "Now I know why Reno said you were becoming aware. I understand a little myself, Tim, becoming aware is to become a man and seeing things as a man sees and putting away all childish things. Tim, let's sit here for a while and keep talking, but, Tim, know this, after all that, I am still afraid." Tim said, "I am too, Paul." Paul said, "Tim, I was not afraid when we were talking about the things that we realize and what we had learn, I had forgot all about it." Then Tim said, "Maybe that's it, Paul, don't think about it, we just have to do it. When the time comes." Then Paul said, "That's it, Tim, you have done it again. We can't let fear come, we have to put our minds on something else. A good thought and don't let fear come in and do it fast, that's the key. Now we know, we can call for Reno, we are ready." Then Tim said, "What are we suppose to think of, Paul." Paul said, "Let's think of how good it will be when all of this is over." Tim said, "That's good, but I want to think of old Daniel, he makes me happy." Paul said, "That's good, Tim, if that's what makes you have peace of mind. Let's call for Reno." Then they heard Big Ben coming. They both got scared, then Tim starting singing that old song of Big Ben's, "Who's afraid of that old bear," and soon Paul was singing, and they were laughing, remembering how Big Ben was rolling in the grass and eating the grass and singing that old song; before they realized it, they were not afraid anymore, then they stopped and started calling for Big Ben and Peter. Soon they were all in the room. Peter said, "What have you guys been doing. Me and Big Ben have been all over this place, exploring, we found some neat things. We saw some beautiful butterflies, you would not believe the colors on their wings, those were the most beautifuliest butterflies I have ever seen, all kind of colors. And there's one cave that talks to you, and one room is like a swimming pool, but it's hot water, can you imagine that, like a big bath tub. Then Tim said, "What about the crayons you guys went after." Peter said, "I realize I didn't need the crayons. Big Ben said I can tell my mom a fairy tale about the fish and everything else I have seen, she will never think it is real. So I can tell the truth like Big Ben said." Paul said, "Only Big Ben could think of that," and laughed. Tim said, "That was great," but he had Reno on his mind, then they herd Reno coming; the sound of his big feet made a lot of noise as they hit against the clay floor. He came into the room and said, "Was it so great, Peter, did you have a pleasant time exploring. And you, Big Ben, did you have fun being a guide." They both said yes. Then Reno said, "There is much more to see, much more and more to learn," as he looked at Paul and Tim. Then Reno said, "It is way past the time for you guys to go." They all said, "It's only been a couple of hours." Then Reno had to remind them of the time difference. Then Big Ben said, "Come on, Peter." They started out the cave to the stairs to the top. Then Reno walked up to Paul and Tim and said, "When you guys have satisfied your hearts, about what is on your heart, Paul." At that moment, Paul knew what Reno meant; he knew he had to find out about Big Ben. Then Reno said, "You guys will come alone, and we will be waiting for you. You guys will leave from your house and come here early and get here before Big Ben and Peter, don't worry about Peter, Big Ben will take care of Peter as he has always done," and smiled. Paul looked at Tim, wondering what did Reno mean by that, "as Big Ben has always done." Paul wondered if Tim had picked up on that, and now he knew for sure they had to find out about Big Ben, and he could not wait until they reached the clubhouse so that they could talk about Big Ben and check out Big Ben's story. Then Reno said good night, and they went out of the cave to the other side of the room and out of sight. Paul and Tim went out of the room after Big Ben and Peter; they had started up the stairs. Paul and Tim went behind them, with their eyes closed; when they opened them, they were at the top. They all climbed out and started for the clubhouse. Paul grabbed Tim and pulled him back and said, "Tomorrow early we will meet at my house and start checking out some of the things that has happen involving Big Ben." Tim said, "But Reno told us to come to the cave," but then Paul said, "Do you remember what Reno said, he said first satisfy what is in your heart and for me that's finding out about Big Ben." Then Tim said, "All right, Paul, we need to do that. Now let's catch up with the guys, all right." After a while they were at the clubhouse. Tim said, "You guys, this has been one of the most interesting days I have. What about you guys." Peter said, "It has been a wonderful day. I have seen so many beautiful things today, and they all made me feel so good, I forgot all my troubles today." Big Ben quickly said to Peter, "I didn't know you had any problems in your life, Peter." Peter said, "I didn't mean it like something bad, it was just a figure of speech, Big Ben." Then Paul said, "Big Ben, leave him alone." Tim could feel the tension between Paul and Big Ben. Tim could see where that was going. And it would not be pretty for Big Ben. Tim thought to himself. It was as if Paul was upset with Big Ben. Big Ben said, "I was only trying to help." Then Tim said, "Don't you guys get started. It's time to go before it gets dark. We had better be going, Paul, don't you think so, Paul." "We have a lot to do tomorrow," Big Ben said to Tim. "Tomorrow, you guys will be in for a surprise when you all start your little hunt for the truth, it's a funny thing about the truth, sometimes the eyes won't let the heart feel the truth or see the truth even when it's right in front of you." Paul got madder and said, "What are you saying, you little freak, anyway how do you know what we will be doing tomorrow, log head Big Ben." And he balled up his fists ready to fight, then Tim said, "Paul, Big Ben is only fooling around with us, let's go, you guys." So everybody said good night, and Peter just stood there with his mouth open and said, "What just happen, did I miss something. Paul, you look like you want to take a bite out of Big Ben, why, Paul, would you act like that, after the day we had together, we had so much fun and I learn so much and, Paul, you of all people the one who has always had the level head, I just can't believe it." Then Tim said, "I don't know what's going on either," then Paul said, "Big Ben knows what it is. I am tired of his little game he has been playing, he pretends not to know what's going down in the cave when he knows as much as Reno." Peter said, "What in the Sam Hill are you talking about. I believe you have been drinking some of Tim's papa's moonshine, man." Then Paul said, "Let's get out of here, Tim, Peter has been brainwash by that little red-spotted face demon call Big Ben." Then Big Ben said, "Take it back, you big old donkey." Tim and Peter started laughing and backing up because they knew what was about to happen. Then Peter said, "That's right, Big Ben, you put it to him, that big old donkey." Tim couldn't help it; he joined in with Peter. It seemed like they wanted to see a fight; they were back together again pushing it on, just throwing logs on the fire, making it hotter and hotter just to see a fight. But then Paul stopped and looked over at Tim and Peter and said, "Not today, boys," and walked away. Then Tim said, "That's a boy, Paul, don't play that foolish game with Peter, Peter is trying to see a fight." It seemed like Tim was jumping from side to side. Meanwhile, Big Ben had started to laugh. Then Big Ben said, "See you tomorrow, big donkey, all right, Paul." Paul didn't say anything; he asked Tim, "Are you ready," and started walking out of the woods for the curb. Tim yelled out to Paul, "Yes, I will be right there," then he said good night to Big Ben and Peter. Then he stopped and said, "Are you coming with us, Peter." Peter said, "No, Big Ben will walk me out, right Big Ben." Big Ben said, "Yes, I will walk you, Peter, to the curb." Then Tim said, "I will say good night," and ran after Paul; he caught up to Paul and said, "What was all that, Paul. I thought you were playing, but I wasn't sure, and I didn't know what to do, I just did what I always do." Then Paul said, "I don't really know why myself, I was just trying to get some kind of reaction from Big Ben. I was trying to make him slip up and say something or do something, so we all could see what he is hiding, but it didn't work. So, Tim, we will check out Big Ben real good, starting tomorrow with the police station first, then we will go down that path he takes to his grandmother's house and see where it leads." "Okay," Tim said, "but Peter and Big Ben will be at the clubhouse, how will we get past them to get to the path." Paul said, "Don't worry about that, we will go around them, we will come in from the little strip mall, where we drop Big Ben off, remember." Tim said, "Yah, Paul, I forgot about that way. Okay then, it is a plan." Then Paul and Tim said good night, and then they heard Big Ben and Peter coming. Paul said, "Hurry, Tim, let's go."

The next morning came. Paul met Tim at the curb and said, "Good morning, Tim, are you ready to put some answer to the mystery of Big Ben." Tim said, "Yah, let's do this." So off to the police station they headed. Along the way, Tim told Paul, "The summer is almost over, only three weeks left of freedom and it seem like I never got out of school." Paul said, "Yes, I know what you mean, the things with Reno, he is always teaching us something and asking us questions. it is fun, a lot like school but better, and I like the things we are learning, but I would just like to be a kid and just be blind to everything that is around me and just have fun and run, play, and don't care about anything but myself. Boy, that would be great." Tim said, "Yes, I can't wait until all of this is over, so we can be kids and act our age and not have to act the age of my dad, 'cause we are only twelve." "Yeah," Paul said and laughed. "Yeah, we sure have grew up fast, and we learn so much so quickly." Then Tim said, "I will be glad when this is over, but in a way I will be sad when all this is over, you know what I mean, Paul." Paul said, "I understand what you are saying about the sad part, we will be in school and can't hang out at the clubhouse or go down below to Salter's Creek or hang out with Big Ben." Tim said, "Maybe Big Ben will go to our school and not let his grandmother homeschool him, what do you think of that, Paul." Paul said, "We are here, let's go in and ask the desk officer about the missing kid that was reported. We will tell the officer it was our cousin who was the kid that was missing and was found down by the strip mall, all right, Tim." Tim said, "All right, Paul, I got it, let's go inside." Tim walked up to the desk where the officer was sitting; he didn't even wait for Paul, and that surprised Paul, so Paul just lagged behind Tim. Tim asked the officer about the report about the missing kid that was played on the radio awhile back; the officer looked at Tim, as if he didn't know what he was talking about, then he said, "Young man, there hasn't been any kid missing here for a long time," then Paul said, "His name is Benjamin T. Powell," then the officer said, "Let me check our files," and got up from the desk and walked to a little room with a whole lot of files and went to a big computer inside. Paul and Tim were waiting, holding their breath, hoping that the officer would bring back the answer that they both wanted to hear. Tim whispered in Paul 's ear, "I hope he can find Big Ben in that computer." Paul said, "He won't find him, Tim, I don't think the whole thing ever happen, Tim." Then the officer came back to the desk and sat down to the desk and said, "Is this a joke, kids. There hasn't been one report of a missing kid in nine months, and there is no record of a Benjamin T. Powell, and there are no Powells living in this area. So what are you kids trying to pull." Tim got scared and got up. Paul said, "Sir, we are not trying to pull anything, we were told that Benjamin T. Powell was missing, and one of my friend heard it over the radio station." The officer said, "What station." Paul said his friend didn't hear the ID numbers of the station. The officer said, "Maybe your friend was playing a joke on you guys. So you boys should go and have a laugh with him. Every child is in their right place as of now, this is a small town, and if there was a kid missing, everyone would have none about it, 'specially if it was on the radio, you guys should have realized that." Then Paul said, "Thank you for everything, Officer." Tim was standing in front of the chair, as if he was in a daze. Paul grabbed him by the shirt, and they walked out of the station. After the boys got out of the station, Tim said, "Paul, you were right. I should have listen to you when you said there was something wrong with Big Ben. What are we going to do now, Paul." Then Paul said, "Now we will go down the path and see where does Big Ben goes when he leaves." Then Tim said, "Paul, I am getting chills all over, and I really don't want to go down the path." Then Paul said, "Let's keep talking like we did when we were in the cave. Then we will forget the fear, because I am a little scared too, Tim, but you know we must do this to satisfy all the question." Tim said, "I wonder what those two knuckleheads are doing. Big Ben and Peter." Paul asked Tim, "Are you worried about Peter?" Tim said, "No, somehow I know, this is the way it has to be, it's like it was a plan, but there is something that's on my mind, how do you explain the report I heard over the radio that day." Then Paul said, "Tell me everything that happen that day, Tim." Tim said, "Okay, I woke up," then Paul said, "I didn't mean like everything, just right before you heard that on the radio." Tim said, "Okay, I am glad you stop me, I was just about to tell you about that little bathroom incident," and started laughing. Paul laughed too as they went down the path that Big Ben took. Then Paul said, "Come on, Tim, go on ahead and tell me." "Okay, I was getting dress, I had sleep late that morning, for some reason, I started playing with the knobs on my little radio, I had just started to listen to one of my favorite songs, when all of a sudden I heard a little static, then that's when I heard it, the report about the missing kid, his name, and that he was the grandson of the founding father of this little town we live in and that he was richest kid in town. Then I finished putting on my clothes and ran all the way to the clubhouse. Where I meet you and Peter, remember, Paul." Paul said, "Yep, I remember that." "So what do you make of that, Paul." Paul said, "That's weird for sure." Then Tim said, "We have been walking for a long time down this path, and I don't see any signs of a highway." Paul said, "Let's keep going, but now let's start counting every time we get to one hundred, we say that is fifteen minutes of walking." Then Tim started laughing and put his hand to his knee and laughed some more. Paul said, "What's so funny, you little jug head." Tim said, "Paul, that is a good idea if they hadn't invented watches, oh wise man. I have my watch on my arm," and started back laughing. Then Paul said, "I forgot that, Tim. So you can keep the time, we will walk for two more hours, and, Tim, I am not scared anymore, are you." Tim said, "No, I am not, it is almost fun, I could say it is a adventure, you know I love to explore," and started laughing. Then Paul said, "You are crazy, Tim," and started laughing; they both kept on laughing as they walked down the path. Then Tim started singing that old song, "Who's afraid of this old bear," and laughed and skipped down the path. Then Paul stopped and said, "Now Reno will have to tell us the truth about Big Ben, no more riddles," and started laughing; he thought he had Reno dead to rights. Then Tim stopped and said, "No, Paul, Reno has you. Reno told us to go and find out what was on our hearts and then come back. Do you remember that, Paul." Paul said, "Yep, I remember that. Reno did it to me again, Tim." Tim started back laughing and said, "There's no need in going any further, Paul, we know what we will find, and that is nothing. We should head back, do you agree, Paul." Paul said, "Yep, you know, Tim, all the things we did to find out about Big Ben. Now we realize we didn't have to do those things. For the real truth about Big Ben, it was in front of us all the time. We just couldn't see it because we didn't want to believe it. We both knew that now that kid should know the things that Big Ben knew and did as much as he did." Then Paul started laughing. "Our mind thought it. But our eyes wouldn't let our heart believe it." Tim said, "I think you right, but I also think Reno had a lot to do with it too. It is funny how everything he taught us, now we can see it because we have live it. Reno is one smart guy and a lucky guy too." Then Paul said, "You left out something. He is a lonely guy too. Anyone that has lived as long as he has and seen all the people come and go and he is still here all alone and all you can do is watch and never act on anything you see. He must be awful tired of watching the world go by and can't really do anything about it because you are bound by a promise, but yet through all of that, if anyone has a question, Reno is the only person that can answer your question, and you won't even realize that he has answer it." Then Tim started laughing and said, "That's for sure." Then Paul and Tim started skipping and laughing. Tim started singing a song he made up. "We are mighty men, and I am he-man the mighty." They kept singing that stupid old song, laughing and skipping and laughing, as they made their way to the creek. For they had become aware of the teaching of Reno. Paul said, "Tim, you know what I said early about this summer was like going to school. I was wrong, this has been a adventure and a good one." Tim said, "I never thought of this summer like that. Now that we have accepted what Reno have taught us, this has been one awesome summer." Paul said, "Tim, I can see the creek. Now let's hurry." Tim said, "Yeah, we can still make it to the creek and go down, okay, Paul, let's put it in overdrive," and they started to run faster, laughing and singing that old song of Tim's. Then they came to a stop; they had reached the creek. Paul and Tim could see the steps that led down to the cave. Paul looked at Tim and said, "Are you ready for this." Tim didn't answer Paul. Paul said, "Tim, I know I am a little scared too, I feel the same way, let's wait here for a while." Then Tim said, "No, Paul, we should go, if we wait, it will get harder," then Tim reached out his hand for Paul. Paul didn't want to grab Tim's hand, but he slowly reached out his hand; they started down the steps hand in hand. Slowly the water came over their heads, and they closed their eyes; in their mind they knew when they open them they would see Reno. That feeling alone made them feel good, and they were glad. Then they opened their eyes, and there they found Reno waiting. He was smiling, then he said, "I have been waiting for you guys, I thought you guys would have been here sooner, but I am glad you guys are here," and started laughing, then Paul looked at Tim, and they just stood there looking at each other. Reno just kept on laughing, then Tim said, "Reno, as many times as we have been down here, I have never seen you like this, it's like you are a fire, that's giving off, this warm feeling." Then Paul said, "It's like we are seeing you for the first time. I can understand when you said you have been waiting for us and that you have raised many generation to get to us, and now I can see how happy it makes you." Then Reno asked Tim, "Why was that?" Then Tim said, "Reno, I can see this in you and can see it, when you laugh you can see the life just spilling out of you, Reno, all that time we spent down here I never saw you like the way I see you today, all that time wasted." Then Reno said, "Hear my words, my young friends, as long as you are learning something useful, there is no such thing as wasted time, time is not lost. Now you can see me now because you are ready for the next level." Tim said, "I can feel the excitement, it is almost overpowering." Reno just laughed and laughed. Paul and Tim started laughing too. Then Reno stopped laughing and turned to Paul and Tim as if he was waiting for something. Reno looked more at Tim, then Paul, but then Paul said, "Reno, tell us about Big Ben, we know he not a real boy like us, yes, he look like us, but he is not like Tim and I." Tim said, "Is he one of you guys, why does he look like a boy, is he like a angel or something." Then Reno said, "Are you guys worried about Peter. He is up at the clubhouse with Big Ben, now that you think you know the truth, are you worried what could happen to Peter." Tim said, "Somehow we knew that Big Ben and Peter are suppose to be together. I think they are meant to help each other." Reno laughed and said, "You are using your gift, Tim. Because you are right." Then Paul said, "Tell us more about Big Ben, Reno. You told us early that Big Ben is not like us, but he has the look of a kid, he must have a lot of power, can he make things happen." Tim said, "Can he fly, can he see the future without coming in the cave, and why did he pretend to be a kid." Then Reno said, "If he had come as me, would you have opened up your hearts and be a friend to him." Tim said, "I don't know." Paul said, "I am sure I would have been afraid of him, even coming down the first time to the cave, I was afraid. But Big Ben made everything okay and fun." Reno said, "Big Ben did a real good job. Now, my friends, it's time to go and see what the future holds for you, when the time comes, you will have a second chance to undo what will happen. After you have seen the future of Peter and yourselves and Big Ben, for you boys must make the right choice. Even Big Ben needs this, just as bad as Peter, you will have seven days to make the right choice, and you will have to rely on what you have learned, and Big Ben will no longer be with you, it was hard keeping the truth from you, Paul. We had to keep you off balance and the truth hidden until the time was right, and now you see the truth and know you see how the truth can be hidden, do you remember what I told you boys about the truth." Tim said, "Yes, the truth can't be hidden, but you guys did hide it from us, so you were wrong, Reno." Reno let out a loud laugh and said, "Were we wrong, Paul." And Paul looked at Reno and looked up in the air, as if he was thinking on the words that Reno had just said, and then all at once he let out a loud laugh and said, "Tim, your ears have heard and your eyes have seen, and yet you still do not get it. Tim, remember the row of lights, the one that shine the brightest, that is the truth, but you have to look for the one that shine the brightest, and if it doesn't feel right, then it's not right." Then Tim looked up in the air, as if he was thinking. Paul said, "Look out, Reno, it is going to hit him any minute now," then Tim let out a loud laugh and said, "Now I get it," and they all laughed and pointed at Tim. Paul called him slow to burn, but when he starts, it's out of control, and they laughed for what seemed to be hours. Then Reno said, "It's time. Now we must go and remember, leave your heart at the door, for you shall see Peter's future from start to end, and it will not be pretty, but you must pay close attention to what happens and the way it happens, for what you see will be the answer to save your friend and the innocent ones. I cannot make it no more plainer for you guys, for I have already told you too much and I will be weighed for my disobedience." Then Reno began to walk past the other doors where all the other animals stood by their doors with their eyes open and tears falling from their eyes. Then Wally the catfish walked over to Reno and dropped his head and walked up to Tim and Paul and said, "My young friends, the weight of the world has been put on your shoulders, although they are small but an ant can move a mountain. Just remember, little by little, and look to the wall, my friends, for what hinges on the wall will solve the parable before you. I must go, for we all must be weighed for our disobedience. Tim looked back at Reno and asked, "Why do they cry." Reno looked at him and said, "For every step a man will take on his journey to enlightenment and to know all the good a man can do but won't when the last step is to be made is a time to cry and rejoice, for you guys are about to take your last step in your journey, that is why they cry and bow their heads to you, for you have earned their respect." And with that, Tim and Paul gave them all a smile and slowly started for the cave. They could hear chimes like a song; it was soothing and relaxing. They were ready. Paul and Tim went on in the cave of the future and left their hearts at the door. Then the screen lit up. Then they saw Peter in his room lying on his bed reading a book. He seemed happy; he was laughing as he read the book, then he put the book on the dresser and started to clean his room and put away his toys and games.

Then he stopped and looked at the door. Tim and Paul could hear screaming and yelling coming from Peter's mom's room. Peter dropped what he had in his hand and ran out of the room; he yelled out, "Mom, I am coming, Mom, he won't hurt you, Mom." And Peter ran in their room, his stepdad had his mom down on the bed slapping her. Peter ran and jumped on his stepdad's back and started hitting and scratching and biting his stepdad; his stepdad threw him off his back and said, "You're just like your worthless mom."

He took the belt from his waist and said, "Today, I will teach you to stay out of my business," and he started beating Peter. Peter tried to fight back, but his stepdad was too strong, then his stepdad stopped and went back at Peter's mom. Somehow Peter got up and went at him again, saying, "Leave my mom alone, you pieces of dirt, come on, I am ready for you." Peter grabbed a candleholder from the floor and went after him, saying, "I will kill you." His stepdad came back at him and said, "So you want to be a man today," and raised his hand; the belt was back in his hand. He ripped the shirt from Peter's back and started hitting with the belt; you could see the blisters rise up from the belt, and then he would hit him again and brust them. His back was red with blood everywhere. But Peter didn't cry; his stepdad said, "You think you're tough, but I will break you or kill you today." His mom was in the corner, in a ball like a little kid, rocking from side to side, crying. Tim said, "Why doesn't she try and help Peter and stop that man from beating Peter." Paul didn't say anything; again Tim asked Paul, "Why does she let him beat Peter like that, and she does nothing but cry. Peter came to her rescue, but she can't help him. She is a witch, get up, you witch, and save your son," and he dropped his head. Paul said, "Tim, fear has her, do you remember what Reno said about fear." Tim put his hands to his ears. Then Paul said, "Tim, remember, leave your heart at the door, we can prevent this if we are strong." Tim moved his hand from his ears, and tears slowly ran down his cheek, then the screen stopped, and Reno walked in and said, "Tim, is the weight too heavy for you to bear." Tim said no, wiping away the tears from his face. Tim said, "This is what I must do, I have to draw my strength from my inner star where my love is stored, it will give me the strength to bear this, for I love Peter like he was my brother, and now I understand what you told us about love, Reno." Reno laughed out loud and said, "It is good to watch the fruit of your labor bloom, so beautiful it is. Come, my young friend, and rest before you see any more. Come with me for everyone wants to pay tribute to you guys for you have done good and have come a long way, my friends, for you guys have put what you have learned to use." Then Paul said, "All right, we will follow you, Reno, for it is good that a man should see the reward of his labor." Then Reno said, "Well put, Paul, I could not have said it any better," and Reno led them to another room; as they walked by the others, they were not crying as they were before. Instead they were laughing and saying, "Well done, boys, well done, but there is more to come, stay strong," and they kept on cheering, saying, "Praise to him that is strong, hooray," and Paul and Tim kept on walking with their heads held high; they were on top of the world. Reno led them into this small room. Paul and Tim had to hold their heads down to get in, but Reno just walked straight through as if he shrunk in size. Paul and Tim didn't, even asked what was going on; there were three stonelike chairs, just like all the other rooms, but there was one difference. The chairs did not look as comfortable as the others did. Reno looked at them waiting for some kind of reaction, but Tim and Paul did not show any emotion about the room or the chairs. Reno laughed. Then they walked up to the rough stone chairs and sat down around a large stone table. The table was rough; it wasn't smooth like the other ones, but Tim and Paul did not ask any question about the way things appeared. They knew it was a reason for this, and all they had to do was wait for the answer. They felt good about themselves, for they had learn to wait and all things will be revealed to them. They sat down. Reno looked at them as if he was looking at the soul of them. Tim asked Reno, "Why do you watch us like that, did we do something wrong." Paul looked back at him with the same look. Reno started to laugh and said, "Paul, why do you watch me like that." Paul said, "When you answer Tim, I will answer you, Reno." Reno almost fell out of the chair with laughter. It was as if the whole cave was laughing. They could even hear Wally and Venges laughing, something they had never heard before; there was so much laughter until Tim and Paul started laughing too. The little room was filled with a feeling of love and cheer that made them more stronger, then Tim said, "Will you tell me now, Reno, why were you looking through me, I felt you." Then Reno said, "Before I answer you, tell me, Tim, do you think that it is right to take a man's life, is it right to kill even if you think the man or woman deserves it." Tim said, "Like Peter's stepdad, or someone like that." Reno said, "Yes, tell me what do you think, Tim, and you, Paul, do you have the right." Tim didn't say anything. Paul just looked at Reno. Then Paul said, "It is no one's right. You should never take anything that you can't give back." Reno said, "Those sound like the words of your father." Paul said, "Yes, those words were told to me when my father talked to me about sex and girls, and now

I realize it fits now and my father was right, that is the way it should be in life." Tim started laughing and said, "Paul has a girlfriend." Paul said, "No, silly, my father was just telling me about the birds and the bees and to take a girl's virtue is wrong if you have no intention of staying for life with her and the same with a woman. Because the first time should be with someone that you truly love with your heart and not with the flesh because once you have taken it and realize that you do not love her, you cannot return what you have taken, her virtue." Then Reno said, "Paul, you have opened your mind and heart, soon you and Tim will know the reason why you are here, and on this day, the sun will not set until you, Paul, and you, Tim, have learned all that you should know, and I will answer all of your questions you have asked me over the months, starting with the last one first, all that I ask of you is that you pay close attention to the answer, because at the end of today, I will give you your last parable. This parable will be the answer to prevent what will happen, we already have told you to watch carefully when you were in the hall of the future, that still is in effect. Know, Tim, I will answer your question early, when you asked me why was I looking through you. I was looking at the colors of your soul to see if what you had just seen had changed you." Then Tim asked, "Was that the reason why you ask me was it okay to take someone life. But if you saw my soul, you already knew the answer." Reno said, "Yes, Tim, I knew the answer, and I already knew what Paul was going to say. In life, you will learn that a man will say a lot of things that are different from what his heart and soul says and what he believes in. In that man, you'll find a divided and confused a man." Then Tim said, "What am I, Reno." Reno said, "You have yet to answer, your soul has no color the same as Paul. Even though he gave a great answer. As I knew he would but those were the words of his father. Right know, Paul is divided, he wants to live the words of his father. But the love he feels for Peter doesn't let him live those words of his father. But I will say this to you, before this is over, you both will have become whole and you will not be able to hide your colors of your soul. Now the time grows near that you might return to the room of the future. But I must tell you this, you heard me speak of your fathers and that they were here and their fathers before them. As I told you, we have raised many of generations to get to you. The reason is we have been watching the men of your world for many of your years and we realized many years ago that man will never reach that higher level of life due to all the evil snares of the world that man has placed before himself, the temptation will be too great for man. In the days to come, the world you know now will change, the people will be consumed with all the things I have warned you of. I have told you of many things like greed, hatred, lust, fame, war, and all the things that a man should not hold to. Man will forget God in the coming years and make his own law, and women and men will even become lovers of themselves, forsaking all. The family values and the innocent ones will be lost and forgotten, even with all of that, man will not destroy the world, they will only make their time shorter here. Your God will be the one that brings an end to all of those things. Until your God comes, there must be people in place to prepare the way and to protect and help and to guide the innocent ones and to help pass new laws to protect them. Just as your fathers, you guys will not remember us when you have finished your task which is at hand, but if the time should come when we need help all that have passed through will remember all that we have taught them. Remember this, change is brought on by one person, not an army, you guys will be that match, you will do the same for the innocents one's so that they want be forgotten are lost to the world for that is one of the reason you guys had to learn all those lesson when you guys have finished this task and your memory of us is gone you will relearn all the things we taught you on your way to manhood just as your fathers but I remind you of this again if we have need of you guys you shall remember all, that will ignite the flames of the fire that burns in every innocent one to stand up and speak out so they want be forgotten, that is the reason why you guys had to learn all those lessons is for this task that is at your footsteps and so that all the things we have done won't be for nothing, remember Peter is only one part of a whole. For what has happened should not have happened. Peter's father should not have died. The forces of evil took him and put an evil one in his place, that is one of the reasons why Peter is so important, and the other reasons I cannot tell you at this time. Now we must move on to more important things. You guys must work together to tackle this task that is put before you and remember that love is the key to all things, now I cannot tell you any more until you finish watching in the cave of the future, if I were to tell you more, you would not understand it now. Right now you guys must prepare yourselves, for we must return to the room." And Reno got up, so did Paul, but Tim was slow in moving, then Tim said, "Reno, how many children will I have." Reno laughed and said, "Tim, you must come, don't delay what has to be you cannot stall for more time, now come." Tim got up, and Paul and Tim slowly walked to the cave of the future. They did not walk as tall as they did when they were leaving the cave, nor were there any music playing in the background, or nor were there any animals outside their doors. Then they reached the door. Tim stopped for a moment and stood in front of the door. Then Paul said, "Tim, we must." Then Paul reached out for his hand. Tim and Paul went inside the cave, and the screen lit up, and they picked up where it left off with the beating and the licks. Peter still wasn't crying; he was taking the licks. His mom was still in the corner in a ball with her hands to her head still crying. Tim still was saying, "She is a bad mom." Paul again said, "No, Tim, she is full of fear." Then Peter's dad reverses the belt and said, "You will cry this time." Peter's mom jumped up and ran out of the room; just when Peter's dad was going to hit Peter with the buckle, his mom came back into the room with a knife. She started stabbing Peter's stepdad over and over again, saying, "I have watched you beat my child for years," as she stabbed him; he fell back on the bed. But that didn't stop her; she came at him again and stabbed him again. "This is for Peter, cry, you bastard, you big pieces of dirt," she yelled at him as she stabbed him; she went on stabbing him, saying, "Never again will you hurt my son again." Then she dropped the knife and went back in the corner and curled up in a ball, saying, "I killed him, Peter baby, I killed him, oh my god, what have I done," and she burst into tears, then Peter ran over to where his mom dropped the knife and picked up the knife and started stabbing his stepdad, saying, "You won't beat me or my mom anymore." Then Peter's mom got up and took the knife from Peter and went out of the room into the kitchen and washed the knife off and went into the bathroom and got a towel and started wiping Peters hand's off, then she went into his room and got him a different shirt and grabbed him and put the shirt on him and took Peter to the corner where she had been crying and started hugging Peter. She was holding Peter in her arm, saying, "I am sorry, son, you tried to protect me, but I didn't protect you, forgive me, my son, I love you. Son, we have to leave this place, son." Then they heard a knock at the door; it was the police. Peter's mom just lost it; she just started shaking and yelling. Peter got up and ran to the door and said, "My mom needs help." The police came inside; only one of the officers went into the room. The other one said that he would call it in; once the officer got inside and saw Peter's stepdad lying in a pool of blood, he ran back outside and called for the other officer to come inside. Once the officer got inside, he asked Peter what happened. Peter told the officer everything. Peter had started talking, and he told the officer everything, all how his stepdad beat him and his mom. Then Peter's mom got up; the officer put his hand to his gun, then he asked, "Who stabbed this man?" Peter said he did it, still trying to protect his mom, then his mom said, "No, he didn't do anything, he is just trying to protect me like he has always done," then the officer took out his handcuffs. His mom started acting crazy; she started screaming. The officer pulled out his gun. Peter said, "Please don't shoot her, let me talk to her." The officer told the other one to get Peter out of the room and started toward his mom, but Peter broke loose from the officer and ran to his mom; she started crying and said, "I am sorry, son, it was all my fault if I would have done something earlier, this would have never happen. I was too weak, son. Don't ever be weak, son." Peter said, "I won't, Mom, you know that, I will never be weak," then the officer came back at Peter and took him out of the room. Then the officer asked Peter's mom, "Is there anyone that can take your son?" The officer told Peter's mom that she would have to come downtown to the station. "You probably won't be charged, but you will have to come with us." Peter's mom didn't say anything; she was only saying, "I am sorry, son," over and over again. The officer said, "Miss, do you hear me, if you do, tell us who do you want us to place the child with, or we will have to call the office of child services, and they will take the child, and it will be harder for you to get him back, do you understand me." But she said nothing, only "I am sorry, son" over and over again. Then the officer put the handcuffs on her and sat her on the bed and went where the other was and said, "We need to call for a medical wagon for her. And call children services for the boy." "They can come to the hospital and take him from there," the other officer said. Then Peter said, "What are you guys talking about." The officer said, "We're talking about your mom. We are going to take her to the hospital to be checked out and then to the station for more questions." Then Peter went crazy, trying to pull away from the officer, crying, saying, "Please don't take her to jail." He pulled up his shirt and showed the officers the marks on his back that his stepdad had put on him. The officer said, "Oh my god, son, that guy got just what he needed."

Then Paul turned away from the screen and said to Tim, "I can answer that question that Reno ask us." Tim said, "Yes, I can too." Paul said, "Yes, Tim, some people need to be killed, but not by the hands of man. Do you agree, Tim." Tim said, "For every bad seed that a man cast, that's what he shall weep." Paul turned and looked at him and said, "Are those your words, Tim." Tim said, "Yep, those are my words, even if they sound like Reno's words." Paul said, "Yep, they do, I think he's rubbing off on us." Then they heard a loud noise saying, "Praise be to them that has been enlightened," and the screen stopped, and Reno came into the room and said, "I see the colors, and I also see that you boys have left your heart at the door and the colors of your soul are shining brightly, and the answer that you all have given is the right one, you boys have just crossed over to a new outlook on life. What I have trying to point out if you are dealing with anything that hurts in order to see it clearly you must leave your heart at the door to do the right thing and to be able to see. I am glad for you guys. Now you must finish watching the screen, for now the beating that you have seen Peter take does not hurt you guys the same way it did when you first saw it." Tim said, "Your right, I didn't realize that, Reno." And Paul said, "Yep, Reno, we can now watch it without the pain." Then Reno said, "Now you shall see," and then he left the little room. When the screen came back on again, Paul and Tim saw Peter sitting in the backseat of the police car. Tim could see that Peter had calm down some, but he was still crying. Tim could see the tears rolling down his face. Peter was wiping the tears with his shirt and shaking his head, and then he put his head in his hand and dropped his head. Then the officer came out of the house with Peter's mom in handcuffs; she was crying and struggling to get free, then Paul looked at the screen again and saw Peter in the back seat. He was going crazy, banging on the windows, and screaming, "Let my mom go," then Peter laid on his back and started kicking at the car window, crying and screaming, then one of the officers went over to calm Peter down; he walked over and opened the door. Peter was still lying on his back, so when the officer opened the door, Peter kicked him, and he fell back a little, then he came back, saying, "Calm down," and reached in to grab Peter, but Peter pushed him and grabbed his gun and told the officer to get the hell back. The officer slowly moved back, saying, "Son, you don't know what you are doing, please don't do this, give me the gun." Peter said, "I will give you what is inside the gun, if you don't let my mom go." Peter was crying and shaking, holding the gun with one hand and wiping the tears with the other hand. When the other officer realized what was going on with Peter, he pushed Peter's mom to the ground and pulled out his gun; the other yelled out, "Don't shoot, you don't want to kill a little boy, because you will never get over it. Let me talk to him." The officer said, "Okay, Dave, I won't shoot, but if he cocks that gun, I will have to take him out, I can't let him shoot you or me or his self, got that, Dave." Then Peter yelled over to the officer that was standing over his mom and said, "Let her go, or I will kill Mr. Dave." "I will," Tim said in a low voice. The officer yelled out to Peter, "Put the gun down, you little fool, don't be stupid. Don't make me kill you, Peter." Tim dropped his head and looked away, and then he looked at the screen again, then Tim saw Peter pull back the trigger on the gun and closed his eyes. Tim could see Officer Dave turn his head. Dave looked back at the other officer that was standing over Peter's mom and gave him the sign not to rush Peter, but the officer didn't give him the sign back to Dave. Dave dropped his head and said, "Don't do this, son," then Peter put his other hand on the gun. He started crying more and said, "Your name is Dave, my real dad was named Dave." Then Dave, the officer, held up his head and said, "Yes, that is my name, the name I was born with, and tonight it will be the name I will die with. Peter, we are just doing our job, no harm will come to your mom, I promise." Peter didn't say anything, then Peter put the trigger back and took one hand off the gun, but he kept it pointed at Officer Dave. Then Dave said, "I understand you, son," then Peter said, "Don't call me, son." Then Dave said, "Okay, your name is Peter." Then Dave went on to tell Peter about his mom and how he had to be the man of the house and help with his little sister and did not get a chance to do the things that the other kids did. Then Peter got mad again, saying, "You don't know anything about me or my mom." And he yelled back over to the officer, "Let her go. I am not going to tell you again." Then Paul said to Tim, "I don't know how much more of this I can watch, for sure Peter is going to get killed." Then he reached out his hand for Tim's hand, then they heard more sirens; there were three more police cars coming, then Dave said, "Please, Peter, give me the gun." Peter said, "No. You will have to kill me first." Then other officers got out of their cars with the guns out. Dave yelled over to them, "Stand down." But no one was listening; they all pointed their guns at Peter. Tim closed his eyes and yelled out, "I don't want to see this." And he started crying; he tried to pull loose from Paul's hand, but Paul held tight and said, "They are not going to shoot him, Tim." Paul cried out, "It's Peter's mom." Somehow she had gotten free from the officer and was walking toward Peter. The officer yelled to Dave to get down, but instead Dave stood up, right in front of Peter. Peter's mom was crying and saying, "I love you, Peter, and I am sorry, you don't have to protect me now, Peter." And she started running faster toward Peter, but Peter didn't see her coming until she was right up on him; she reached for the gun, but Peter did not realize it was his mom and held tight the gun. The gun went off; she fell right at his foot. It was the strangest thing. None of the officer fired their guns; it all happened so fast. Peter, realizing what he had done, pointed the gun at Dave again, then you could hear all them pulling back the triggers of their guns. Dave dropped his head. Peter was screaming, "Look at what you made me do. You made me kill my mom, and all you had to do was just let us go. I am going to kill you now." He put his other hand on the gun. All of the officers were crying out, "Please don't do it, son, we don't want to kill you." Then Peter stopped and said, "Now there's nothing here for me, my mom is dead, my father is dead, so I might as well be dead too," and he pointed the gun at his head. Paul cried out for Reno. Paul said, "Reno, we don't want to see any more, please stop this," and grabbed Tim and hugged him tight. Then they started singing, "The sweet chariot of God is coming to take Peter home," and started crying. They both were crying; they were not watching the screen anymore. Then Paul said, "What do we have to do to keep this from happening, tell us." They both started calling for Reno, but Reno did not come, then Tim said, "Look, Paul." Peter was still holding the gun to his head, but they saw his mom move her arm; she was trying to get up. She was covered in blood. This time it was her own blood. She got to her knees and grabbed the gun from Peter's hand and threw it to the ground and said, "Son, you will never have to protect me again, I should have been the one protecting you," and she put her hand over his head and hugged him. The officers ran in fast and tried to grab Peter from his mom. She started fighting with the handcuffs still on her, saying, "Leave him alone," but she went limp with her arm still around Peter. The officer ran up and took the cuffs off her and said, "She is still alive." "That's one tough lady," one of the officer said. Then one of the officers came up and slammed Peter to the ground and pulled back his hand and put the cuff on him. Dave said, "Come on, man, he's just a kid. There's no cause for that." The officer told Dave, "That's why you got your gun taken by this little kid, you're too soft," and he picked Peter up by the pants while Dave just stood there watching. He put Peter in the backseat again and told him, "If you try that with me, I will come back and tie your feet and put a rag in your mouth." Then he closed the door and went back over to Dave to find out how all of this happened. Dave was waiting for him with all the rest of the officers. Dave asked, "Had anyone called for a medical wagon?" One of the officers said, "Yes, it's on the way." Then Dave went on to plead his case for Peter; he told all the officers, "This is not a bad kid, he was just confused and scared and trying to protect his mom, give him a break, don't take him to juvenile, those kids will eat him up. Even when he was pointing the gun, he still said 'yes, sir,' and 'mister' and 'please,' he was real respectful. He was not going to shoot me, you all know that, he had plenty of chances. Let's just call the children service to take him, I will take him, let it be on me." Then one of the officers said, "Dave, why are you willing to put your whole career up for this kid." Then Dave said, "I was a kid once, and if I had went through what this kid have been through, with the abuse of his stepdad. Have you guys seen his back and stomach and legs, his whole body looks like a pincushion. What if it was your son and you were not here to watch out for him. Wouldn't you want someone to give him a break." Then his partner said, "Dave, I agree with you, you can make the call, I am with you, but I can't speak for the rest of the guys." Then Dave put out his hand and said, "What about it, guys, will you all look the other way." Then they all said, "I don't know what you're talking about. When we got here, it was all over." Dave walked over to the car and called for child services. Then he walked over to Peter and opened the door, but he did not take the cuffs off. Dave said, "Peter, your mom is going to be all right, you hit her in the shoulder, the ambulance is on the way. Now listen to me, Peter. I know you are not a bad kid. I stood up for you. The other officer wanted to take you to jail. But I talked to them, and they are willing to do things my way. Now, Peter, here is the deal, we will put you in foster care until your mom gets better, but you have to promise me you will act right and no more crazy stuff. No more fighting and cursing and all that other stuff, all right, son." This time Peter didn't tell Dave not to call him son; instead Peter asked him, "Why are you doing this. I heard what you said to the other policemen, and you were right, Mr. Dave, I was scared, I didn't know what to do, and I didn't want to be alone, and I could feel that you are telling me the truth, and I believe you, I know you will do all that you can for me and my mom." Then Dave said, "Peter, there is something that I didn't tell you. I grew up here. This is where I was raised, when I was a little boy in school all the other kids uses to call me the hand-me-down boy. My family was dirt poor, my mother could not read or write her own name, and my father died when I was eight years old, when he was alive, he showed me plenty of love, and we always had something to eat and new clothes, but when my father died, my mom had to work in the fields picking bean and peas and working in packing house packing vegetables, my mother did not make that much money. She had to take other people's old clothes that they were going to throw away and fix them for us, those other kids that used to call me names were mean and hateful except for one kid, that kid treated me with respect and used to let me come over and play with his toy and games, and sometimes I would spend the night, and his mom would watch my brothers and sister when my mom had to work late or go to work. Do you know that kid's name. It was the same as mine." Then Peter said with a smile, "My dad." Dave said, "Yes, we lived next door to your dad and grandmother and grandfather. We stayed there for a while. Then my mom met my stepdad, and we moved away. Me and your father stayed good friends, we wrote to each other every week. He was my only friend and my best friend, I remember the last letter I got from your father. He had just finished high school, your dad was on his way to New York to go to college, after that, we didn't write that much, and as time went on, we lost track of each other, the last I heard of your father someone told me that he got married to this black lady. His parents hated it and disowned him, and I heard the girl's parents did the same to her. Later I heard that they had a little boy together. I always wanted to visit him, and I had planned on it, but I heard that he had an accident and died, so I guess I am doing this for him. I am sorry, Peter, if I would have known you and your mom had moved here that pieces of dirt of a stepdad would have never put his hand on you, I can guarantee you that that lowlife, your mom did the right thing, I am glad she killed him, and I promise you, Peter, she will not go to jail." Then Peter said to Officer Dave, "Can you take the handcuffs off. I promise not to take your gun. I just want to give you a big hug. Now I feel better, and I am not alone." Paul and Tim started dancing around and signing, "We know what to do. We know what to do for Peter and his mom, hooray for Officer Dave." Then Reno walked in the room and said, "My, how the mood has changed." Then Tim said, "Reno, we know what to do for Peter and his mom, all we have to do is to find Officer Dave, and he will take care of Peter's stepdad, that's for sure." Then Reno said, "My young friends, sometimes in life the simplest answer is not the right one, ask yourselves this, you heard the words of Officer Dave, there was emotion in his words, but most of all there was anger. Now what do you think Officer Dave would do to Peter's stepdad." Tim said, "Kill that jerk." Reno said, "You're right, Tim, and that's not good, because more innocent people will be affected. Officer Dave would go to jail, and his children would not have a father, and his wife would not have a husband, and friends of Officer Dave would be affected too, their wives and their children would be hurt, and that would not be right." Tim said, "No, Reno, that would not be right to put that many people through all that pain." Then Reno said, "Paul, by your own words, that would be wrong. Do you remember." Paul said, "No, Reno, I don't remember saying anything like that." Then Reno started laughing. Then he stopped and said, "Paul, it was when I asked you does anyone have the right to take the life of another. Even if it is a person like Peter's stepdad. Do you remember now." Paul said, "Yep, I remember, and I still believe that" Then Reno said, "Why would you and Tim plan to murder Peter's stepdad. By using Officer Dave like a gun, it would be true, you and Tim wouldn't be the one who committed the murder, but you and Tim would be the cause of it, and that is the same as doing it. Dave will be one of the keys to this puzzle, but not the main key that will set Peter and his mom free. Everything must be done in order, and there is only one way, and it is the way we have planned it to be, because we are at war with the evil things of your world. We have to be careful not to fall into the traps of the ones that the forces of evil have set for us. For we have already lost Peter's dad too soon. Tim, do you know what war I am talking about." Tim said, "Yes, you mean the war overseas and all the innocent people that have been killed for no reason." Paul said, "No, Tim, how stupid can you be. He means the war of good and bad, the unseen battle that's going on every day." Tim said, "I didn't think of that." Reno smiled and said, "Many of men don't think of that war," and he turned and started out of the room, and Paul said, "Wait, Reno, why didn't you come when we call you when Peter was at one of his low point, we needed you. We really wanted you to come," then Reno said, "You didn't need help, and you didn't need me, you were not chained to a chair, and you were not locked in this room. No one made you stay in the room of the future, but you stayed, and it was not fear that held you in the room, it was love, and that is a good thing, now you see that love is stronger than fear. Take this as another life lesson learned." And he left the room, and the screen came back on. They saw Peter sitting in the front seat of the police car. It was pulling up in front of this big building. Tim said to Paul, "Looks like Peter got a break. But it is too early to tell." And Paul and Tim looked back at the screen and saw Peter and Officer Dave walking up to the door of this big building; a big man answered the door. He was wearing a suit; he was big and tall and fat, but not too overweight, just big. Tim said to Paul, "Peter better be good, because that guy is a giant." Then Paul said, "Right, that guy is big, but Peter can take him, with Officer Dave's gun and smile." Then they looked at the screen again and saw Peter and Officer Dave going in the door. Then Reno came back in the room and said to Paul and Tim, "From this point on, you will not see everything that happened to Peter, because time will not allow it to be so. So you will only see bits and pieces of Peter's future, only the parts that mean something to you, but be of good cheer, what you see will not be all good. For you, we see greed and lust and all the bad things the world has to offer. These things a child should not see, but this you guys must see in order to save Peter and yourselves. You guys have done well thus far, but there is still more pain for you to see, what you guys have learned will help you through this. And pay close attention to Peter's appearance, for his face will change through the hard times he will go through. But of all things, remember you guys have left your heart at the door and watch this with your eyes and mind and make no images of what you have not seen when the door is closed. You, Tim, and you, Paul, asked me no question, for you will get no answer." And then Reno left the room, and the screen came back on. They saw Officer Dave talking to the big guy, but they didn't see Peter. They heard Officer Dave ask the big guy had he had any luck in placing Peter in foster care. The big guy said no, whose name was Bill. Officer Dave said, "It has been two weeks." Then Bill the big guy said, "It could be even longer. I was hoping that Peter's mom would get better." Then Officer Dave dropped his head and started kicking at the carpet and said, "I don't want to think about her, but I guess, I will have to. So I might as well tell you Peter's mom is doing fine from the shot in her shoulder, will be well enough to go home, but she won't be going home, her mind is gone, all she has been saying is "Peter, I am sorry and I love you, Peter" over and over again. When she leaves, she will going to a mental hospital, and you know when you go in one of those places, you don't come out that easy." Then Bill dropped his head and said, "Are you going to tell Peter." Officer Dave said, "I don't know what I am going to do, I know I should tell him, but I don't know. If there was just a way to help him keep the faith, if Peter loses his hope and knows that there's a big chance that his mom won't be coming for him, he might try and hurt himself, or something worse. That's why I need to find a way to help him to hold on. I have an idea, why don't you have Peter write a letter to his mom, and you or I will answer him back, all we have to do is read the first letter and go from there." Officer Dave dropped his head and put his hand on top of his head and started shaking from side to side and said, "If we do this, we will have to pay for what we'll do one day, but for now, we must live for the day, so let's do this." But then Bill asked Officer Dave a question, "Why don't you take Peter home with you." Officer Dave dropped his head very low and said, "I am ashamed, and I wish I could do it, but I already have three kids of my own, and we live in a two-room house, and I just don't have the money for another kid, I wish I could do it, and my wife will have a problem with Peter's color, he's half black, and she will not want him around our kids, she is stuck in the forties. When I married her, I did not know she was a racist, if I would have known that, I would have never touched that witch, if it wasn't for our kids we have together, I would leave her in a blink of an eye, but, Bill, I don't want to talk about that anymore." Then Bill said, "I can see that this has put a lot of pressure on your relationship, and one day it will break up your home, if you let it. So we need to find Peter a good place, so you can put this behind you. There's something I have to tell you about Peter, he had an accident last night, some of the bigger boys jumped him and roughed him up pretty bad." Officer Dave said, "Was it Peter's fault." Bill said, "No, Peter didn't even fight back, he didn't even let out a sound, he took all the licks they had to offer." Then officer Dave said, "We have to get him out of here, because he will never fight back or try to protect himself, he made a promise to me that he wouldn't fight, and he won't." Then Bill said, "Don't get angry when you see him, it is not as bad as it looks, I have already dealt with those boys, they won't be bothering Peter anymore." But Officer Dave said, "Yea, those boys won't, but what about the next boys that want to have some fun with the new kid, 'cause they know he will not fight back." Bill dropped his head. Tim told Paul, "I do not want to see Peter like that," and put his hand to his eyes. But just then the screen jumped. Then Paul saw Peter sitting on a bed reading a letter. Tim said, "That must be the letter from Officer Dave or Bill." Then Paul said, "Tim, we are not suppose to make any assumption of what Peter is reading or what he will do when the screen jump, remember that is what Reno said, Tim." Then Tim said, "I remember, I won't do that again, Paul. He looks good, no scars." Then Paul said, "Yea, on the outside he look like old Peter, just as mean as ever," and they both smiled, then they saw a lady come into the room. Tim said, "She looked mean," then she said to Peter, "Get off that bed and put away that old letter away and clean this room, you lazy do-for-nothing kid," puffing on a cigarette. Peter put away the letter and picked up pieces of blank paper and sat back on the bed. Then the lady came back in the room and snatched the paper from his hand and ripped it up and said, "No food for you tonight, you lazy good-for-nothing," and pushed him off the bed. "This room better be clean when I come back." Then Tim said, "Paul, I don't see anything wrong with his room." And Paul said, "Tim, for once you're right. I think that old bag just doesn't like Peter." Then the screen jumped again. They saw Peter in this white van pulling up to this old brick house; a man in a suit got out of the van and walked up to the door and rang the doorbell. A baldhead fat guy answered the door; they shook hands, and they both looked back at the van, then the guy that drove the van came back for Peter and took him inside. They saw a lady in a wheelchair; she had long black-and-white hair and kind of skinny, with a dirty white dress on. The man that drove the van had them to sign some papers. The fat guy showed Peter to his room and said, "I will be back later, sweetie," and went back to where the lady and the guy that drove the van were sitting over by the TV. They all shook hands, and the guy that drove the van left. The lady in the rolling chair was over by the TV, and the fat man sat in a chair by the lady and started watching TV for a while. Then he got up and gave the lady some pills. He sat there for a while, then the lady fell asleep. Then the man got up and went over to Peter's room; he opened the door and said, "I told you I would be back, sweetie. It's time we got to know each other, and this is the way things are going to be, and close the door." They heard Peter saying, "Get away from me, you freak, don't do that, put your clothes back on," and he screamed. Then the screen jumped. Tim didn't say anything; neither did Paul. They both dropped their heads. You could see the tears falling from their eyes, but they didn't cry, and they did not try to imagine what happened to Peter in the room. Tim looked at the screen again and saw the same white van parked in front of a house. Tim said, "That looks like the same house, where the old lady with that same old dirty white dress and the old bald fat guy." Paul said, "It looks like the house, Tim." Then Paul said, "That is the house." Then Paul said, "Look, Tim, there's the old fat guy at the door." But when Tim looked, he didn't see the old fat guy. Instead, Tim saw police cars coming; they pulled up to the house and got out fast and went up to door and went inside. They didn't see what was going on in the house. Tim said to Paul, "I want to ask what is going on inside. But I won't, and I won't wonder what it is, so I will cover my eyes so I don't see anymore." Tim was scared that Peter was dead; that old man killed Peter, or Peter killed him or the old lady. Those things were on Tim's mind, but he didn't say that to Paul; he only covered his eyes. Then Paul said, "Look, Tim, that old bald-headed fat man is coming out, and he is in handcuffs." That made Tim shut his eyes tighter; now he knew Peter was dead. Tim wanted to cry, but he didn't. Paul told him to open his eyes, but Tim didn't. Then Paul said, "Tim, look, they are bringing that old lady out, and she is in handcuff too." Then Paul said, "Tim, I know what you are doing, you are doing just what Reno told us not to do, imagining what went on with Peter, you have to stop that, Tim, you are only hurting yourself. Now look at the screen, Peter might be coming out next." They both waited watching the screen, but no Peter. Then the screen went off; they both said, "What happened to Peter." Then the screen came back on, and they saw the same white van in front of this beautiful house, with dark green grass all over the yard. With a white fence all around the house, there were two little kids playing in the yard, a boy and girl. The little boy looked to be about seven or eight; the little girl looked to be about five or six. Then they saw a lady coming out of the house. "She was pretty," Tim said; she walked up to the gate and stood there looking down the street like she was waiting for someone. Then they saw that white van pulling up in front of the house. Tim said, "Here comes that log-headed Peter." A man got out with a briefcase and a tall kid got out. Tim and Paul could not see the kid's face; he had curly brownish hair and a big head and big ears like Peter, but they were not sure. Paul said, "Could that be Peter." Tim said, "No, it's too tall for Peter." Then Paul said, "If that's not Peter. Then what happen to Peter." Tim said, "Maybe that old guy and old lady kill Peter, that's why the police was at that house." Paul said, "Peter is not dead, I don't believe it, Tim. Let's just watch the screen and see what happens, all right." Tim said, "Okay." Then they looked at the screen and saw the tall kid get out of the van and open the gate; he had turned his back to them and started to go inside, and they still didn't see his face. Tim said, "He's taller than you, Paul, he probably could take you, Paul." Paul laughed and said, "If that's Peter, he wouldn't stand a chance," and they both laughed a little. Then they heard the lady say, "Welcome, Peter," as he was going inside. Paul and Tim just looked at each other and looked back at the screen. The lady gave Peter a hug, but Peter didn't hug her back; he kept his arm to the side. It looked like Peter was sleepwalking. Tim couldn't see his face yet, but Tim said, "He looks like he's lost and lonely." Tim dropped his head for a moment, then he looked back at the screen. The lady told Peter to go inside, and then he turned, and they saw his face. Tim said, "He sure looks bad, Paul, look how sad he looks." Peter started walking toward the front door; the little boy threw his ball and said, "Catch," but Peter didn't even try and catch the ball. It hit him in the stomach; the little boy ran over and picked up the ball and said, "I am sorry. Maybe later," and went back to playing with the little girl. The lady told Peter to go on inside the house again. "Make yourself at home, my house is your house for as long as you want it." Tim said, "Maybe this will be the one, a good home. I wish Peter didn't look so helpless." Tim was remembering Peter at the clubhouse how happy he was, so was Paul; he reached out and grabbed Tim's hand and said, "This hasn't happen yet, Tim. Let's finish looking at the screen." But Paul began to wonder about Tim; how would he act when they got back to the clubhouse where Peter would be waiting, but Paul pushed his thought aside and started back watching the screen with Tim. The lady was still at the gate with the van driver, she was signing some papers for Peter. Then the van driver told her, "Good luck with that one, he's a strange kid, he never said a word the whole trip here. He didn't even ask where was he going. I don't believe he can talk," and he started laughing. Tim could see that the lady did not like what the man said. She answered the van driver, "Maybe Peter didn't like the company he was in. Good day to you, sir." Then the man said, "I am leaving, but mark my words, you will regret this." The lady turned to go inside of the house, and the little boy came up to her and said, "Mom, what's wrong with Peter, doesn't he like us," and the little girl came over too and said, "Yea, Mom, what wrong." She gave them a big hug and said, "Peter is sick." The little girl said, "He doesn't look sick." The lady said, "This kind of sickness you can't see it. Peter has a broken heart, and his soul is weak, he has given up on people and life. He has suffered so much in the past, he has been bounced from foster home to foster home and has been used and abused for four years and has no one to love him, and no one is worth his love he feels. So it's up to us to try and show him love and let him know that there are still good people in the world. This will be my hardest case ever, this is where all my training will be called on. So, kids, you will have to be brave and strong and don't give up on him and help me to watch him, okay, guys, can you be strong for Mommy." They said yes. Then she gave them a hug and said, "Go and play, let me go inside and check on Peter." Then the screen went blank. Tim turned to Paul and said, "It doesn't seem like we have watching this, for four years of Peter's life, and now he is sixteen years old, no more little kid with dreams being a star." Paul said, "Tim, why did you say that." Tim said, "It's the look on Peter's face, for sure he has stop dreaming." Before Paul could say anything, Reno came into the room. And Reno said, "You guys have done well this far of your journey, and you have suffered plenty. You have awakened feelings and emotions that you didn't even know you had. But there is more to come. I came here to prepare you for what you will see and to let you know that the feeling that you will have is normal for mortal man. So don't be ashamed and feel low, for all the feelings that you will feel is the right thing. Now I must go." And he turned and left the room. Then Tim said to Paul, "Did Reno seem upset to you, Paul." Paul said, "He sounds like the same confusing guy I have known." Tim said, "I don't know, but something is different about him."

While they were talking, the screen came back on; they both turned and looked at the screen. They saw Peter coming back into the house and going down the hall to the bathroom; he was walking real slow and soft like he was trying to sneak past everyone. He came out with his hand in his pocket; he yelled out toward the next room, "Mrs. K, I am going to the park to do some reading and relaxing for a while." Mrs. K was the lady's name whom Peter was staying with. She yelled back, "Okay, Peter, but don't stay out there too long, you keep track of the time, you know how you lose track of time when you're out there at that park and be careful, baby." Peter said, "All right, Mrs. K." Mrs. K was in the next room playing with the other kids. Peter started out of the room, but he stopped, like he wanted to say something else, but he didn't; he turned and went out of the house. Then the screen stopped. Tim and Paul looked around for Reno, but he was nowhere to be found. Tim said, "That's funny, Reno always come." When the screen came on, they saw the little girl come out the room and go to the bathroom; she didn't stay in there long. She ran out yelling, "Mom, Mom." Mrs. K came out of the room where she was playing with the kids; she met the little girl in the doorway of the bedroom. The little girl pointed to the bathroom. Mrs. K ran to the bathroom; she went inside, and she screamed out, "Peter, oh my god, why, Peter, why." And she ran out and ran back to the bedroom where the kids were; she grabbed the little boy and said, "Son, you have to go, son, and try and catch Peter, you must run as fast you can. Do not stop for anyone, if you hear someone call your name, do not stop, keep running, you must not stop, keep running, can you do it, son." The little boy said, "Yes, Mom," then she said, "Peter won't do anything as long as you are with him, and once you catch him, stay with him and don't let him out of your sight." She gave him a hug and a pat on the back, and the little boy was off and running. Then Mrs. K put her hands to her head and started shaking and pulling her hair, then she took her hand and made a fist and punched herself in the head and said, "Oh my god, what have I done, I don't want my son to see Peter if he has already done it. Oh my god, I have to catch my son." She ran out the front door with the little girl. But she knew she could not catch her son with the little girl, so Mrs. K went to the neighbor and knocked on the door, but no one answered; she was stomping her feet, then she heard someone say, "Just a minute." She told her daughter to stay right there and when the door opened to go inside and stay there until she returned with her brother. The little girl said, "Mom, save Peter, I love him just like he was my real big brother." Mrs. K almost started crying, but she didn't; she jumped off the porch running. She could see her son running; he was almost at the park. He was running like the wind; she felt like she couldn't catch him. She started crying and started saying to herself, *How could I have been so stupid, Peter fooled me, why didn't I see that, I made a big mistake, I even put my own child in danger, I am stupid.* And she fell to the ground and said, "Lord, I made a mistake with Peter, because I was blinded by all the bad things that happened in his life, and I was so proud of myself of what I thought I had accomplished with Peter, I was too egotistical. I thought I did something that no one else could do. I was stuck on myself, and I didn't see the warning signs, please, Lord, give me the strength to catch my son." She got up and started running; she was running like the wind, like she had wings on her feet. She could see that she was getting closer to her son; she yelled for him to stop, but it seemed like he got faster. I tell you that kid really could move. Mrs. K kept on running, screaming his name. His name was Bobby. Mrs. K kept on screaming his name, crying and running. She could see the people in their cars looking at them wondering what was going on. But she didn't care what people thought; the only thing she wanted to do was to catch her son, and that is what she was trying to do. Mrs. K was almost in reaching distance to her son; she knew Bobby was close to the gate. He was about to enter the park. But Mrs. K knew she couldn't grab him, so she dove and tackled him like a pro football player. "It's a shoestring tackle," Tim said. Mrs. K rolled when they hit the ground to keep from falling on her son. When they stopped rolling on the ground, she grabbed her son; he was still trying to run and saying, "I have to save Peter, Mom, I have to, Mom, I just have to get there, Mom." Mrs. K said, "I am sorry, son. I never should have sent you after Peter. That was the wrong thing to do." Bobby was still crying, saying, "I have to save Peter, Mom." Then Mrs. K hugged him tighter and said, "Now listen to me, baby, and you listen good, son. I am sorry, son. Mommy made a two mistakes, son, and it might be too late to fix one, but I sure can fix this one with you. I should have never sent you after Peter, listen, baby, do you remember when we had Cricket and when Cricket got hit by that car. We took him to the doctor. The doctor did all he could do for Cricket, but it wasn't enough, and the doctor came to us and said, 'Cricket is in great pain.' Do you remember that, Bobby." Bobby said, "I remember that, Mom." Then Mrs. K said, "Do you remember what the doctor said." Bobby said, "Yes, Mom." "The doctor said it would be the best thing to let Cricket go to God and let God keep him for a while and let God play with Cricket like you did. Remember, Bobby." Bobby said, "Yea, Cricket was a good dog, and he did not need to suffer and be in pain like that because I loved Cricket." "At first you didn't want Cricket to go, remember, Bobby." Bobby smiled and said, "Yea, Mom, I really acted up." Mrs. K said, "Yes, you did, but after you thought about it, you said maybe God needs a dog too. You let him go, let me ask you this, do you miss Cricket." Bobby said, "Yes, I miss Cricket sometimes, not all the time like it was at first." Then Mrs. K said, "Do you cry, are you sad when you think about Cricket." Bobby said, "No, I don't cry, and I am not sad, because I know where Cricket is, and I know she is having lots of fun with God." Then Mrs. K said, "You hold on to that and know this, sometimes people can hurt and be in pain just like Cricket and they too want to go to God and ease the pain and stop the suffering, even if it's not real and in their head. Some people are real sick and need help, but sometimes all the help in the world is not enough." Then Bobby said, "You mean like Peter, he is in pain and he is suffering, right, Mom." Mrs. K said, "Yes, he has been in pain for four years." Then Bobby said, "Mom, are you going to let Peter—Peter is not a dog, right, Mom." Mrs. K dropped her head, and she held her head up again and said, "Bobby, I want you to play here over by the swing, but first let me look and see if I see someone out here to keep an eye on you." She looked and saw her old neighbor from their old house. She yelled out, "Marry, will you keep an eye on Bobby for me, I have to check on someone." Marry didn't answer her back; she just threw out her hand and nodded her head as to say yes. Then she grabbed Bobby and said, "You play, son, and you play hard, son, and make this the best play day ever, you enjoy yourself and play like you never played before, and no matter what you see or what you hear don't stop playing, do you hear me, son." Bobby said, "Yea," and he went over to the swings and started playing. Mrs. K headed for an area where there were a lot of oak trees; she knew she would find Peter there. Mrs. K was walking real slow, like she didn't want to go. She walked for a while; you could tell she wanted to stop, but she kept going on like something was pulling her toward Peter. Then she stopped and looked at Peter from a distance. Peter was sitting under that grand old oak tree. It was a large tree about the same as the one at the clubhouse. Peter had some letters in his hand, but he was not reading them; his hand was by his side. Then she started walking again; when she got closer, she yelled his name, "Peter, Peter." But Peter didn't answer her. She started crying as she walked toward him with her arms folded; she finally reached him. She stood over him and said, "Peter, my love, why did you do this, my lovely son, why. You fooled me, baby, I thought you were getting better, but you were just going through the motion and showing me what I wanted to see that you were well. You were just giving me what I needed to believe that you were getting better. Why, Peter." Then she started crying. She was crying so much until her shirt was wet with her tears, then she called him again, "Peter," but still there was no answer. Then she saw his hand move a little; she reached for her cell phone to call 911. She held the phone up to dial the numbers, but then she stopped and looked down at

Peter, but he wasn't moving his hand anymore; she put the cell phone back in her pocket and sat down beside him and leaned him over on her lap and said, "The world let you down for four years. You were abused, many people have let you down and used you, and the ones that could helped you have forgotten you, how many more children must suffer, my love, while men of this world play war games with guns, like kids play with toys, rather than find ways to protect the innocent ones in this world, the ones that are too young to help themselves. So they let the children of this world be sent off to unsafe homes where people just use them and abuse them for their own selfish reason. I see now, Peter, I see clearly. No more, Peter, no more. I will make the world know your name. What happened to you won't happen to another child. I will be your voice, Peter. I see now, Peter, I see clearly now, my beloved son." She started rocking him, crying and saying, "No more, no more will they have to suffer." Tim looked at Paul and said, "Maybe Mrs. K is going to lose it too, like Peter's mom." Paul didn't say anything right away. Then he said, "Maybe that wouldn't be so bad. Let's just watch this lady play God." Tim looked at Paul; he wanted to say more, but he just started watching the screen. Mrs. K was still rocking Peter on her lap; she was still crying. Then Mrs. K kissed Peter on the forehead and started singing this song. "Hush, little baby, don't you cry. God's angels are coming for you, no more pain, no more suffering. God's angels are on their way. Soon you'll be home with God, you'll see. Now go to sleep and cry no more. Here comes the angels to carry you home." And she burst into tears. Her eyes were red as fire, and her face was just as red to match her eyes. Then she screamed out. Then she stopped and said, "Peter, my love, some people will say I could have saved you. But you and I both know that it was too late. I know you don't blame me for anything, my beloved son. Everything that you love was taken away from you, and you didn't have a choice. You were forced to do the will of other people. What you have done is your choice, and I will not take that from you now. Man can fix any part of the body. They can do transplants and reattach parts of the body. But all the doctors and kings' and queens' men and the presidents' men could not fix this little child's broken heart." And she started crying again. Then the screen went blank. Tim said, "Peter is gone, he's on his way home." Then Paul got real quiet, like he was going to explode. Then it happened. He went crazy; he was punching the air saying, "That witch kill Peter, why did she have to play God, she should have call the police. That witch, I could kill her," then he fell to the floor on his knees; he put his hands together and said, "Why, God, why. Peter never done no wrong to nobody, he was innocent. Even when everybody else was mean to him, why, God." Paul was still fighting at the air. "That old lady Mrs. K did wrong, God, nobody has the right to say who lives and who dies, that's wrong, Tim." Tim didn't say anything; he was quiet. Then Paul said, "Right, Tim." But Tim still didn't say anything. Paul said, "What's wrong, I am right, aren't I, Tim. Please say I am right, I know I am right, you don't have to tell me, God is on my side." Then Tim took a deep breath and said, "Paul, I think Mrs. K did the right thing." Paul got from the ground and ran over to Tim and grabbed him and said, "I will kill you. I should knock your head off, you little fool." Tim said, "Paul, you can hit me or even beat me to death, but that won't change my mind." Paul said, "Why, Tim, I thought you love Peter like I did, he was a asshole sometimes, but I love him like a brother, and why are you not crying, Tim. It seems like you don't have any feelings, what has happen to you." Tim said, "Paul, I feel, I just don't know what to feel, hurt or joy, I am confused. Man, I want to cry, but at the same time, I want to say hooray, not because Peter is dead, but that he won't have to suffer anymore, maybe I am not saying it right, but you know what I mean. If Mrs. K would have save Peter, you and I both know that when Peter has his mind set on doing something, he is going to do it, and Peter had made up his mind to kill himself. Maybe the next time he might take someone else with him. Sooner or later, Peter was going to kill himself, because that is what Peter wanted. Paul, don't you see that." Paul did not answer him. Paul still had Tim in his grip. Paul turned him loose and walked away and said, "Tim, you tougher than I thought." Tim smiled and said, "If I only knew what to feel, my heart is full." Then they heard cheering, the same music that they had heard early, then Reno walked in and said, "You boys have done well, you have done what few men have done, and no man could have done better. Everyone is proud, and we have decided that you guys should receive a gift, and when this is over, you shall have it this day." Tim said, "Reno, my heart is trouble about what I have seen." Then Reno said, "I warned you of this and fret not, Tim, soon you will feel what is normal to you, and maybe this is all you will feel. Maybe you will feel more, give it a minute." Then Tim said, "Reno, what Mrs. K did, was it right." Reno said, "In my world, there would be no question, for the answer is in plain sight, but in your world there has to be rules to help keep order and to protect those who can't protect themselves. Man has not yet evolved enough to be his own keeper. So in the law of man, she was wrong, but now I ask you, in God's law, was she right. But remember this, God gave every man the right to choose. Was it Peter's life or God's life. If you have not figured it out, Tim, I will tell you now. The answer is in every man, it will not be the same for every man. Because every man is different, so there is no right answer or wrong answer. It is up to each man and what he believes in. You guys have come far, but there is more to see." And the screen came back on, and Reno walked out of the room. Paul and Tim saw two young guys driving in a car. They could not hear any sound; they only saw faces, but the guys weren't anyone they knew they thought. Then they saw that one of the guys had red hair like Tim and the other was black like Paul. Paul and Tim looked at each other, but they didn't say anything. Then they looked back at the screen, and they saw the young men smoking a rolled cigarette and drinking from a liquor bottle. They were passing the bottle of liquor back and forth to each other, laughing for a while and crying. Then something ran out in front of the car. The black guy was driving; he turned the wheel. The guy with the red hair yelled. Paul and Tim could see his mouth wide open and he was pointing down the road. They were headed for the edge of the road in the woods. Then the screen went blank, and Reno came back into the room and said, "Now it is over. You have seen it all. Now we will rest for a while. Then we will talk. Come and follow me, my brave young men." As they followed Reno, they could still hear the cheering and the music. The music sounded so strong, but yet it was calming. The sound of the music made Paul and Tim feel proud of themselves. They started to walk a little taller. But as good as they felt, they still had Peter on their minds. Tim wanted to ask Reno all the questions that were in his head. Tim put his hand to his mouth. Tim was really trying his best not to ask Reno any question, but he couldn't hold it. Tim said, "Why, Reno." But Reno didn't say anything. So Tim asked him again because he thought Reno didn't hear him. Tim said, "Reno, why did Peter have to die and what about me, I don't know what to feel, Reno." Then Paul said, "Reno, Tim ask you a question." But Reno still didn't answer. Reno just kept on walking. Paul turned his head back to Tim and looked at Tim. They both knew that Reno heard them. Paul turned his head back toward Reno's large shell on his back. Paul made a fist with both hands. Paul was getting angry. Then Paul started talking to himself in a really low voice to himself, saying, "This old turtle of a man is going to push me too far. Lord, I am really trying not to go crazy on this foolish old turtle of a man." Then all at once Paul let out a loud scream. Paul said, "Reno, not another step, Reno. Reno, this is the end, it all ends here now, Tim ask you a question, and you didn't answer him back, and that wasn't nice, and I also ask you. You acted as if you didn't hear us, but I know you heard me and Tim. What's going on, Reno." Reno stopped and turned around real fast toward them. Tim looked like he wanted to run, but he stood there waiting for what was going to happen. Paul jumped back in a boxer's stance and said, "Bring it on," and Tim said, "I am with you Paul so bring it on, old Reno and also got in a boxer stance and put up their fist's in front of their face and they stood ready for Reno. As Reno got closer, Tim could see that Reno was smiling and Tim drop his hand to his side and call back to Paul to let him know that Reno was smiling. Then Reno let out a loud laugh. Paul dropped his hands, and Reno walked closer and said, "I thought you guys would never get angry. I was getting tired of walking." He pointed behind Tim. "Look behind you, Tim, there is your feast. The table has been following us." Tim turned and looked and said, "That was not there a minute ago. Where did it come from." Paul said, "Stupid, Reno just said the table was following us." Then Tim said, "Why, Reno, why did you have to get us all work up." Reno said, "You guys were holding in all those questions, and it had to come out. In life, it is not good to bring the pot to the stove and bring it almost to a boil and not let it boil. It is not good for the food inside the pot, because the food in the pot will spoil. And the same is for man, or the soul will spoil." Then Paul said, "Of all the thing you have said, that was the plainest." Reno just laughed and said, "Your feast awaits you." Tim said, "Let me at it. I might save some for you guys." The table was full of fruits and vegetables and cookies and cakes and all types of juices. Tim was so shocked of the food, he yelled out and said, "I am in heaven. There is so much food until I don't know where to start," then Tim stuffed a mouthful of grapes in his mouth, then he went to work on the cookies, then he took a bite of cake. Paul and Reno were just standing there in amazement at Tim; he was eating like he had never eaten before. Paul told him to slow down 'cause he might get a ticket, 'cause he was eating so fast. Then Tim said, "I have learn not to let a free good meal go by, because you guys know, my mom can't cook, she can't boil water, but she tries awful hard. So I have to eat enough to last me until the next one comes," and he laughed and went back to eating. Tim was putting the food away like a garbage disposal. Tim stopped long enough to wave his hand to invite Paul and Reno to come over and join him. Paul joined in and started eating too. Reno was still standing; he started to walk around them, saying, "Eat, my young friends, and be of good cheer. For we have decided that you guys will not have to bear all of this, what you have seen. We have broken our promise and our oath we took many, many years ago to only watch and not participate in the life of man. But we have and more, we will be weighed for what we have done. We have even played with time and events to protect what we have done for the future of mankind. Remember what I have said about the pot on the stove. That is why we must go all the way with you guys, because the world is ready to boil. That is why I must speak to you guys about the failure in man, even today we have held the sun in one place to give you guys time so that you would understand why you are here in this world of man, they have ears but they hear not the cries of the innocent ones, they have eyes but see not the injustice that is done to the innocent ones. Of all the things that man has done to himself, we still see hope for man if man finds himself. In this world you will find out that there is more blindness than sight, and in the same people their ears are just as blind as their eyes. Soon I will tell you guys much more things, and I will relieve you guys of that burden that you are carrying, but for now you must listen, while you eat. First thing, Tim, be not ashamed of the way you feel, you know what Mrs. K did was right in your eyes, because you felt the pain of Peter more than Paul. For that is your talent, to feel the pain and suffering of others, and you also know the true answer to the question I asked you earlier, but you are ashamed of your belief and that people will laugh at you. And you are in denial to what you want to feel. You will learn that it is okay to feel good when someone else feels bad. That is why, Tim, your talent has not yet come full to you. One day you will learn all that matters is what you think and what you believe and not what other people think about you. Now eat, Tim, when you swallow, swallow those words with your food. Soon, my friend, I shall give you peace. Open your heart to the truth and be not ashamed to what you feel." Then Reno said "Paul, do you want to save Peter from that fate you saw." Paul dropped his head and stopped eating; it seemed like he wanted to cry. Then he held his head up and said, "Reno, I have feelings too. Tim might feel more than me, but I have feelings just like Tim. I love Peter just as much as Tim. You did not ask me the same question as Tim about Mrs. K, what she did was right or wrong. Does it matter what I think." Reno said, "My friend, you are Paul the mighty, you are stronger than Tim, and you always think about the questions put to you and the things that happened to you, and you look for the truth in the words not spoken, and the words you hear you weigh them and look for the answer in the word not said, to see if it is the truth. When you hear the truth, you know it in your heart, and you can see the truth when you see it, that is your talent, to find the unspoken truth. But like Tim you have not fully learned to keep your heart out of your decision. You will know the truth when you put your heart aside. All things will come to you, and understanding will appear to you. And, my friend, Paul, I did not overlook you, my friend. We knew your heart will not let your eyes see what your mind knows to be true. You will learn sometime in life it is good to hold your peace and speak not what you know to a person. It is better to wait and let that person come to you. Then you can speak the truth." Then Paul said, "Reno, I do not want Peter to die, what can we do to prevent this from happening. I do not want to die either. Tell us Reno." Then Reno said, "Yes. I will tell you, but I cannot tell you straight, it will be in a parable. But yet there is more, I want to tell you why we interfered in the life of man and why they will not reach the next level of life. Let me give you guys this, we have given up on mankind because they have fallen in the simpliest of things. Some men are so into themselves until they believe that every other man should walk and talk and look like him, forgetting that every man and woman are different and every man, woman, and child must be judged for the things they do, and not by them that hold themselves in the seat of judgment. They have forgotten the simpliest of things, and that is respect of others, for some try and force their will on others, they have also forgotten that old saying, 'Let every man be held accountable for their actions.' If a woman should kill her unborn child, what will man have of her. Some would say kill her, and some would say it's her right, and some would say take her to jail and bring her before the judge. In all of this, man is divided, and a house that is divided cannot stand, no good will come of that. But remember it is good for a man to bare his opinion and what he believes, but that same man will force his will on others, forgetting the words of his God. For the answer to that is simple. But man does not see it." Then Tim said, "Reno, what is this simple answer." Reno said, "A man that knows the law of his God knows it, but they are like you, Tim, he is ashamed and afraid of the rest of the world will not agree with him and will laugh." Paul said, "Reno, that is not a answer." Then Reno said, "Even you, Paul, you know the answer, and you are a child in the words of God, for the words of your father are in your heart and mind, for you have heard your father say it many of times in church." Paul dropped his head in shame. Then Reno said, "Fret not, Paul, soon you will realize what you already know." Then Reno said, "We must move on, there is more to listen to. This parable of man is for you two so that you might understand the ways of man. Now take this, there were two men of different colors who went out for a walk in this special neighborhood, and they came upon a burning building, and everyone in the building was out, but a child. Everyone got outside safe and had given the child up for dead.

One of the man asked, 'Is everyone out.' The people of the neighborhood said, 'Yes, but there is a child in the building. And by now the child must be dead now.' Then one of the men that was out for a walk started running toward the burning building. The other man grabbed him and said, 'I cannot let you go inside, you will be killed.' But the man broke free. Then the people of the special neighborhood started to chase him, saying, 'Don't go inside or you will be killed, like the child,' and they tried to stop him from going into the burning building. They all tried to hold him, but the man broke free and went inside the burning building. The building was totally in flames, but the man soon came out with the child. NOW Paul I ask you how would you feel if everyone in the special neighborhood was black and the child was black and the man who risked his life was white." Paul dropped his head in shame, but Tim had a little smile. Then Reno said, "Now you, Tim, close your eyes and see the people in the neighborhood, can you see them." Tim said, "Yes, I see them all." Then Reno said, "What if everyone in the neighborhood was white and the child was white and the one that risked his life to save the child was black, how would you feel." Tim dropped his head in shame also, and Paul gave a little smile. Then Reno said, "Man has forgotten the thing that matters the most, for a man only sees the color of a man. For each race wants to be better than the other, and in doing that they have lost sight in the things that means the most." Tim said, "What is that, Reno." Reno laughed and said, "If everyone was blind in this world, what would they say about the man that risked his life to save the child and what he did, and let me also ask you this do you think that same blind man would have felt the same shame as you guys felt, the blind man would only say this man that risked his life to save another life was a brave man and cared more about the life of another than himself and he would not be a shame for he would only be proud of the man. That is what matters the most. Soon, my young friend, you will be able to understand all that I have said. But yet there is a little more I must share with you before I give you your gift. Let me give you one more, take this, this is part of the first one I spoke of early, Paul. The one that I said you know the answer to, now listen, for in this you will see the truth and the answer, Paul. A young women goes out in the world for a week and loved four young men, for she loves the worldly things and finds out that she is with child, so she calls the first one and says, 'I am with child, and I tell you now, I have been with more than you,' and then she asks him, 'What will you have me do?' The first one tells her nothing and hangs up the phone. So the young lady calls another and tells him the same as the first, then she asks him, 'What will you have me do?' The second one unlike the first said, 'If it is mine, I will be there. And we should get married, I know you won't stop partying and I like to party too. We can take turns going out and partying, nothing will change for you or me.' The young lady says okay and moves to the next one, telling him the same as the other ones. This one says, 'I will pay for an abortion.' Then she says, 'I will let you know.' The third one says, 'All right, call me when you know.' Then she moves on to the last one. She tells him the same as the rest, but this one was different from the rest, he asks the young lady, 'What did she want.' The young lady said, 'I want to have it. I want to keep it regardless who is the father. I can get more with a kid than by myself. I will get more tax money, and I can get a check from the government and a nice place to live and not pay a lot of money for rent. I can get food stamps and more. So in a way it's like winning the lottery.' Then the man said, 'Will you stop going out and be a stay-at-home mother and raise your child, or will you still be a party girl and leave the child home with anybody willing to watch it.' The young girl said, 'Yes, I will still go out, but I won't leave the child like that.' Then the man said, 'You should get an abortion, because you are not ready to bring a child in this world. The child would only suffer, and you are too stupid to give it to someone else, so if it is mine, you should have an abortion, and if it is not mine, you should have one, and I will pay for it. I made a mistake, and the child should not have to pay for my mistake, I should have had some type of protection on, but in my haste to satisfy my own selfish lust, I didn't. But I know you are too stupid to realize what's best for the child, if you don't get an abortion, I know you want to even put the child up for adoption, because you have already seen how you can live easy off of the child, through the government. Whatever you decide, call me and let me know.' Paul, which of these young men are right in man's eyesight, and who of them are wrong in God's eyesight." Tim said, "I know, Reno, the first guy was wrong." But Reno didn't say anything; he kept waiting for Paul, but Paul dropped his head as if he was ashamed because he didn't know the answer and he was also wondering why Reno asked him and not Tim. Tim already seemed like he knew the answer. Then Reno said, "Paul the mighty, you act as if you are unhappy because I asked you this." Paul still had his head down; he was thinking he heard the words that Reno said, but there was only one word Reno said that answered the question in Paul's head. Paul said, "Reno, I was unhappy that you ask me which of the people was right, but it was the word you call me that help me to understand and also give you this answer. I can see no wrong in them because I don't understand and cannot reason it out." Reno laughed, and he laughed hard and long and said, "That is the answer I was looking for, and the answer I expected from you, but there is no wrong and there is no right in any of them, for that is one more way man has fallen and will not reach the next level of life for he has fallen in the most simple of things, let me tell you why, this is a question that is up to every man and their belief, for there will not be one man that can agree on what is right in man's law, for this did not need to happen. For your God knew that this would happen and gave man the knowledge to prevent things like this, but man will not even use that which God has given him, he will not even use it to save his life and not spread disease throughout the land." Then Reno got real quiet and dropped his head; it seemed like there was a tear falling from his eyes. Then Tim said, "See Paul, you jerk, you made Reno cry, you always have to have the right answer." Then Tim walked over to Reno and said, "Don't cry, Reno, Paul will figure it out, and I bet you, Reno, he will come up with the right answer." But the tears kept falling from Reno's eyes, and Paul said, "Tim, he is not crying because of what I said, you little nut, it is what he has been saying all the time. Don't you get it." Tim shook his head and said, "No, Paul I am sorry, but I can't make the connection." Paul said, "You are really stupid, Tim. It is like a young kid who is real good at football and could be a superstar, but he won't play because he is doing all the wrong things in life, that's what Reno has been trying to tell us about man. Man could be so good, and this world could be so perfect, but man will not do the right thing, he has put money and all the worldly things before the things that matter the most in life, he can't even do the simplest of things in life. And to watch these things and you have the power to change mankind, but you can't because you are bound by a promise and a oath, but yet you must watch man destroy himself and do nothing but watch. And to see all that man could be go to waste because of their greed and lustful ways of selfishness and their foolish pride. That is enough to make anyone cry and more. You go ahead and cry, Reno, now we understand, Reno." Then Reno held up his head and said, "You see, life is so simple, a baby could understand life, but yet so hard that a full-grown man can't see how simple life is." And he started crying, then he stopped and said, "My young friends, I have taught you much and you have learned much, and you have learned much more than your little hearts can carry. It is time for us to release some of the pain and discomfort from your heart and mind." And Reno called Tim and Paul to come close; once they got close to Reno, he reached out his hand and put his hand on their shoulders and said, "You will not remember what I have shown you about man and his downfall, and you will not feel the full feeling of Peter's fate, you still will know what happens, but the pain of it will be more bearable for your little hearts. Now, my young friends, how do you feel." Tim said, "I feel good, Reno. But it feel like I lost something, but I don't know what it is, and I am hungry." Paul said, "You're always hungry, Tim." Then Paul said, "Reno, what are we going to do about Peter." Then Reno asked, "Tim, how do you feel, do you want those things to happen to Peter, do you still want to save Peter, and you, Paul, how do you feel, do you also want to save Peter." Paul said, "We will do whatever you say or whatever you ask of us, we will do it, right, Tim." Tim said yes. Then Reno said, "Listen to what I say and open your heart and open your mind, I will give you this parable, and once you guys figure it out, you will know what to do to save Peter's life and you already know the answer to this parable, but if you guys do not figure out this parable and don't realize that you already know the answer, you will have lost it all and the chance to save Peter and yourselves and Big Ben's life also. Are you guys listening and watching me." Then Tim said, "I have my eyes on you like a hawk on a field rat, and my ears are to the floor. I won't miss anything you say." Then Reno laughed and said, "That is good, my friend, because you will need it. Because as I have said early, Big Ben will not be at the clubhouse anymore, for he has done all that he can now, it is up to you guys. Here is the parable. This has been around for as long as the world has been here, and he can be your best friend or your worst enemy, it does not respect any person, nor does it show favor to anyone, and it will change two times in an hour and will change more time than the hairs on both your heads, and he is known by many names, and some call him father to us all, but all the names mean the same. Let not the last words I said mislead you, it is not your God. My friends, this is a long parable, and there is much to remember, but I will give you this, all that matters is how many times he changes, there you will find the answer. Now, my young friends, the hour goes late, for we can no longer hold the sun in one place, it is time to go." Tim said, "Reno, this day has been rewarding, and we will solve that parable, you can bet on that, Reno." Reno said, "Now, my young friends, you have seven days and six nights before Peter starts that terrible journey. Now, my friends, go in peace, you will not come back until you have solved the parable." Paul said, "We understand," and headed for the stairs back to the top. Tim said, "We will see you, Reno," and reached for Paul's hand; they walked holding hands to the stairs, humming that old song of Big Ben as they went up the stairs to the top. Once they reached

the top, Tim said, "Paul, do you think we should go to the clubhouse."
Paul said, "We can, but you know everyone is gone, it is late, Tim." Tim
said, "You're right, Paul, but I just wanted to see Peter." Paul said, "I know,
Tim, I want to see him too, I wonder what Big Ben did with Peter while
we were down with Reno." Then Tim said, "Paul, about that parable, we
have to solve it, and I don't have a clue of what it is, do you, Paul." Paul
said, "No. I don't have any answers. We better be getting a move on it. We
don't want to get caught out here in the dark." Tim said, "All right," and
started walking a little faster. Then Tim said, "Are you afraid." Paul said,
"No, but there are things out here that we don't know." "You sound like
Big Ben. I wonder where is Big Ben and what is he doing right know. I am
going to miss him. He was the life of the clubhouse, he taught us so much,
and I will never forget him, he was more than my friend, he was my brother,
are you going to miss him, Paul, do you think he is with Reno down in the
caves, I wonder are they watching us right now, what do you think?" Tim
asked Paul as they got closer to the highway. Paul said, "Tim, I don't know,
and right now my mind is on that parable because we only have seven days
and six nights, and I am worried that we might not solve it in time." Then
Tim said, "Don't worry so much, the answer will come to us. We are at the
curb, do you want to go over to Peter's house and check on him." Paul said,
"His dad might be there, and he might answer the door, and I don't know
how I will feel about him, so it might be better not to go." Tim said, "You
probably right, Paul." Then Paul said, "Anyway, it is late to go to someone's
house, and I better be making it to my house, I have been gone all day, and
you too, Tim, you better be making it to your house too, we will have all
day tomorrow to try and figure out that parable and catch up with Peter,
so, Tim, I will say good night." Tim dropped his head and said, "I guess
you're right again, Paul, so I guess I will be going to see you tomorrow."
They both went home, but they had Peter on their minds, wondering what
Big Ben had told him and taught him.

That next morning, Tim got up early and headed for the clubhouse.
He stopped at the curb and sat on the curb waiting for Paul or Peter to
come. Then Tim heard someone singing, it was that old song that Big Ben
had made up, "Who's afraid of that old bear." It was getting louder and
louder. Tim started tapping his foot to the beat of the song, then Tim got
up and started dancing around. That old song had Tim by the ears; he
couldn't stop dancing. Tim could hear the sound of the song getting
stronger and louder, but he kept on dancing. Then Peter walked up on Tim

dancing and said, "What are you doing, are you having a fit, are you going crazy, and why are you up so early, and why are you here." Tim said, "I was waiting on you or Paul to come, but I am glad it was you that came first, Peter, I have a lot of question to ask you about your day with Big Ben, how did Big Ben treat you." Peter said, "It was the best day ever, I never meet anyone that know as much as Big Ben about the woods. By god, he is one true wilderness man." He smiled. "He taught me so much and showed me a lot of things and told me a lot of secret things that I cannot tell you until we are all together." And he started laughing. "Big Ben told me to enjoy the secrets that he told me." Then Tim asked, "Peter, what is in the bag over your shoulder." Peter said, "It's a surprise, don't you know boy," and laughed. Tim said, "Peter, the way you talk about Big Ben, it seems like you know something about Big Ben that you are not saying. Big Ben will be here today." Then Peter said, "Don't you know, boy," and started laughing. Tim heard the way Peter was talking and the way he was acting, and he thought to himself the new way Peter was talking was strange, but he didn't say anything. Then Peter asked Tim how was their day and what did they do. Tim didn't say anything; he just stood there for a minute, then he said, "Not as good as your time with Big Ben, we didn't do that much." Peter said, "Big Ben told me not to ask you guys anything about yesterday. Because you guys wouldn't tell me anything, but you know me, I never do as I am told," and he started laughing. Then Tim and Peter heard someone coming down the path. Tim yelled out, "Is that you, Paul." Before Paul could answer, Tim yelled back to Paul to let him know that Peter was with him, then Peter said, "Why don't you go and meet him, I know you guys have a lot to talk about." Tim just stood there in shock; he couldn't believe what Peter said, then Peter said, "Go ahead, Tim, and meet Paul." Tim turned and started to run down the path. Tim was beginning to get a little scared, so he ran, but then he stopped and looked back at Peter. Peter was smiling and laughing; he was down on his knees laughing. Tim started running a little faster calling Paul. "Paul." Peter had lost what little sense he had; he's gone plum crazy. As Tim was running yelling to Paul about Peter, he almost ran straight into Paul under the long branch overhanging the path. Tim ran up to Paul and started telling him everything that had happened to him with Peter. Then Paul said, "First thing first, Tim, good morning, did you think of the parable. Did you think of any answers." Tim said no, then Paul said, "I have, and I think it is a man, but I need more time to put it together." Tim said, "That's good, Paul, but we need to talk about Peter and the way he is acting." Paul said, "Tim, we will just have to play along with Peter and not say too much, just let him do all the talking. Tim, do you think he knows that Big Ben won't be back." Tim said, "He acts like he knows, but he is not saying a thing. He was laughing to himself and acting all crazy, like he was playing around, and Peter has this big bag over his shoulder, as crazy as he is acting, I hope it not a gun in the bag and he tries and kill us." Paul said, "You are such a drama queen and a motor mouth, Tim. Let's go and check on this crazy man you say that is at our clubhouse, and, Lord, don't let Tim's tongue go to speeding and talk too much." Then Tim said, "Paul, do you think Big Ben has put some kind of magic spell on Peter." Paul said, "Don't be silly, Tim, man, I tell you, the more I listen to you, the sillier you sound." Tim smiled and put his hand to his mouth and said, "I won't talk anymore." Paul said, "Now it's too late, we all have seen your stupidness," and he laughed. "Come on, we are almost to the clubhouse." Tim ran on ahead and said, "Paul, that little nut is not here." Paul called out, "Peter, are you here," but there was no answer. Tim yelled out, "Peter, are you here," but there was no answer. Then Paul said, "Let's look over there, maybe he's hiding." Tim said, "All right," and they walked away from the clubhouse. Paul had his head straight ahead looking down into the woods for Peter, but Tim was looking back at the clubhouse, and he saw Peter climbing down out of that grand old oak tree; he could hardly calm down for laughing. He fell to the ground, rolling on the ground laughing. Then Tim said to Paul, "Wait, Paul, there's Peter by the clubhouse, he was in the tree. Paul, let's get him." They ran back over to the grand old oak tree. Peter was still on the ground laughing, pointing at Tim and laughing. When he saw Paul and Tim running back at him, he knew he was in for it; he waited for them to get closer. When they got closer, he started to run around the tree laughing. Tim started chasing him around the tree, so did Paul around, and around they went for hours just laughing, then Paul stopped and said, "You pull a good one on us, Peter." Peter had stopped running as well as Tim. Then Peter said, "I did pull one on you guys, Tim, you should have seen your face, what did you think, Tim, that I had got eaten by your water turkey," then they all looked at Tim and started laughing all over again. Then Paul stopped and walked over to the stump where Big Ben always sat and picked up a stick and started drawing on the ground. Peter and Tim walked over to where Paul was sitting. Peter said, "What's wrong, Paul, I didn't mean to make you mad or upset you." Paul said, "It's not that, I just have something on my mind that I have to figure out, all I need is time." Then Peter said, "Maybe you need to tell someone or me, maybe I can help you, or maybe someone else can." Tim said, "Paul, can handle it, Peter. Peter, what was in that bag you had over your shoulder. And will Big Ben be here today." Peter said, "That bag, the things inside are a surprise." Then Paul said, "What type of surprise is it." Peter said, "It's food, we are going to cook something very good, you guys, and you're going to love it." Tim started smiling and rubbing his stomach. Peter just had made Tim the happiest man in town. Tim had this rule. He would never pass up a free good meal when it was offered. Because everyone knew that his mom can't cook, and sometimes Tim goes for a month without a good, tasty meal. His mom tries offer hard to cook good, but it's not good or tasty. Tim has gotten to the point he doesn't even chew; he just swallowed. Then Tim said, "What do you need for us to do, Peter." Peter said, "You guys need to gather some dry wood." Tim said, "All right, Captain," and started off. Then Peter said, "Wait, you guys, I have a better idea. Tim, you gather the dry wood and stick and be careful, you don't want to pick up a snake, I know how you city boys are." Tim laughed and said, "One day with Big Ben and you are a expert woodsman." Peter said, "That is the truth, you know, Tim," and Peter laughed. "Tim, you better get a move on it, those sticks are not going to pick themselves up." Tim said, "Don't you know, boy, you're right," and he started laughing, as he walked away to pick up the dry wood and sticks. Paul was still sitting on the stump drawing on the ground, the way Big Ben used to. Peter walked back over to him and said, "Me and you, Paul, will do something else, the most important part of the whole thing." Paul seemed like he didn't hear him; his mind was still on the parable that he knew he had to solve to save Peter from that terrible fate he would suffer. Peter called to him again and said, "Do you hear me, big man, I mean boss man." Paul looked up at him, remembering that Big Ben sometimes called him by that name. Then Peter said, "Do you want to talk about it, Paul, it might help. Sometimes it's good to talk, Big Ben says even if there's no one there you can talk to the trees and the flowers and the birds and the bees and to God, and you don't have to worry about them repeating it to someone else. That's if you don't want to talk to me." Paul said, "It's nothing, Peter, thanks for that, it was good to hear, now what about this important thing you and I have to do or find, what is it." Peter said, "Get ready, brace yourself, we are going on a hunt for a special limb." "Paul said, "A limb, you mean a piece of a tree." Peter started laughing and jumping up and down and rubbing his hand together like Tim was rubbing his stomach about food. Then all of a sudden Paul put his hands to his head and started smiling, and then he went to laughing, realizing that he had heard someone else tell a story about the prince and the special pony, then he said, "Peter, I hope you don't be like the prince and the special pony." Peter said, "I never heard of that story, but it must be funny." Paul just laughed and laughed and walked up to Peter and said, "You have made me feel good, and for a moment, you made me forget my problems and thank you for that," and he put his hands on Peter's shoulder. "Come on, Peter, let's go and find your special limb, this might be what I need." They walked for a while, then they came up on this little tree. Peter walked around it, looking at the limbs and shaking his head no, then Paul started making pony sounds like a horse and said, "Yep, this is the story," and started laughing. Peter went to laughing too, and he didn't even know the story; they laughed and walked for a while. Then Peter said, "Paul, I know where we can find the limb." Paul said, "Are you sure, Peter, Tim is waiting for us, and we have been gone for a long time, you know how worried Tim can get." Peter said, "I know, Paul, and you're right, and I know exactly where it is." Paul said, "I don't believe you, but I will follow you a little longer," then Peter said, "You won't be sorry, wait until you see it." Paul said, "You act like you have already seen it." Peter said, "Damn right, Big Ben got it for me yesterday." As soon as Peter said that, Peter realized what he had said and how stupid it was to say it, but he held his breath and kept on walking. Paul stopped walking and said, "What did you say." Peter got a little scared; he didn't want to get a beat down from Paul. Paul was very big for his age. So he didn't want to make him mad. Paul said, "You knew where the limb was all the time, and you had me all over the place looking, why, I should bash your head in," then he stop and started laughing. "But it was fun, Peter. So I give you a break, but tell me something, are you and Tim related." Peter started to laugh, and Paul said, "Let's go, the drama queen is probably crying by now," so they headed back to the clubhouse when Peter had the limb; once they got there they saw Tim walking around looking foolishly for them. He ran up to them and said, "You guys are so stupid and careless, you could have told me you would be gone this long." Tim was mad and upset. Tim kept saying, "You guys left me." Tim gave Paul the evil eye. Then Peter said, "Those magic words that made everything all right. Tim, in my bag, I have a pot and butter and lemon juice and hot sauce and some cocktail sauce and some crackers and punch, and for dessert I have my mom's famous blackberry doobie, man, I tell you, it is good, and now we have everything we need to catch the main course and that is crawdads, there are thousands of them in that little creek over there, Big Ben showed me yesterday, and he taught me how to catch them, we have to muddy up the water a little with this limb and get in the water, it's not deep, it only comes up to your ankles, and grab them with your hands, then we make a fire with the wood, but we don't put the pot over the fire, only on the side of the fire as close as we can, that way, it won't get all smoky. And then we will wait for a little while and then eat." Tim said, "I love you, man, no, I really do, that sound so good, I can hardly wait." Then Paul said, "Yea, let's get at it." So they went over to the small area of the creek and did as Peter said; man, the crawdads were in there like bees in a beehive. They filled up the pot with crawdads, and Tim said, "Where are we going to get water from." Peter laughed and said, "All this water and you ask that, we don't need a lot, Tim, maybe none at all, we are going to steam the crawdads, you don't boil them, stupid." Tim said, "I knew that, I was just testing you," and he started to laugh. So they made a small fire, then Peter broke a peace from the limb and pushed it in the ground close to the fire. Tim asked, "Why are you doing that." Peter said, "Don't you know, I am going to hang the pot up on this limb close to the fire, it is the best way to steam things or cook in the woods." Tim said, "I knew that, I was just testing you again to make sure that Big Ben taught you good," and they all started laughing. Then Peter said, "We will sit around the fire and talk." Paul said no, because he didn't want motormouth Tim to get started talking. Then Paul said, "We can play the cloud game." They all said, "Yea, that's the best game." Then Peter said, "We will have lunch when it is ready, all right." They all said, "That was a good idea," and walked over to where the sun and shade met and lay on the ground in their usual spot; they left the spot for Big Ben, even though he wasn't there. Peter said, "Who will go first." Tim said, "Hey, you guys, let's just lay here for a while and enjoy the peace and quiet and see who can hear the sound of the waterfall first." They all said yea, so they lay back, each of them clearing their minds and opening their ears to Mother Nature. Paul was trying awfully hard, but he was having trouble getting his mind cleared. Paul kept shaking his head as he lay thinking. Then Paul started talking real soft to himself, saying, "I will not." Then Paul rose up to see if anyone heard him; he saw that Peter or Tim didn't hear him. So Paul lay back on the ground looking up at the sky at the clouds. Then Peter asked, "Are you all right, Paul." Paul didn't say anything. Peter didn't ask him again. Tim started making groaning sounds. Paul said, "What's wrong, log head." Tim said, "My stomach knows there's food over there, and it won't let me think." Paul said, "Tim, you are really stupid." Then Tim said, "Paul, there is something I have to tell you and Peter." Peter rose up and said, "Go ahead." Paul held his breath. Paul didn't know what was going to come out of Tim's motormouth. Paul only hoped it was not what they learned down in the cave. Then Paul said, "Go ahead, Tim, and speak your mind." Tim said, "Paul, do you remember when I came over to your house about a month ago and you were in the kitchen eating and you put that Cajun seasoning on your food and your father call you and you left me in the kitchen alone. Well, I kind of borrow that seasoning from you guys. I have been putting it on my food at home. I was going to pay you guys for the stuff. But I hadn't got around to it, I am sorry, Paul, for that. But man, I just couldn't take the none-tasting food my mom cooks." Peter started laughing and called Tim a food thief and a kitchen bandit and laughed. Paul said, "Peter, leave him alone." "It's okay," Paul said, "I would like to know if the seasoning make the food taste better." Tim started to laugh and said, "It taste good, so good until sometimes I can't wait until supper time. My sister was watching me real close for a while, she knew I was doing something to my food, but she couldn't figure it out, 'cause I was eating my food with a smile. She kept watching me, one day she caught me, and now I have to share it with her, or she will tell. But that's not the problem. We are running out of that stuff. Do you think I could buy some more from you guys. And you can keep this little matter between us, Paul." Paul started laughing and said, "Sure, kitchen bandit, you little thief," and they all laughed. Then Peter said, "Look, you guys, I see a horse in the clouds." Then Tim looked and said, "It looks like a horse." Paul looked and said, "It is a horse, maybe Tim can ride him like a real bandit." They all laughed; by that time, the lunch was ready. They got up and sat Indian style around the pot. Tim said, "I think I will eat twelve with cocktail sauce and twelve with the other sauce, and I will even try some catsup on them. Then I will eat some with crackers." They all laughed and dug into the pot of crawdads, eating and laughing; once they finished the crawdads, Tim said, "Now let's get to the blackberry doobie." Tim served them the doobie, and they ate and laughed. Paul ate so much until he was groaning, holding his stomach, and he said, "I know I won't eat any supper tonight." Tim asked Paul, "Can I come over to your house, I will eat your supper tonight for you. I will help you out any way I can, even if I have to eat your dinner for you, 'cause you're my friend, and friends help each other, right." They all laughed and said, "You just can't let a free meal go by, can you, Tim." Peter said, "Tim, where do you put all the food you eat, are you part camel." Paul started laughing and put his hands to his knees and said, "I can't let this one pass, no, he's not part camel, he's part jackass." Peter and Paul started laughing. Soon Tim started laughing too and started making donkey sounds; that made it all the funnier. It was getting late. Paul said, "Well, you guys, it's almost time to go, we had better start putting things away." Tim asked were there any more crawdads left. They laughed and said, "No, Tim." Peter started putting things away, then Peter started humming that song of Big Ben. Tim joined in humming and dancing, then Paul started humming and dancing too. But Paul was dancing real crazy; it seemed like Paul was trying to dance his troubled mind free. Then Peter said, "Hey, you guys, it is getting late, we best be getting a move on it." But for the first time, Paul didn't listen. Paul kept on sing and dancing, as if he had all day and nothing to do. Then Peter said, "Paul, you go ahead and dance and you can sing. You can even pretend that there's nothing bothering you, but it is. I have been watching you all day, and I can see there's something wrong. But I know you won't tell me, and that's okay. Big Ben told me that you guys had a secret and for me to help you guys through it and to have as much fun as I could. Big Ben told me a lot of things, and when the time is right, I was to tell you guys a little at a time, to keep you guys on track and to give you peace of mind, when you need it and for me not to say too much. That I would know when to speak and when not to. So I hope this was the right time. But here is something Big Ben did not tell me. We all have learn more things this summer than some people learn in a lifetime. Whatever problem it is, you, Paul, already know the answer. All you have to do is listen. I know you guys think I am crazy for talking like that, I said what I felt in my heart. You know I haven't had that feeling since that night my dad died, it seem like that feeling died with my dad. Guys, I remember I had a little friend, he kept me company after my dad died. He would talk to me and play with me. I never saw him, but he talk to me. I could hear him in my ears, laughing and telling me things. But the older I got, the less I heard him talking to me, after a while I didn't hear him at all." Paul looked at Tim really strangely, because Paul also had a little friend and Peter described him exactly, and Paul was wondering did Tim had a little friend too. In Paul's mind, he knew it was Big Ben. Then Peter said, "I knew my father was dead before my mom did. When she said let's go to the hospital, you guys, I didn't want to go. Because I knew my dad would not be there." Peter had tears in his eyes. "You guys are the first guys that I have told this to. I never told my mom, hell, you guys, I couldn't even talk about it. It has been as if it didn't happen to me but to someone else, and I was watching it through someone else's eyes. God, I am sorry." Then Paul stopped singing and dancing and just stood still with his mouth open. Tim waved his hand at Paul. Peter didn't see him. Tim was remembering what they had learned about Peter as a child and how Peter knew certain things. Paul lowered his head back at Tim. Then Paul said, "Peter, why did you say you were sorry to God." Peter didn't say anything; he just kept his head down. Then Paul turned and started to walk away to finish putting things away, when Peter said, "I will tell you guys. Only if you tell me what you meant when we were playing the cloud game laying on our backs looking up in the sky. I saw you, Paul, when you look around to see if anyone heard you or not. So tell me, Paul, what did you want to ask me, I could see the way you looked at me. You said 'Oh my god, what are we going to do,' I think those were the words you said, and then you looked at me." Tim's eyes got big as a silver dollar, and he looked like he wanted to run. Paul looked at Tim. Paul knew he only had a little while before Tim started telling everything. Then Paul said, "I will tell you, Peter." Then Tim put his hands to his heart and held his breath; it seemed like he was bracing himself for what he thought Paul was going to tell Peter about what they had learned back in the cave. Then Paul said, "Peter, I thought no one heard me. When I was talking to myself when we were laying under the old oak tree, it has been bothering me." "Paul," Peter said, "it's you. You change so fast, and that is strange, you got to admit that. And how did you know what to do for me when I was feeling sorry for myself." "Peter, you had me looking for a silly limb, and you had it all the time, but the whole trip made me forget my problem and made me feel good, Peter, somehow you have learn what to say, like now." Tim took his hand from his heart and started breathing. Then Tim started laughing and said, "Boy, things have really changed. It use to be me who asks the stupid question trying to ease Peter's mind of the words that had slip out Paul's mouth," and then Tim burst into laughter. "Paul, you know Peter is not that smart to realize those words you just spoke, he's a log head, you know." Tim looked at Paul and gave him a smile; he knew that they had took that question from Peter's head. Now Peter was on defense, then Tim said. "There's no way Peter thought of all of this on his own. It had to be Big Ben's idea. I don't mean that in a bad way, Peter, but you're like me, we are not the brightest bulb in the box." Peter said, "I understand, Tim. Big Ben had told me all those things and how to act." Then Tim said to Paul, "See, I told you, Peter is not that smart." Peter just laughed and said, "Yea, Tim, you're right. Now let's put everything up and head home." Then Paul said, "You're not going to get off that easy, Peter, you have yet to tell us why did you say 'I'm sorry, God' early when you were talking about your dad." Peter dropped his head and said, "I thought I did when I told you guys about my dad, but maybe you didn't understand, what I was saying for a long time, I was upset with my father, he didn't have to die, all he had to do was to stay home with me, I beg him to, but he wouldn't, he had to leave, and he died. I didn't even cry at the funeral, my anger just wouldn't let me." Then Peter started to cry a little, but then he stopped as soon as he started laughing and said, "I am all right, now no more worries, the pain has been paid for, so let's pick up." Paul and Tim said, "All right." They hurried and put up all the things 'cause Tim gave Paul the eye and they both wanted to talk about Peter. So finally everything was put away, and they all headed for the path. Tim was walking ahead. Peter was in the middle. Paul was the last. Then Peter started to sing that song, "Who's afraid of that old bear," and Paul and Tim joined in. They sang all the way to the curb, then Peter said, "You guys want to walk the rest of the way alone, I want to think about the day and plan for tomorrow. I have a lot of surprises for you guys." Tim said, "After today, Peter, nothing you do will surprise me." Paul just laughed and said, "See you tomorrow, Peter," and walked away with Tim following; they both stopped and looked back at Peter. He was standing there just smiling as if he knew that Paul and Tim wanted to talk about him. Tim said, "Go home, Peter, we will see you in the morning." Peter turned and waved and said, "Good night, jug heads." Then Paul said, "Tim, this day was very strange, and a day I'll not soon forget. I didn't even have time to think about the parable. Tim, we have to solve this parable to save Peter from that awful fate. He will endure if we do not solve that parable." Then Tim said, "You said early that you thought it was a man. Paul, tell me where did you get that from." Paul said, "Remember the words, it will change two times in a hour, and it can be your friend or your worst enemy and is call father to us all and it is not God, that it has been around forever, and it is known by many names but yet all the names mean the same. Maybe there was something else, I don't remember. Those are the important things. And a man change two time from a child to a man, and he has been around forever and man can be your friend and he can be your worst enemy and is father to us all and it is not God." Tim looked at Paul and dropped his head. Paul said, "Yea, I know, it doesn't feel right, Tim, but it can work." Then Tim said, "Remember what Reno taught us about the truth, that the truth will feel all parts of the body like food to the body and your answer does not do that, maybe after we have had time to digest the answer it might, but right now it does not. But we were all off guard today and could not really think about it. Tonight I will think about that answer too." Paul said, "Yea, Tim, I am, I am wipe out, I can't think anymore, I keep thinking about Peter and today." Tim said, "I know what you mean, Paul." Then Paul said, "Are you coming over, Tim." Tim said, "No, Paul, I somehow lost my appetite, I just want to get somewhere and be quiet and think, 'cause the days are moving fast." So they said good night.

That next day was the same as the first one. Peter had tricks and surprises for Paul and Tim that went on the rest of the week; he kept them so busy, and the days were full of fun. He even showed up one day with short pants and a T-shirt and no shoes. Peter said, "It was a pool day." It was things like that that kept Paul and Tim guessing. They didn't have time to work on the parable. Five days had went by, and Paul and Tim were no closer than when they left the cave with Reno. It was on the fifth day at the end. Paul was sitting on the same stump that old Big Ben used to sit on. Tim and Peter were playing around, playing freeze tag. Paul just was looking, shaking his head, saying, "Peter, you and Tim are so silly, what will happen when one of you tag each other, who will be left to play, you guys are really stupid," and he dropped his head and started laughing. And then he got real quiet and started looking strange and sad. Peter said, "Yea, Tim, Paul is right, I am going to check on the crawdads, do you want to come." Tim said, "No, you go ahead." Peter said, "See you knuckleheads later," and he walked away, then Tim walked over and said, "Paul, don't be so sad, I finally feel sad too. It has been like we were held up and kept off balance by Peter. But and all the strange things that Peter did, I believe that somehow Big Ben had it all plan to keep us from solving the parable. But, Paul, remember what Reno said, if we do not solve the parable, Peter will find the treasure he has been looking for, he will find peace. "I have tried my best, Tim, to answer that damn parable," Paul said, "but it seems like my best isn't good enough, I feel like I want to cry." Then Tim looked at Paul and saw that he was crying. Tim could see the tears falling from his eyes. Tim walked over and put his hands on his shoulders and said, "Paul, are you giving up, you can't, we have to try, Paul." But Paul just sat there shaking his head and crying. Tim sat down beside him and just looked at Paul, then Tim started humming this song his mom sings while she's cooking. Tim kept on humming with his hands on Paul's shoulder and started rocking side to side as Paul cried a little harder, saying, "I don't want my friend to die and to go through all that we have seen in the cave of the future, it's wrong. Damn you, Reno." And he stood up. "Do you hear me, damn you straight to hell," and he sat back down and cried some more. "I can't figure it out,

Tim, I just can't. That stupid ass Peter, if he wouldn't listen to Big Ben and just let us find our own way." Then Tim said, "Now, Paul, you listen to me. Be quiet and cry no more, just as Peter said, we already know the answer, all we have to do is relax and the answer will come." Paul stopped crying and said, "You're right, Tim, we do know the answer." Then they heard Peter coming up the path, smiling and laughing, and looked over at Paul sitting on the log that Big Ben sat on, with Tim beside him. Peter could tell that Paul had been crying, but Peter didn't say anything. Peter just said, "I am back, and I think we can catch more crawdads later, eggheads," and he started to laugh. "We had better start putting things away so that we can head for home." So they picked up their things and went down the path.

That next day, Paul and Tim got to the clubhouse early; they both sat on the stump that Big Ben used to sit on. They both hung their head down low because they still were no closer to the answer, then they heard Peter coming up the path. Peter greeted them in the usual way by saying, "Good morning, eggheads, you guys are here kind of early aren't you, guys, maybe the early bird pull you sleepyheads out of bed." Then Peter walked toward them and said, "You guys, I have something to tell you guys, something that Big Ben told me and the things he had me do to you guys." Paul raised up his head with a smile, a feeling of relief that Peter was going to give him some answer, so did Tim. He felt the same way as Paul. Paul always had that feeling that Reno would not let them fail in saving Peter from that horrible fate he would suffer and Reno would not let him and Tim die that way. Paul knew time was running out for Peter and himself and Tim, and they still didn't have any good leads on solving that damn parable. Finally, Paul was feeling good about the situation they were in. And Peter had not told them anything yet; it was just a feeling of hearing some answers, and truly they had labored for the answer, and the expectation of the upcoming answers that Peter had in his mouth and was about to tell made Paul feel like he was going to burst into little pieces. Then Peter said, "Big Ben told me to tell you guys on the sixth day and this is the sixth day, Big Ben told me to tell you guys everything he had me do to you guys, but he didn't tell me how to tell you guys, so I am going to tell you guys something, I have always wanted to preach like a preacher and preach a sermon, so we are going to have church. Paul, before you say anything, I know we shouldn't play like this, but we are just having fun and we are not using God's name in vain, so this is all right. Paul, you and Tim will be the deacons, and the trees and the bushes will be the people. Now listen, boys, every time I say something good or something you like, you guys have to say amen and stuff like that." Then Tim said, "Like the people at Paul's daddy's church." Peter said, "Yea, and I will be the preacher. You guys wait here," and he went into the bushes and rolled out a log and rolled it beside Paul and went back in the woods and came back rolling another log. Peter rolled the log in front of Paul and Tim and said, "This is my stand, I will stand on this log when I preach the truth about Big Ben." Tim said, "Tell it like it is, Preacher, and preach on, that sound so sweet to my ears." Tim started to laugh a little, so did Paul. Then they both looked at Peter standing on the log, and Tim said, "You look real good on that log, Pastor Peter." Then Paul said, "Amen to that. Now tell us more about Big Ben and give it to us straight, Preacher." Then Tim started to laugh. Paul tried to hold it in, but he couldn't; every time he looked at Peter standing on the log, he laughed harder. Then Peter said, "When the sermon is over, we will take up a collection from the members." After saying that, Peter suddenly burst into laughter and fell off the log, and Paul and Tim started rolling on the ground laughing. Tim was holding his stomach laughing. Paul was on his knees; they had forgotten all about their little troubles, and Peter had not told them anything yet. They were lost in laughter and fun. That went on for hours, with Tim and Paul making jokes about their new leader, Pastor Peter. Then Tim said, half laughing, "Pastor Peter, what is the name of your church." Peter said, "The church of the woods." Then they started laughing again, but Peter stood back up and back on his stand and said, "Let the church come to order." Paul stopped laughing and sat on the log and looked at Peter waiting for him to start, but Tim was still rolling on the ground laughing. Paul said, "Pastor, looks like Tim has a demon in him." Then Peter said, "We might have to lay hands on Tim." Then Paul said, "Yea, it might have to be a fist upside his head." Then Peter said, "You're right, Deacon Paul, we might have to beat it out of him," and the laughter started all over again and lasted for hours, back and forth, one little joke after another, then after a while the laughter stopped. Peter got back on the log. Paul sat back on his log, and so did Tim, feeling happy and carefree, no worries, and their minds were open and their hearts were set free through the laughter. Then Peter said, "My friends, as I said, as I said, my friends, this week has been the most happiest of my life, I have been through a lot, my mom and me. But for the first time, I somehow feel that things are going to be better for me and my mom, this summer with you, Paul, and you, Tim, and Big Ben and even Reno, I can't understand him when he talks or says one of those stupid saying of his. It has been a blast, you guys, and I learn a lot that will help me. I guess, I just wanted to say thank you, guys." Tim dropped his head, and Paul pushed him in the side. Then Tim held his head back up and smiled and said, "Preach on, Preacher, you are certainly telling the truth, preach on, elephant boy, I mean, Preacher elephant boy. Paul said, "Amen to that, Deacon Tim, 'cause Pastor elephant boy sure do have some big ears, he looks like he could fly with those ears, they're like giant wings." Then Paul and Tim started laughing. Then Peter raised his hand and said, "Thank you, Deacon Tim and Deacon Paul, for those remarks, but we will not stop this time for a laughter break, we must move on." Paul and Tim stopped laughing and looked at Peter with excitement in their eyes. Then Peter said, "I would like to preach to you all tonight about Brother Big Ben." Tim raised his hand and said, "Excuse me, Reverend, Preacher, Pastor man, but it is daylight, matter of fact, it is morning." Paul almost pushed Tim off the log he was sitting on and said, "Stupid, it's only pretend, silly." Peter said, "That's all right, Deacon Tim, 'cause somewhere in the world, it must be night." Paul stood up and said, "You go on ahead and preach the truth, man. Amen, Pastor Peter. Preach, Pastor Peter, tell us more about Big Ben." Tim yelled out, "Come on with it, Preacher Peter, set my soul free." Pastor Peter started laughing a little, but he kept on talking. Tim stood up at that point and said, "Shit, man, this is getting good." Paul pushed Tim and said, "Tim, that's not good to say bad words in church, I don't play like that, Tim, you should always respect the Lord, we didn't do anything wrong until you said that word, now I don't want to play church anymore, you took the game too far, stupid." Tim said, "I'm sorry, Paul and Peter, but I got caught up in my own little joke, I didn't mean anything. Forgive me too, Lord. All right, Paul." Paul didn't say anything, but Pastor Peter said, "The Lord forgive you, and so do we. But I am getting hungry and a little tired, so let's take a break, Big Ben showed me a interesting snack, I would like to share it with you guys, it's call sour grass, and its name says it all. Tim, I bet you won't be able to eat a lot of that sour grass." Paul started laughing and said, "I just can't let this one go by, I know it's wrong, but, Peter, it is so funny when you said that Tim won't eat a lot of that sour grass, I see him like a cow in the field just grazing through the field of sour grass." Then Peter said, "You might be on to something, Paul, he does has a iron stomach and a cow has two stomachs." Paul and Peter burst into laughter; even Tim had to laugh too. He even started making cow sounds; that made all the joke funnier. Then Tim said, "Where is this field of sour grass." Peter said, "Come on." And he led them across the way beyond the field of bushes to this clear field of sour grass. Then Peter said, "Wait, Tim and Paul, I must tell you guys a couple of things before you guys start chewing on the sour grass, Tim, you cannot swallow the grass, you must chew it like gum, once you get all the juice out, then you spit it out and start over, and, Paul, you must pick the ones that have a reddish tint in the stem. The biggest ones, those are the one that has the most flavor to them, now you guys got it." Then Peter said, "One more thing, don't eat them until we get back to the clubhouse, we will sit and talk, and I will tell you guys more about Big Ben and the thing he taught me and the secrets he told me about you guys, all right, you guys." Paul said, "All right," but Tim did not say anything. Paul said, "What's up, Tim, that's sounds like a good idea, don't you think so." Tim still didn't say anything. Peter said, "Paul, it's okay, he doesn't have that look, we don't have to run." Then Paul said, "What's wrong with the little nut," then Tim said, "Hey, you guys, I don't think that's such a good idea, that doesn't work for me." Paul said, "You little nut, why doesn't it work for you." Tim said, "I was trying, but my stomach wouldn't let me. My stomach keep saying taste it. Just a little taste. Just a little bit, that's all I want. That's why I didn't answer you guys, I was doing battle with my stomach." Paul and Peter fell to the ground in laughter and said, "All right, Mr. stomach, just a little bit, only one." Tim started picking the sour grass; he picked a handful, so did Paul, then Tim walked away with his sour grass. He put a piece in his mouth and chewed, then he let out a scream and started popping his lips together and said, "Boy, that's sour," and spat it out. Paul and Peter laughed, and Paul said, "Finally Tim has found something he doesn't like and can't eat." Peter said, "I told you, Tim, it was bitter." Tim said, "For once, you really have spoke the truth, you frog head fool," and he kept on spitting and said. "Peter, are you sure we can eat this grass." Peter said, "Yes, Tim, Big Ben wouldn't let us eat something that wasn't any good." Tim said, "Yea, you're right, Peter, I think I will take another chew," then Peter said, "Wait, don't eat any more until we get back to the clubhouse, I have some salt back at the clubhouse." Then Tim said, "What do you mean you have salt, are you going to cook some food or something." Peter started laughing and said, "No, stupid, you can dip the end of the sour grass in the salt, and it will taste better." Tim said, "What are we waiting for, let's go." Paul started laughing and said, "You just love punishing yourself, Tim." Then Peter said, "Guys, it's time, we should be heading back, everyone has some sour grass." Paul and Tim said yea. Peter said, "Let's head back." They all walked back in a line, with Peter in the lead. Peter started humming their song and dancing, then he turned and looked back and said to Tim and Paul, "Whatever I do, you guys have to do it too all the way back to the clubhouse." Paul and Tim said, "All right, let's do it." Peter started walking with his hands in the air and waving them from side to side. Then he started singing and dancing, then he put his hands under his arm and started walking like a duck and started quacking like a duck. They kept on doing strange things like that all the way to the clubhouse and laughing and joking with one another. Once they got back at the clubhouse, Peter told Tim and Paul to sit on the ground, and he went inside the clubhouse and came back with a box of salt and sat on the ground with Paul and Tim and put a small amount of salt in his hand and said, "Now, Tim, do as I do." Peter bit the tip of the long straw like grass, and then he dipped the tip of the sour grass in his hand with the salt and then put it in his mouth and chewed with a smile. Tim started to smile and said, "Give me some of that salt, let me try." Paul didn't try it; instead he put the sour grass in his mouth and chewed it and said, "This is not that bad, I don't know why that little sissy boy was crying," and he started laughing. Then Peter said, "You know, guys, that was fun, this has been a fun-filled day, I hate for this day to end, but it must, if not there will be no tomorrow." Then Paul and Tim dropped their heads. Peter had just reminded them of the thing that was before them; they kept their heads down thinking of how lonely it would be without Peter and also they too didn't want to die. Then Peter said, "Cheer up, you guys, there's no need of looking like you have just lost your best friend." Then Paul got up and walk away with his head still down. Peter started getting up to go over to him, but Tim said, "Leave him alone, he's okay, it's the sour grass, it's too bitter." But in Tim's heart, he knew that that was not the case. Paul was feeling like he had let everyone down, including himself. Then Peter called over to him, "Come back over here and let me finish telling you about Big Ben." Paul came back over and sat back on the ground with that same piece of sour grass in his mouth and looked at Peter. Peter said, "Big Ben had me play some bad trick on you guys, I still don't know why, but I guess it doesn't matter, we had fun, Big Ben said that we would have fun, and he also said that you, Paul, you would be the hardest one to trick, but, Paul, you wasn't that hard to fool, and he also said that Tim would follow, even if he thought it was wrong, he would go along, just promise him food and Tim would go wherever I lead him and you," then Peter started laughing. Then Peter stopped and looked at the face of Paul; he knew for sure he was going to get an old-fashioned butt kicking and said, "Don't you hit me, Paul, I was only doing what Big Ben told me to do to you guys, and you know what,

I still don't know why he had me do those things, but that is what Big Ben said and that I had to keep you guys busy and your minds full of question and off balance, Big Ben said once I got you guys hook, all I had to do was to reel you guys in slow, just like fishing, Big Ben said. That's why I was doing those things, like with the crawdads and with the berries and now with the sour grass, oh yea, and the swimming in Salter Creek, and talking all funny and trying to be this big problem solver, tell you guys the truth, Big Ben told me whenever I saw one of you looking sad to do something funny or do what come natural to me. I bet you guys thought I was crazy or something." Then Tim said, "I liked it better when you were preaching about Big Ben." Paul said, "Tim, one thing hasn't change." Tim said, "What is that, Paul." Paul answered him, "You're still one crazy stupid white boy, I mean, if you put your brain in a bird, it would walk instead of flying." Tim laughed and said, "What's wrong with walking." Paul just put his hands to his head and yelled out, "Lord, take him please," and they all started laughing. They laughed for a while, then Paul said, "Peter, I was going to answer your question you ask us about, did Tim and myself were thinking that you were crazy, before Mr. smart guy Tim open his trap, I did think you were crazy, but we couldn't figure out how could you learn all those things, only in the time we were gone. It didn't seem possible." Peter laughed and said, "But I did, but come to think of it, it seem to me that Big Ben talk the whole time we were together. And we didn't move off these logs. Wait a minute, you know I have never seen these logs in those bushes before, you guys, and how did I know they were over there." Then Tim said, "Stop it, Peter, you're not making any sense, of course, the logs were right there, and yes, Big Ben must have showed them to you." Then Paul changed the subject and asked, "What else did Big Ben say and do." Then Peter said, "Yep, there is one more he said or did, but he told me to tell you guys only at the end of the day." Tim said, "This is the end in a little while, we will be leaving in a couple more minutes." Peter said, "I guess it's time. Big Ben told me to tell you guys this. What you have seek for in the day, it shall be reveal to you in the night and that you guys already know the answer, only you have to be still and you will discover the answer." Tim said, "What kind of fool thing is that. It sound like something Reno would say." Then he looked at Paul and smiled. Then Paul and Tim got in hurry to leave; they wanted to talk to each other about what they had just heard Peter say. Paul and Tim realized that it all made sense to them. In the words of Reno, it meant all things in their proper place and time, something Reno had said many of times, and they felt good because they knew that they were not alone. Then Tim said, "It's time to go, you guys, right, Paul." Paul hurried and said, "Yep, it's about that time, we should start getting ready to go. Tim, why don't you start rolling the logs back over where they belong." Tim said, "All right," and started rolling the logs back. Peter said, "Why are you guys in such a hurry." Tim looked at Paul, and Paul said, "It is just time to go, Peter, that's all." Peter said, "Okay, but I know there's more to that than you guys are saying, but that's all right." Soon the boys were done putting away everything and tidying up the clubhouse. Peter was moving around slowly with his head hung down low, with a sad look on his face, as if he knew it would not be the same again after tomorrow. That there would not be any more tomorrow for him. Tim saw that Peter was looking downhearted and sad, so Tim called over to Paul in a low voice and pointed over at Peter. Once Paul saw the look on Peter's face, Paul asked Peter, "What's wrong, Preacher man?" Peter didn't answer; again Paul asked him, "What's wrong, you did such a good job on telling us the thing Big Ben had you do to me and Tim, you even preach a sermon on it, we had so much fun, I have not laugh like that in a long time, so, Pastor, you did good today, don't end the day in sorrow, when it began with fun, let us end it the way we started it, with fun and laughter." Then Tim said, "Damn right and amen to that, Deacon Paul, tell it like it T. S. is, and that there is straight talk, Pastor, I mean, Preacher elephant boy." Then Peter held his head up and fell to the ground in laughter, so did Paul; even Tim was laughing at his own words. They laughed for a while, pointing at Tim and calling him the voice of comedy. Then Peter stopped and said, "Well, boys, it is time to go that egghead Tim just won't let a man feel sorry for himself for one minute, with his words of wisdom." Paul said, "It was me who spoke all those words to you, Peter, not Tim." And Peter said, "Yes, and they were good words that felt my heart, but it was the words of that egghead that made me forget why I was sad and made me laugh." Then Paul said, "I understand, sometimes all you need is a good laugh to make everything all right." Then Peter said, "That's right." Paul said, "See, Peter, you have taught us something else in the words of Reno, you have taught us a life lesson," and they started laughing all over again, calling Peter Junior after Reno. Then Tim said, "Come on, Junior, let's head for the path" Paul and Peter and Tim went down the path laughing; they had ended the day just as they started it, just as Paul had said they should. Soon they were at the curb where Peter started up the street and Paul and Tim started down the street, then Peter stopped and said, "Paul, Tim, I was going to ask you guys to walk me home, but somehow I feel you guys need to be alone, you lovebugs." And he turned and headed down the street to his house. He left Paul and Tim standing at the curb watching him as he walked down the street to his house, then Peter stopped and yelled out, "I didn't say good night, so good night, you eggheads," and gave them the finger. Paul and Tim just laughed, and Tim yelled back at Peter, "He's back, Peter the terrible," and they all laughed, then Peter turned and went on home; they saw his mother come to the door and give him a hug and take him in. Tim dropped his head and said, "I hope Peter doesn't get a beating tonight," then Paul said, "Stupid, that's not until tomorrow night, and we still have time to save him, remember, Peter said that the answer will come to us tonight, but we must remember the thing we have learn this summer from Big Ben and Reno tonight, Tim, I am going to be quiet, just like the day when we learn how to hear all the sounds in the woods and discovered the waterfall, but I tell you, Tim, it is going to be hard because my AC is out, I will let the windows up and be quiet." Then Tim said, "I didn't want to say anything, but my AC is out too, it's strange, right, Paul." Then Paul said, "It is, but I think it is all Big Ben and Reno doing." Then Tim said, "Paul, I am scared, I don't know what I will hear or see tonight, and that's makes me afraid, I guess it is the unknown that is shaking me up." Then Paul said, "Remember what Reno said about fear, it is a tool of the wicked and not a good thing and not from God, so when you feel that fear coming, just start humming or singing our song, all right, Tim." Tim answered Paul, "Okay, that sound like it will work. Paul, what if you understand the parable before me, will you come over and let me know." Paul said, "If it is not too late, I will sneak out through the window and tell you, and you will do the same for me, but if it is too late or something happen that we can't meet, then we will meet here in the morning, let's say about five thirty, so set you clock for that time, all right." Tim said, "Good." Then Paul said, "Tim, now I am getting scared." Tim said, "So am I, I guess that's normal." "Well, I guess I will be going on home," Paul said. Then Tim said, "Paul, you wait here for a minute and give me a head start, before you go home, I want to walk by myself, that old preacher man Peter was right. This night I must go the rest of the way on my own, 'cause tonight you won't be with me, and I need this little time to get stronger for what awaits me, good or bad." Then Paul said, "Somehow I understand what you are saying, it doesn't make any sense, but I understand. So go ahead, I will wait here for a while," then Tim said, "Good night, Paul, I hope to see you soon, and I pray that whatever we will discover this night, it won't be too bad." And Tim gave Paul a hug and turned and walked away with tears in his eyes, almost crying. Paul was doing the same; he was about to cry as Tim was walking away. He stopped and said, "This should be a happy time, for weeks we have worried about that parable and what it meant and about Peter, now that the answer that we have labor for and worried about now it is upon us, we are afraid of it." And Paul just dropped his head and said, "Good night, my friend," with tears falling from his eyes. Paul stood there for what seemed like a lifetime, as he watched Tim make his way home; as Tim got to the sidewalk of his house, Paul started his journey to his house. Paul was walking like he didn't want to go home, but he knew he had to; he finally reached the porch and opened the door and went up the stairs to his room, and just as he said, he let the window up in the room and got ready for bed. He knew that he would not sleep, not because of the hot summer night, but because of what was on the way, he lay across the bed waiting; he lay there for hours, but nothing happened. He heard no sounds, nor did he see anything. Then he started to wonder about Tim; maybe he had found out the answer and would soon be at his window. He got up and went to the window and looked out and shook his head and said to himself, "No Tim, I guess he is having trouble too," then he lay back in the bed and lay down with his hands under his head. Paul started getting sleepy; he could feel his body relaxing, then he started hearing sounds as he was about to enter dreamland. He heard some frogs by his window croaking for rain; that's what his dad always says when he hears the frogs, then Paul said, "No, Mr. frog, you're not the answer that I am looking for," then he heard the limbs of that old tree outside his window. "No." He shook his head. "You're not it either," then he heard some laughing through the window from the neighbor's TV, and he smile and said, "No, not you, Mr. TV," and started drifting off to sleep. But out of all the noise, there was one sound getting louder and louder, then he heard his father snoring. Paul smiled and said to himself almost asleep, "No, not you, Pop, no, not you," and he laughed softly as he was almost asleep. Then Paul said to himself in a sleepy voice, "There is another world, I have never paid that world any attention before, the sounds of the night, there are so many sounds." And he smiled. Paul was almost there in dreamland, a place where anything can happen, but that noise kept getting louder; it just wouldn't let him cross over. He thought to himself half sleep and half awake; he never paid that sound any mind before, and it was never that loud. It seemed like the quieter the night got, the louder it became, then in a sleepy voice, he said, "Tic, toc, that old clock on the wall." And he turned over to cross over, then Paul said to himself, "That old clock has been hanging on that wall for a long time,

it's funny it never bother me before. Tic, toc, that old clock on the wall."
Then Paul started saying it over and over again on the wall. Paul was
remembering something on the wall. Then he said, "That old crazy old
catfish, so that is what he meant when he said, 'What hang on the wall is
the answer,' it is time," and he jumped up out of bed and ran over to the
clock and said, "Old friend, you have been here all the time, right in plain
sight," then he started repeating the parable. "You can be my best friend or
you can be my worst enemy, you have been around forever and let me see,
minutes is one seconds is two, you are always changing, never stay the
same, and you are a person 'cause everyone call you Father Time, a father
to all, and know I know the answer and it is time and now I know just what
to do for Pete, it has been so damn easy." He ran to the bed to put on his
pants, but then he heard a voice in his head, saying, "Rest easy, my friend,
just as the answer has come to you, the same will come to Tim," and Paul
began to dance around and around just like Tim when he was really happy.
Paul stopped and got down on his knees and said, "Thank you, God, for
helping me to save Peter," and then he got up and got back into his bed
listening to all the noises of the night. He said to himself, "They all make
beautiful music together," and closed his eyes and crossed over to that
awaited land of sleep with a big smile on his face with the expectation of
tomorrow. Then just as Paul was getting ready to cross over to that awaited
land of dreams, the clock went off; it was time. He raced out of bed and
put on his clothes and washed the sleep out of his eyes and went down the
stairs; his father was up and in the kitchen. He asked Paul why was he up
so early and told him it was too early to go out. Paul started to plead with
his father, saying, "Please let me go, I have something that is very important
to do today, and I have this problem that I could not answer, but last night
the answer came to me, please let me go, please." Paul's father saw the look
in his son's eyes and the excitement and he listened to him how he told him
how important it was to him; he knew if he said no that Paul would sneak
out anyway, so he told Paul to go ahead. Paul said, "Thank you, Dad, I owe
you one." And he ran for the door, then he stopped and turned and said,
"Dad, I love you and thanks again. Today is a special day for us, me and
Tim and Peter. Can you cook us breakfast, please, Dad, please." Paul's
father said, "I will make a breakfast fit for a king." Paul said, "Thank you,
Dad, now I owe you two." And he laughed, and his dad laughed with him,
and out the door he ran; he jumped down the steps from the porch and was
off to the curb. He saw Tim standing at the curb. Tim had not seen him
yet. Tim was dancing around just like Paul was that night. Then Tim turned

around and saw Paul. Tim stopped and started his Indian dance; he started dancing, putting his hands to his mouth and singing just like in a war dance. Once Paul saw him doing the dance, he stopped and started doing the same dance, Indian war dance, then Tim stopped and reached out his arm, then he started running in place, moving his feet faster and faster, and Paul was doing every move that Tim was doing, then they both let loose at the same time, like two trains crashing. They ran into each other, hugging each other, just like they had been apart for years; they fell to ground rolling on each other, then they helped each other up and started telling of the night they both had. Tim said, "It was so strange, Paul, I couldn't sleep, I just toss and turn, then as I started to drift off to sleep, I realized the answer. I tell you, Paul, I discovered a whole new world, and it is the sounds of the night." Then Paul said, "Now, Tim, you know what we have to do now." Tim said, "Yea." Then Paul said, "Let's go over it. Now, Tim, what time was it when the beating started with Peter." Tim said, "It was seven thirty." Paul said, "Are you sure." Tim said, "Yea, 'cause I remember looking at the clock on Peter's table." Then Paul said, "You're right, I saw the clock too, I just wanted to make sure." Tim said, "That's all right. At this point, we must check and recheck to be sure." Paul said, "You're right." Tim said, "Paul, what time was it when the police came." "It was about eight thirty," Paul said. Tim said, "You're right, Paul, 'cause I look at that clock, it's funny I didn't even realize I was watching the clock like that. What time was it when his mom came back in the room with the knife." Paul said, "That I didn't look, I was focus on her, I didn't see the clock. That's okay, 'cause we will call the police station in time, I know we will. Now, Tim, we have to figure out how long it will take for the cops to get to Peter's house. Do you want to make any changes to the time we just talk about." Tim said, "I don't think so," then Paul asked Tim, "Do you have any change to make a call to the police station to see how long it will take them to come, so do you have any change." Tim said, "No, but I know where I can get some, come with me, my sister has a jar full of change, I will sneak into her room and borrow a couple of quarters, she sleep like a log. She will never know, I was in her room, I have borrow from her before, and she has never caught me yet." Paul said, "Okay, let's do it, but I will wait out here." Tim said, "That's okay, let me go in." Tim went in, and then he soon came out with a handful of quarters in his hand, then Paul said, "That's good, let's go," so they headed for the strip mall. Then Tim said, "We can't call the police to Peter's house." Then Paul said, "You're right, let's use the address to that empty lot on the corner, okay." Tim said, "Now let's get to the strip mall."

So off they went; they soon came to the strip mall. There they saw a pay phone. Paul said, "Tim, I know you won't call because you are scared of the police, so I will call this time, but when we do it for real you will have to call too, all right." Tim said, "You can count on me, Paul, I will call now if I have to." Paul said, "No, I will do it, only you listen, and when the time comes, you will know what to say." Paul calmly walked over to the booth and went inside; he left the door open so Tim could hear. He put the coin in and dialed 911; he told the operator that there was a fight at the address of the empty lot on the corner and hung up the phone and said, "Tim, mark the time," and they took off running back home to get there to see the time it would take for the police to come to that empty lot. They were almost there when they heard the sound of the sirens of the police car." Tim said, "Can you see them, Paul." Paul said, "Not yet but the sound is getting stronger, so they must be close, what time is it now." Tim said, "I got it mark," and they kept on running toward their houses. Then Tim said, "I see the car," then Paul said, "We can see from here, let's stop and rest and see what happen, we don't want the cops to see us." Tim said, "You're right, let us hide in the bush over there." Then Paul said, "That's good, we can see everything from here." They went inside the bushes and hid and watched the police as they pulled up to the lot, then Paul said, "Tim, how long did it take." Tim said, "Fifteen minutes from the time of the call." Paul said, "That's good time, now let's go over all the events and times and get the right time to call the police, so they can catch Peter's stepdad in the act." Then Tim said, "I love this, this is fun." Paul said, "That's good, Tim, it is fun for me too, but we have to keep our mind on the time. Now we know the beating started at seven thirty, so if we call at seven, the cops should get there at seven fifteen." Tim said, "Then they will get there too soon." Paul said, "You're right, so if we call them time the beating starts, then they will get there at seven forty-five, but we don't know when his mom came back with the knife." Then Tim said, "Let me think for a minute, seven forty-five and the cops got there at eight thirty." Then Paul said, "Are the cops still at the empty lot." Tim said, "No, they're gone." Then Paul said, "Why are we still hiding." Tim said, "I don't know, but I like it in here, let's finish the plan before we move." Paul said, "All right, Tim, continue." "Okay," Tim said, where was I, oh yea, seven thirty and they will get there at seven forty-five, since we don't know what time the stabbing was, I think if the cops get there, when the stepdad start the beating, give or take a few minutes, it would be fine, the only thing we will have to tell the police station that a child is being beaten and a woman is being tortured by the stepdad, the cops will insist on seeing Peter and his mom, they will see the bruises, and that will be the end of stepdad. What do you think of that Paul." Paul started to smile and even laugh a little and said, "I didn't know you had that evil part in you, Tim, that's super, but let's not say stepdad, let's say a stranger broke in and is doing all those terrible things to those innocent people." Tim said, "You're not bad yourself, Paul, you too have a evil side. So we will call that police station at seven thirty, okay, Paul." Paul didn't say okay right away; he turned to Tim and said, "Tim, it's like you said, it is better to call a little early as long as they catch his stepdad in the act, so let's make it seven twenty-five, it's only five minutes anyway, something might happen, it might be traffic." Tim said, "Paul, we live in the country, there won't be any traffic, but I understand. Okay that's the plan, and we are going to stick to it no matter what, no more changing our minds, all right, now let's get out of these woods and go by and pick up Peter, my dad is going to cook breakfast for us." Tim stopped in motion and said, "What did you say." Paul said, "My dad is going to cook for us." Tim grabbed Paul and hugged him and said, "You are my one true friend, I love you, man, you sure do treat your friends good, buddy. If I had some money, I would pay you or buy you a surprise, 'cause you are such a good friend." Paul said, "Stop it, Tim, the food is free, and you don't have to say all those thing just because I am going to feed you, we both know it's the food you love." Tim laughed and said, "I laid it on too thick." Paul said, "Yep, so thick until you could cut the bullshit with a knife," and he started laughing. "Come on, world's greatest bullshiter, let's go and get Peter, he should be up by now, 'cause my dad is waiting on us." So they were off; they passed by the empty lot, and Tim said, "Thank you, Mr. empty lot, for being empty and with address on you," and he started laughing and singing one of his stupid songs, "I'm on my way, I'm on my way to eat not at Grandmom's house or Grandpop's house, I'm off to eat at Paul's house." And he started laughing, rubbing his stomach, then Tim stopped singing and said, "We are at Peter's house." Tim started yelling for Peter to come outside. Paul hit him and said, "Don't make a lot of noise, you might get him in trouble, stupid." Tim said, "Oh yea, you're right," and walked up to the door and knocked. Peter came to the door and said, "What are you knuckleheads doing here so early." Tim said, "Paul's father is going to cook for us, so come on, or I am leaving without you, egghead." Peter said, "Paul, why did you bring this fool here, he's crazy for food. I am saying this 'cause you're my friend, if you feed him, you will never, I mean, never, I mean, never, never, get rid of his greedy behind." Tim started laughing and said, "Paul, that egghead might be right, I just might run away from home, you know a man can only take so much of bad cooking before he start looking elsewhere, and I am out of that Cajun seasoning to put on my food my mom cooking so I can eat it. That egghead Peter ain't that far off." Then Paul said, "Stop clowning around, you guys, let's go." Peter said, "One minute, I have to tell my mom where I'm going." Peter closed the door and went back inside and then came back out and said, "I left a note, my mom was still sleeping, and I don't want to wake her." Then Tim said, "All right, let's eat, I mean let's go." All of a sudden Peter began to run; he took off like a bullet fired from a gun. Paul yelled out, "Peter, stop, why are you running." Peter stopped and said, "I am trying to beat Tim to your house 'cause when he get to the kitchen, there won't be anything left, he will eat everything in sight and maybe even you." Paul yelled at him, "You are crazy, Peter." Then Peter started back running and laughing. Then Tim started running too; he took off after Peter, then Paul started running too, laughing, saying, "You guys are crazy, totally mad," and kept on laughing and running. They all were running. Soon they reached Paul's house; they got to the door and opened the kitchen door. You could smell the bacon and the ham and the eggs and the sweet smell of potatoes. Tim stopped and just stood at the door and said, "I don't want to go in, don't make me, guys. This could be very dangerous for me, I might hurt myself real bad, guys. I need a eating buddy, someone to stop me and help me not to overdo it, okay, you guys. Please, I just need a little help." Then Peter said, "I will help you with your greedy self, but you got to promise me something." Tim said, "Anything, just name it." Then Peter said, "You got to promise me you won't bite my hand if we both reach at the same thing on the table." Tim started to laugh and said, "You got a deal. There is one more little problem, now, Paul, don't get mad, but it's like my granddaddy says about a black man, if you want him to work, don't feed him a good meal, 'cause he will get lazy and go to sleep, well, I am the same way, I get sleepy and lazy when I eat a good meal, like this." Then Paul said, "That's all right, Tim, don't get mad now, I know you don't get much sleep, 'cause your mom can't cook a good meal like this." And he started laughing and pushed him inside, and Paul's dad did not disappoint them; there was so much food, they had to hold Tim up by the arms. He acted as if he was going to pass out; he kept on acting like he was going to pass out from the sight of the food. He asked Peter to feed him one spoonful just to get him started. Paul's dad asked Paul was Tim all right. Paul told his dad that Tim was not used to real food and started laughing. Peter had put a spoonful of food in Tim's mouth, and it was on. Tim started eating like there was no tomorrow. Paul's dad just stood at the end of the table in amazement, watching Tim go at it with the food. Paul's dad said, "Son, in all of my years, I have never seen anyone eat like that and so small, my god, son, we have to put you in the next county fair eating contest, you will win hands down." They all laughed. They all ate and ate and laughed. Then Paul said, "When breakfast is finish, Dad, I want to take some money from my saving and buy the biggest watermelon that fruit market has on the corner." Paul's dad said, "That will be fine, son, but the way that kids there eat, I don't think you guys can find one big enough, so I will buy one more." Paul told his dad thanks, so did Peter, and Tim said thanks too, with a mouthful of eggs. Then Tim asked Paul's dad, "Do you cook like this every morning," then Peter said, "I see where this is going," and looked at Paul and laughed. "Welcome to Paul's family, I told you, Paul," and they all laughed, and Paul's dad said to Tim, "Son, you are welcome here anytime." Tim said, "Gee, thanks, sir, I will be back, you can count on that," and let out a big burp. "A little more room," and they all laughed, even Paul's dad. Soon the fun was over. Tim had started slowing down, saying, "I could not eat another bite," still pushing food in his mouth, then it was over. Tim said, "No more." Paul and Peter cheered and said, "The cow is full, both stomachs are full." Paul's dad said to Paul, "You shouldn't talk like that to your friend, that's not nice." Then Tim said, "Sir, it's okay, we play like that all the time, he didn't mean anything by it, it's just that I am always hungry and it seem like I do have two stomachs like a cow. Moo, moo, see, sir, it's okay." Paul's dad looked at Tim and said, "If you're okay with that, son, then it's okay with me. And let me get some money for the watermelon." Paul said, "Yea, get my money from my room, you guys, wait here." Then he stopped. "Peter, don' let Tim near my father's seasoning, all right." Peter said, "You can count on me," and started to laugh. Paul came back fast and said, "Dad, we are leaving," then Paul's dad said, "Here, son, here's a little more money," then they all thanked him one by one for his cooking. Tim promised he'd be back real soon, then they were off to the market laughing and skipping. Peter said that they better had run for a while 'cause Tim was going to get sleepy soon, then Peter and Paul started to run, but Tim said he couldn't 'cause he was too full, full like a tick on a hound dog's back and started laughing. Peter said, "Only a country pumpkin could quote a lovely poem like that," and burst into laughter. Soon they reached the market; they picked out two nice watermelons and headed to the clubhouse. Tim said, "We will put the melon in the creek, like always." They all said, "Yea, then we will go off and play and explore these here woods." Tim said, "Spoken like a true country pumpkin," and started laughing, and off they ran.

That was one day that would go down in history; the boys played like there was no end. They played the cloud game and ate watermelon and played; they even went skinny-dipping in the creek. But Peter didn't take off his clothes, but that was all right. Paul and Tim didn't expect him to, and Tim did not try to tan his ass like last time; it was a glorious day, but like all days, things must come to an end, and that day was winding down. Then Tim said it, those words that none of them wanted to hear, "It is time to go, boys." Paul said, "You're right. Tim, we had better be cleaning up things." Peter was still running around like he didn't hear them, just like he was when they first got there. Tim yelled out to him and said, "Hey, crazy, it's time to go, come and help us to clean up, it's almost time to go." Peter stopped and said, "Can't we stay little while longer. I want to make this a day to remember. I wish I had a video camera, so that I could always have this day to remember you guys. And I will tell you guys this, I will not say good night to you guys or will I say bye. Because that will mean I am ending the day and I never want this day to end." Then Paul and Tim looked at each other in a wonder that Peter should say that. Because Tim and Paul knew what was going to happen tonight, but the words Peter had just spoken made them wonder if Peter knew what horrible thing awaited him later tonight. Then Tim dropped his head and looked at Paul. Paul looked back at Tim and said, "Chin up, everything is going to be all right. Peter, remember, what Big Ben taught us, you have already made a movie. It's all in your head. When you get home or if someday you get lonely, just close your eyes and remember this day and all the days here at Salter Creek and you will be right back here, with us and Big Ben." Peter smiled and said, "You're not so stupid after all, but you, Tim, you are still a country pumpkin and stupid," and started to laugh and walk over and help putting away the supplies. Once all the supplies were put away for the day, they gathered in front of the clubhouse, just standing there looking at what they had built and feeling that same proud feeling they felt when they first built it. Then Peter said something that shocked Paul and Tim. Peter asked them, "Where do the dead people go, do you guys think that there's life after you die. Paul, do you think everybody goes to heaven." Paul didn't answer, and Peter asked them, "Will I go to heaven when I die." Tim yelled out at Peter, "What in the hell are you talking about, son, you talk like you're going to die or kill someone," and then Tim pushed Peter to the ground. "You look here, friend, don't be talking like that around here." Paul just stood there looking at Peter lying on the ground, then Paul reached out his hand and said, "Pay no mind to Tim, he's just afraid of death, that's all." Then Peter got up and said to Paul, "What was wrong with the question I ask, I wasn't asking for myself, but for someone else, and it's like Reno said, Tim, if one does not die, then he has never lived, death is not the end, only another step in the cycle of life. Tim, you all know death could come at any time or to anyone, death is the master prankster, that is why you should live every day to its fullest and full of so much fun so there are no regrets for anyone, and this what I think, death could be a party no one knows 'cause no one has ever came back from death to tell. So that is why people think it is the end and a bad thing, maybe if people really knew, maybe they wouldn't feel the way they do about death. So, Tim, don't be afraid of death, just know that death will come to everyone sooner or later." Paul looked at Peter and said, "You were paying attention to things Reno said and the things he taught us." Peter laughed and said, "Someone had to 'cause that square-headed Tim wasn't," and he looked at Tim and called him a baby. "We better be going, so I am going to go," and he turned and left just as he said he would. Peter didn't say good-bye are good night; he just turned and left. Paul and Tim stood there as he walked down the path. Then Tim looked over at Paul and said, "Paul, will this work. Will the plan work, I am sure Peter knows something, he might not know what we know, but he feels something for sure, you can bet on that." Then Paul said, "Maybe you're right, Tim, but now is not the time to wonder about what Peter knows or don't know. We had better go over the plan now, Tim, you have to call the station and do what we said and call twice, and I will do the same, you got it, Tim." Tim said, "I got it, Paul, but I am really scared about this, I hope this is the right thing to do." Tim turned and started down the path with Paul following him, with his head hung down low. Soon they reached the curb where they would part. Even though they lived in the same direction and almost neighbors, they always walked together, but on this night, they went home alone. Then the hour came. Tim called the station, and he called it twice like they had talked about, then it was Paul's time to call; he also called twice. They waited for a while. They weren't watching the clock, then they heard the sirens of the police cars coming around the bend, then the stones began to glow; they knew they had to go to the cave. Paul headed for the door; he just knew his father would stop him and ask a lot of questions on where he was going. His dad was sitting in a chair by the door. Paul's dad ask him where was he going. Paul said he was going over to Tim's house. Paul's dad only said, "Be careful, son." Paul couldn't believe it; his dad let him leave and without a lot of questions and with all the police cars coming down the street. Paul was in shock, but he hurried out the door to the curb. Then his mind fell on Tim; could Tim get out as easy as he did? Then Paul looked up and saw a light shining at him from the curb. Paul wondered who was that, then the light shine down at the ground, and he saw it was Tim holding a flashlight; they met each other and gave each other a hug, and Tim said, "The timing was perfect, the police got there right as we plan it, Paul, aren't you happy." Paul didn't answer, then Tim said, "Paul, did you hear me, we save Peter." Then Paul said, "Did we." Tim said, "What are you talking about, Paul." Paul said, "My dad let me leave the house without drilling me on where I'm going, he has never done that before. And you, Tim, you were already here with a flashlight before me, I should be the one asking question." Tim said, "Paul, don't be silly, my stone started glowing, and I had this overpowering feeling to get to the cave, same as you, but I grab this flashlight and brought it with me, I keep it with me at night, I sometimes use it when my mom makes me turn off the lights, that's all to it, and my mom and dad did me the same way, they never let me go out at night, but this night was different, I thought just like you, no way, especially when there was police cars in the neighborhood, Paul, you know who is behind all this, it is Big Ben and Reno." Then Paul said, "You're right, Tim, I guess I knew it all the time." Then Tim said, "Tell me what did you mean when you said did we save Peter." Paul answered him, "We don't know for sure until we get to the cave, now, log head, shine that night-light so we can get to the cave." They made their way through the path. Paul said, "We really didn't need a flashlight," 'cause he knew his way through the woods blindfolded. Anyway, it is a full moon, and it almost looks like it's daylight. Then they passed the clubhouse; it looked more beautiful at night than at day, Tim said. They kept on going, then Paul said, "We are here. Look at the water. It is so clear, I can see right through it, way beyond the steps almost to the other side." Slowly they started down the steps holding hands as they stepped down the stairs in the crystal-blue water, as they made their way down one step after another. Tim said to Paul, "The water looks like a million fireflies on top of the water, how the moonlight reflect off the water." Then they both stopped with the water at their necks and looked at each other; they didn't say a word. They both nodded their heads and took a deep breath and closed their eyes and made that last step; they knew when they opened them, they would see Reno waiting for them and Big Ben, that they knew when they opened their eyes there stood Reno laughing, and he greeted them with a big hug and a smile and said, "You guys have come full circle, and you shall know all there is to know, all will be reveal to you this night. You guys will meet and talk with all of us, even Venges and Wally, but Venges is not here, but he shall return soon. My little warriors have won the war, and now you all shall taste the victory, for what you all have done. For many have fought a war, but few have had the chance to taste the victory." Then Reno led them into the room with the stonelike chair and the large flat rock table; they all sat at that table in the stonelike chairs. Then Tim asked Reno, "Did we save Peter, is everything going to be fine for him." Reno said, "For what you guys have done and what you have been through, for me to say the words will not do you justice, but you shall see the fruits of your labor." Then the table began to glow and got brighter and brighter. Paul took his hands off the table real fast and stood up as if he was afraid of what was going to happen, then Tim did not move his hands; he left them on the table. Reno remained sitting at the table, laughing and smiling. Tim said, "Shit, man, what's going on, man." That seemed to make Reno laugh more and smile more at them. Then Paul yelled out, "Stop it, Reno, what's going on," and the table got even brighter and brighter until Paul and Tim had to cover their eyes from the brightness of the table; when they opened them, the stonelike table looked just like the water of the creek. It was crystal clear and blue; it also seemed like it had little fireflies on top. Then Reno said, "Look into the pool of water and see what your labor has done, you shall see what you have labored for, behold, my friends." Tim didn't want to look, and neither did Paul; that made Reno laugh out loud again and said, "You guys have took a million steps and have traveled many miles to get to this point, and now there is but one step left to take, and you guys are afraid," and he laughed and laughed long and hard. Then Paul said, "I am not afraid of anything you have to show me." Tim said, "Damn right, you tell him, Paul." Tim was steadily moving behind Paul; from behind Paul's back, Tim said, "We can take anything you have to show us, right, Paul. Paul, will look at anything, tell him, Paul, you tell that old Reno something, go ahead and let him have some more, you're the man, Paul, you are Mr. John Henry, the strongest man in the whole damn world, that's who you are, Paul, and you're not afraid of a damn thing, who can comb his hair with a tree limb and drink muddy water to cool his thirst. You go ahead, Paul, and tell that old man turtle a thing or two." Reno was almost crying from laughing so hard at

Tim and pointing at him. Then Paul turned and looked behind him at Tim and said, "Yea, Tim," and started laughing at the things he had said. Even Tim started laughing at himself, saying, "I kind of got carry away." They laughed and laughed. Everyone was laughing and pointing at Tim. Paul called him his backup man. Tim said, "It's like you said, Paul, if something happens, there has to be someone left to tell the story of what happen to that fool, man, if something would have happen, I would have been running so fast, I would have outrun my own echo, I would have been out of sight and out of mind. That's how fast I would have been moving." They laughed even harder at Tim, and Tim had this serious look on his face. Paul could tell that Tim was serious. Then Paul said, "Tim, are you sure you're not one of us, listening to you talk, it sounds like me." Then Tim laughed and said, "I finally made it, I am a soul brother, and I didn't even have to get a tan." Paul just went down to the ground off that one, 'cause he knew what Tim was talking about, when he tried to give his ass a tan, when Peter made the comment about his snow-white ass, when they were swimming in the creek and swinging from the rope on that old oak tree. Paul was down to his knees in laughter, so was Reno. While Paul was down on his knees laughing, Tim looked over Paul's shoulder and said, "Paul, I see Peter." But Paul didn't answer; he was still caught up in Tim's remarks on running out of sight. Tim said it again, "Paul, I see Peter in the pool of water," but again Paul didn't answer. He was still laughing at Tim, then Tim put his hands on Paul's shoulder and pulled him up to the pool of water and said, "Look, cabbage head, there's Peter," then Paul stopped laughing and said, "Yea, Tim, I see him." Tim said, "Yea, that's that fish-eyed fool, look, Paul, he's talking to that same cop we saw in the room of the future, what was his name." Paul said, "Officer Dave." "That's right," Tim said. "I hope Peter doesn't take his gun this time," and started laughing. Paul told him to shut up and watch the pool of water. They saw Officer Dave walk over to Peter's mom; she was bleeding from her mouth from where Peter's stepdad had hit her. Officer Dave asked her, "Did your husband do that to you and was he beating the boy?" His mom didn't say anything. Then Dave said, "Are you okay, ma'am, do you need to go to the hospital." The lady shook her head no. Then Officer Dave said, "Son, can you tell me what happen here, why was this man beating you." Peter also dropped his head. Peter's stepdad was sitting on the bed with another officer standing over him, with his hands on his shoulder. Peter's stepdad started smiling and said, "Officer, there's nothing going on here, the boy just got out of control and hit his mother, you can see the blood coming from her mouth and when you guys got her and saw me beating the boy, I was only punishing the boy for his action, I think the boy has been smoking pot or something." Officer Dave turned and looked at Peter and then looked at his mom and said, "Ma'am, is this true." His mom didn't say anything, then he turned to the man and said, "Well, that seems to be the case. Then all of a sudden, Peter's mom started shaking her head no. The other officer that was over Peter's stepdad pointed over at Peter's mom so that Officer Dave could turn and look, then the officer put his hand on his gun. Peter's stepdad said, "See, I told you guys, she's crazy." Peter's mom was shaking her head no and waving her hands. Officer Dave asked her, "You all right?" Officer Dave moved closer to the officer that was standing over the bed, then Peter's mom started saying, "Not this time, I am tired of you, no more, I tell you, no more. You won't fool these people that I am crazy, you have held me here against my will for years, threatening me that you will kill my son if I tried to leave and beating him when he tries to stop you from beating me, no more, you worthless piece of dirt, you won't ever lay your hands on me or Peter's money that his dad left him." Then Officer Dave said, "Ma'am, what are you saying, you mean to say that your husband has held you and your son against your will and beat you both." Peters mom yelled out, "He's not my husband, he's just someone that I hired to work for me remolding the kitchen, he was very nice at first, asking a lot of questions about what happened to Peter's dad and my husband and was there any insurance money, I made the mistake of telling him, it was close to three million dollars left to Peter and me. The next thing I knew he had moved in and told me that I better tell everyone that we are married or he would kill my son, whenever he wanted money or wanted me to do something, he would start an argument, he knew that Peter would come into the room to save me and that would give him the chance to beat him and to keep me in line, but I only gave him pennies, I fooled him, I keep on telling him that the money was not ready, but the little I gave him kept him quiet, but he still said I better not tell my son or he would kill the both of us. He never let me go anywhere, he would let Peter go and play to make things seem like we were a happy family, but what could Peter say, all he knew is what I told him. That was that we had gotten married. That's all that he could say or tell anyone, that's all he knew." Then Peter said, "She is telling the truth, he beat me all the time." Then Peter pulled up his shirt. "Look." Peter's back and stomach were covered with marks from the belt, and his back was bleeding from the new marks; the officer that was standing over the man that Peter knew as his stepdad told him to stand up, and he put the handcuffs on him and said, "No one has the right to do what you did to this kid, my god, man, you have no sense of what is right and what is wrong," as he put the handcuffs on him tight. Then Peter ran over to his mom and said, "Mom, I am sorry, I didn't mean to cause you any problem, I was only trying to protect you. I knew he was hurting you. I just knew it." Then Peter's mom grabbed him, and they hugged each other, and they both cried. Then wiping away the tears, Peter's mom said, "Peter, that night after the accident, when your father was at the hospital and we were on our way, you told me that your father was not at the hospital, how did you know that, Peter, I always knew that you could see things and knew certain things." Peter said with tears in his eyes, "Mom, I could, but now it's not the same, I don't have it anymore." Then Peter's mom grabbed him and held him and said, "That's okay, son, I knew you had that gift, and I didn't do anything to help it grow, son, I should be the one saying that. Son, after your dad died, I was pretty messed up, I was lost in my own sorrow and self-pity, son, I let you down and myself down, now I know what we have to do, we have to face what happened. Son, that man didn't do anything that I didn't let him do, everything that happened I let it happen, because of my self-pity. Son, you know when this is over, we are going back to New York, this time we won't be running away from yesterday and the things that happened we will be running to tomorrow, and know this, son, everybody goes through their problems and comes through good, and together we will have to put yesterday behind us and start living for tomorrow and all that it holds for us." Then Dave put his hands to his head and said, "Oh my god." Then he looked at the other officer and said, "Take that piece of dirt to my car, do you hear me, and go ahead and start writing up the report just as this lady said it. You got it." The officer said, "Yea, Dave. I understand what you are saying, buddy," and then the officer led the man out the door and whispered in his ear, "I would hate to be you when Dave gets through with you." After the officer had left the room, Dave started asking Peter's mom about her husband and said, "I knew your husband, we grew up together for a while, until my mom got married again to my stepdad." Peter's mom put her hands to her heart and said, "Are you." Then Officer Dave said, "Yes, that's me, old patches," then Peter said, "You knew my dad." Dave said, "Yea, I can tell you some things about that guy." Then Peter said, "I want to hear it all, sir." Then Peter's mom said, "Soon, Peter, he will" and went on to talk to Dave. Peter's mom said, "I remember you wrote my husband a while back, he was so happy to get that letter," then Dave dropped his head and said, "I am sorry that I missed the funeral, I didn't know he had died, and I didn't know you guys were down here, if I would have known, that piece shit would have never hurt you or Peter, but he will pay for his action, and I will fix everything so you and Peter can leave in the morning, but you will have to come back for the trial, if there will be one." He smiled. "I will have to be going soon, but if it is okay with you, I would like to check Peter out before I go, I was a medic in the army for a while, and while I am checking him out, I will tell him what his father did for me when I was a kid." Then Peter's mom called Peter over and told him to do what the officer said. Peter said, "Okay, Mom." Dave looked at his mom and said, "You're right, Peter is tough, just like his dad, and he is a rich little kid too." Peter started laughing and said, "I was rich yesterday before I knew about the money. I don't want it, I already have everything that I need in this life, I know the things that matter the most in life, and it is not money for sure." Then Dave said, "Come, Peter, and lay on the bed." Peter said, "Yes, sir." Dave felt him in the stomach and put his ears to his back and listened to his breathing and touched him all over to see if he was in any pain. Then Dave looked at his mom and said, "Peter is fine, he will be a little sore for a while, but he will be fine, when you get back to New York, take him to your doctor and give the doctor this card, it has my phone number and the case number." "All right," his mom said. Then Dave said, "Come here, Peter, and let me tell you a little about your dad, he was a crazy little dud." Peter started laughing and said, "Go ahead, please I have been waiting my whole life for someone to tell me something about my dad." Then Dave started laughing and said, "Peter, I was like you when I was little kid, I was known as patches, 'cause all my clothes were patched, and all the other kids at school used to make fun of me and laugh, calling me the poorest kid in town, it was true. 'cause we was, when my dad was alive, he provided for us real good, but when he died, he left us with nothing, my mom didn't know that much, hell, she didn't even know her name if it was written in lights at night, she couldn't read or write, so it was hard for her to get a job, so she worked in the fields, while she worked, we stayed at your father's parents' house, it seemed like we spent more time there than we did at home, and your father didn't make fun of me, he treated me like a brother and my sister like a sister, I played with his toys more than he did, he made me feel like I was richest kid in town, I didn't hold my head down in shame at his house. I held my head up high. He gave me the courage to keep going on and to know that there are good people out there. He was my best friend. Now, Peter, tell me was that a good guy or not." Then Peter looked at his mom and said, "I am glad we came here, I am not glad about what happen to us, but I am glad we came, it seems as if it was for me to learn 'cause if I would have stayed in New York, I would have become what my father hated, and that is a snob, a rich little snob." Then Peter's mom said, "Peter, get your thing together." Then Dave said, "Listen I get off at seven, I can come by and pick you guys up and drive you all to the airport, maybe we can stop by my house and you guys can meet my family, I will cook breakfast for you all, and I will take care of the tickets, they will be waiting for you at the airport, I have a buddy that owns a travel agency." Peter's mom said, "That would be great, let me check with the man of the house." She called Peter and told him what Dave had said. Peter was happy and went over to the dresser and took out an envelope and said, "Mom, my other friend gave me this envelope, and he told me not to open it until the bear was gone, I didn't understand what he was saying at the time, but now I do, I am not afraid of that old bear, the bear is dead. You never met him, his name is Big Ben, and he told me that I would know when the time is right to open it, and he was right, the time is now, the bear is dead, but I don't have to open it. I already know what's inside." And he started laughing. "It's Paul and Tim's address and phone number." He laughed. "It's just like one of those things Reno would say, all things in their proper place and time, and everything must proceed in order. Then Dave said, "Those seem like smart kids, I would like to meet them, that Big Ben and that Reno kid someday." Peter said, "You have already meet one of the them, behind the strip mall," and he started laughing. "My other friend, you would have to be a kid to hear or see him, for only the heart of a kid can see or hear Reno." And he walked away humming that old song, and then the screen went blank. Tim asked Reno, "Is there any more to see, Reno." Reno said, "Yes, there is much more to see, but you guys will not see the rest. You must live it. Soon the others will be here, and they will show you guys more. I have shown you all that I can, the rest that you must see will be shown to you by the others that are on their way. Now listen to me, you guys, what they have to show you and tell you may not be what you want to hear, but I know you guys are strong and tough." Then Paul said, "Reno, will we ever see Peter again." Reno said, "You cannot erase what has been planted in the heart, even if he is a hundred miles away, in this life you will learn sometimes the best friend is the one that is the farthest away. And to answer your question in plain talk, yes, my friend, you will see him again, every summer, and you all will have many more adventures together." Then Reno dropped his head and walked away. Tim asked him what was wrong. Reno smiled and said, "Nothing, my little funny man." Then Tim asked him again what's wrong. Then Reno said, "I have known all the time that this day would come, but even knowing does not make it any easy, I have been around for hundreds of your years, I have seen man do some bad things and some good things, I have been an obedient servant, but at the end, I wasn't, and I must pay for that, we must pay for that one mistake that we made many years ago, even though we have turned that one mistake into something wonderful, that can do way more than we could ever do for mankind, none of that matters now, my friends, soon, I must go to whom that sent me and cash this check that I have written for myself and the others, but you know what, my friends, I wouldn't change a thing, my friends. My heart is full of sorrow and happiness. Happy that I can feel all the things that you guys feel and to be able to share them with the people of my home world, for that was our job because they had grown tired of their own lives. You guys must know this, you have given pleasure to many even to those that you have never met, I tell you this because I am proud of you as a father to a son that has done a good deed. But the sorrow I feel is greater than the happiness I feel, because of you guys, I will miss those funny little things you say, Tim, and you, Paul, I will miss your strength, I have known many over the years, but you guys are different, you guys have yet to ask me why I came to you as a turtle and why all the parables. I can tell you my part, and the others will tell you theirs. First of all, I am from the future in my world way beyond the clouds in the sky, a place just like your earth, and no, Tim, I am not an angel or your God. I was once a man just like your fathers, but our world got so wicked with greed and lust, and with all the things that will come to your world in time, our world was out of control, men and women were out of control and our leaders decided to end all the evil things of the world, our scientists evolved technology until they could do anything, so city by city they went transforming the people into cells of energy, a place where when one person laughs a million others laugh and when one person is sad the whole city is sad, they said it would be like heaven we now know that no man can make heaven, only God can make such a place. The people of my world would give anything just to cry or to be sad or to have just a smile to themselves, those little things that so many think nothing of, to know that somewhere someone else would give anything for those things, those little things must be priceless, and, Tim, we have learned that there will always be good and bad, Tim, and that there are two kinds of men, that's the good man and a bad man, those people will not decide the world's fate, it will be the people in the middle who have not chosen, those will be the one that will make the difference in your world, those are the ones that hold your fate in their hands, those will be the ones that decide your fate, and those are the ones that evil follow, offering them whatever they desire, we know now that, you see, Tim, we do not have bodies, and we have no emotion, we cannot feel as you guys do or do we think as you guys do, we do not speak. We hear each other's thoughts in our minds, we don't need clothes or any of the things your world hold so dear, for we learned many years ago that those things are the things that corrupt the soul and cause problems, and the most important thing of all is a man's faith, the belief that there is a higher power, now we know that to be truth, we have learned to believe that your God will free us from this hell that we have made for ourselves, that has given us hope. Now I cannot tell you guys everything of my world, but the little that I told you is enough. Now why did I come as a turtle, I could have been anything, but that is what your heart could believe at the time, the first encounter, do you remember, Paul." Paul said, "Yea, I remember, Reno, it was when you brought Big Ben to the edge of the creek." Then Tim said, "Here come Wally and Venges." Wally walked over and said, "I knew you guys could do it, and you have done well, I hope that Reno has taken good care of you guys." Paul and Tim said, "Yea, Reno has done a good job," and looked at Reno. Reno just smiled, then Wally said, "Come with me." He took them over to the cave of the past; they had never been there before. Wally said, "Come, my friends, don't be afraid, this you have earned, now behold." They looked at the screen; it was the same as they had watched in the cave of the future, then the screen jumped to when they saw the two young men in the car. It was them, then they heard what they were saying, something they didn't hear in the cave of the future. One of the young men said, "Damn, Tim." Then they both knew it was them; he said, "If only we would have call the cops early, Peter would not be dead now." And they passed the bottle and smoked that pot, and just as it was in the cave of the future the car ran off the road, and they were killed. Then the screen went blank. Tim said, "It was us that call the police that night just as we did this night, but this time we did the right thing." Wally laughed and said, "Yes, boys, you did, that is why you could not solve the parable because you guys would have change the plan so many times until you would have made the same mistake. You guys got a second chance, and you made good of it, but in your world many of men get a second chance every day to do the right thing, but they don't, they still make the same mistake, soon, my little friends, man will not get another chance, the time is right for man to see his mistakes and make the right choice, but there is yet one thing man must learn, when he realizes that thing, he then can make the right choice, for he is running out of time. Your world grows meaner and harder by the minute, it is as if the whole world has drank from the worldly cup of bittersweet nectar, and soon the whole world will be drunk in their own confusion, not knowing what is right or wrong and losing themselves in themselves, but you were given this second chance because of your fathers and what they have done, we selected you because of your fathers, your fathers were picked because of their fathers, and so on and so on, I can tell you this, because as your fathers and their fathers before them, you will not remember this, will you remember the things that you have learned this summer, you will only remember what a great summer this was, you will know the things you did for Peter and all the fun times you guys spent exploring the woods, and that is all." Then Venges walked over; he didn't seem as mean as he looked for some reason and said, "Come," and he led them back to his cave that had no name on it. "Behold." They saw Peter's stepdad; at least that is what they had thought. Now they knew the man that they took for Peter's stepdad was not; they knew better now. They saw him take a sheet off the bed and threw it across the rafters of the ceiling, and he hung himself. Then the screen went blank, and Venges said to them, "This man has done other men a great thing so that no other man should have his blood on their hands. For he was not worth it, that another should be stained with blood on their hands. He was not born a bad man, he was once a good man, he worked hard and did the best he could, he even went to church every now and then, but he let greed and lust rule his heart, he drank from that cup, that worldly cup of bittersweet nectar that the world offered him. It made his heart black and cold, he let the love of money rule his life and an easy way of living with all the things it offered him. And for that is death, no one took his life, he took his own. For regret is a hard thing to live with. When you realize what is in that cup of bittersweet nectar, some men that have a good heart but can be drunk from that bittersweet nectar and when they sober up, cannot bear the regret of what they have done, when they realized they have made a big mistake. So let that be a lesson to you." And he laughed. Then Wally yelled over, "Speak directly to the boys, because they do not fully understand those things that you speak. Every man will one day pay the price for his actions, just as we must pay for breaking our promise to only watch. We have been here for many of years, and we bent the rules in our favor to protect what we had done." Then from the other side of the room they heard that song, "Who's afraid of that old bear," and they knew it was Big Ben; at last he had come. Tim said in a low voice, "Big Ben," then Big Ben walked over. Venges bowed his head in greeting to Big Ben, and so did Wally and even Reno. Then Big Ben said, "It is good to see you, old boys," and he reached out and hugged them. "It is I. I am the reason why they must pay, it is what they did for me, many years ago. Come with me and I shall show you guys. I have never lied to you guys. I don't have a mother or a father, I am the last of my family, and I have been alone here for many of years. Many kids have come through here. But none of them were able to help me to become what Reno and Wally and Venges intended for me, when they saved me, I became one of them, but I could not let the past go and evolve into what they intended me to be. But in order for me to evolve into what I am supposed to be, I had to let go of the past and let the hurt heal. As you know, there has been many kids that have come to these caves, we have let them find the steps, hoping that I could bond with them and be as a kid and live as a kid and help me to heal from the past, but out of all those kids that have came through, you guys were able to do what no other could do for me. You see, guys, I was a real boy like you guys at one time, before the bad man came and before I found this place, soon your eyes shall see what I am saying, but I will attempt to tell you guys. Reno and Wally and Venges raised me, they did their best, but they knew little of what a little human boy needs, I was so lonely, as you guys know, here in this cave time does not go as your time. One day here is like a year in your world. I became stuck, I could not let go of the past, I longed for my mother and father. All I ever wanted was to have a family, and you guys were the first ones to make me feel like I had a family, you guys were even willing to share your mother and father with me, your brother, I could feel the love from you guys, and that love was enough for me, and you all gave me that family I was longing for, you see. In Reno's world they do not have bodies, and I could not lose mine. I could not evolve into what they had made me and what I was meant to be. That is why they kept bringing kids here so that I might find what I had lost, so that I could evolve into what I am meant to be. I am a time traveler, I can go to the future and to the past and the present, I can do and go anywhere and anything, but because I could not let go of the past, I have been a prisoner in this cave." Then Paul said, "So it was never about Peter or me or Tim, it was all about you. Then Reno started laughing, so did the rest of them, then Tim said, "Why are you guys laughing at Paul." Big Ben said, "We are not laughing at him, it is what he said, he still does not understand. I will tell you straight, Paul. If there was no you or Tim or Peter, there would be no me, our lives were woven together many years ago through your fathers and their fathers before them." Then Tim said, "I understand, Big Ben." Then Big Ben said, "I know you do, Tim, and now Paul understands now. Wally told you guys that man will get a second chance, now let me tell you how, when man realizes that he is his brother's keeper and that the action of one will affect them all and when man realizes that, then he will receive his second chance, and maybe this is his chance and he has not realized it yet and remember this, time will wait for no man to get ready. Come with me and see what I have told you." Big Ben pointed at the wall, and it lit up, and they started seeing this family living in this log cabin, a woman and a little boy and a man with a squirrel cap on his head; the man told the woman he was going out to check the traps and that he would be gone for a day or two. He said there's enough meat in the cabin to stay inside until he returned. Then he walked over to the little boy and said, "You watch out for your mom." The little boy acted like Peter, when he was a kid. Then the man left; the little boy was running around in the cabin playing, then the door got kicked open. There were three men coming in the door with fur coats on, with long breads and long hair; the woman grabbed the boy and put him out on the side through the wooden window and said, "Run and get your dad." The little boy ran to the front; there he saw his dad lying facedown in the dirt, trying to crawl to help his wife; the little boy tried to help his dad, but he was too little. The man pushed the little boy away and said, "Run and hide yourself, son, and don't make any noise and do not come back here, do you hear me. Do not go in the house. Go in the woods and wait for your mom, if she does not come to you in a day, leave and find your way, son. It is not much, but that is all I can do for you. You know the way to the township, boy, that is where you must go, it is with great sorrow that I leave you, son." And then he pushed the boy away and made it to his knees and then to his feet and ran in the house; the boy turned and ran and did not look back or did he go back to the house, then they saw the little boy hiding in the woods waiting for his mom, but she did not come, so he did as his dad told him to do and started for the township, but the little boy was crying and had gotten lost. He was running in circles, then he came upon to this creek and fell in. Then they saw Reno take him, then the screen went blank. There was total stillness; the air had gotten hot. Wally moved real softly to Big Ben, so did Reno and Venges; they made a ring around him, and they told Paul and Tim to close their eyes and to keep them closed until they told them to open them. Paul and Tim could hear Reno and the others speaking in a strange language. Then they heard Big Ben cry out, "Why, my mom and dad, why," and they heard this awful sad cry; it lasted for what seemed to be forever, then there was laughter, and they herd Reno say, "It is done, the past has passed him by. You guys can open your eyes now, Big Ben has something to say to you guys." Then Big Ben said, "That was the first time I saw that, Tim and Paul, over the years it seemed like a faded picture, you want to see but you can't, thank you, my friends, now I can transform, and you guys will see this body no more, I am happy, but yet I am sad that I will not see you guys again, but I know that is not the case, for I can see you guys whenever I want, but you won't be able to see me, nor will you guys remember me, soon it will be time for you all to leave and do your last task, Reno will tell you soon, now, my friends, I must go, I want you to know what you have done for mankind, I can do what Reno and the others couldn't do. I am not bound by an oath or a promise, where every innocent one is wrong there is where I will be, and when they leave this world and cross over to the next one, I will help them to cross over, I will be their friend when they need one and nobody cares." And with that, the room started to grow lighter and lighter. Wally came over and put his hands over Tim's eyes, and Reno did the same for Paul, and then it was over. Tim asked Reno, "Where did Big Ben go, was he invisible." Reno laughed and said, "Big Ben is in the air, he is the star that shines the brightest in the sky, he will always be there for you guys and the rest of mankind." Then Paul said, "Reno, before we go, tell me of the punishment that await you guys and will it be painful, will you guys have to suffer and why won't Big Ben help you guys, you guys help him when he needed help." Then Tim said, "We will help you guys, if Big Ben won't, because you have help me and Paul and Peter and many more, so it is right for us to help you guys." Then Reno dropped his head and said, "With those words, you have just won us favor in the one that sent us here. We see now that there is hope for mankind, if man is to have a second chance, it will be through men like you and Paul, Tim, now you boys can see anything you want. Tim, you once asked me about your wife, would you like to see her, or you, Paul, would you like to see anything." Paul looked at Tim and said, "No, there is nothing that I want to see, all that I want is to be as a child, to run and play and to take little thought of tomorrow." And then Reno said, "And you, Tim." Tim said, "By your own words Reno everything in it's proper place and time for we have looked into the sun and saw inside ourself's and became men's and if we were men we would never see ourself's the same for we saw our faults and fears and the desire's of our hearts and we face them now it is time to be as a child to run and play and to take little thought of tomorrow just as Paul said" Then Reno said, "Come here, you do a father proud. You have learned the true things that matter the most in life. You have made me proud, now go and do not look back, for we will not be here, once you guys get back to the top, you must tear down the clubhouse and throw the wood back in the creek, with every piece of wood you guys take down, so shall your memory of us and Big Ben and all that you have learned down here in the caves, once it's done, all that you will remember is what you have done for Peter and all that Peter shall remember is the fun he had this summer with you guys, for you all will share the same memories. Now go, my friends. We hope that you enjoyed this parable of life and hope that it has helped you guys in some way. And like the boys in this parable you to have become a man or a woman, and now you know the thing that matters the most and can help save mankind and give them a second chance."

Now, my friends, I must tell you one more parable, but this one I will explain it before I tell the parable. This parable deals with the politics of this world, now let's just imagine that Mom is the Democrat and Dad is the Republican and the mistress or the other man could be the Tea Party or some other special interest group or even the lobbyist that has come between Mom and Dad, causing Mom and Dad to fight, causing the Republican and Democrat to fight between each other, causing each party to say that one is better than the other and that they have nothing in common. I hope this will help you understand the purpose of this book and why it has no ending 'cause the ending has not been written.

A Child's Prayer

Hear me, O Lord, for I am your child, help me, O Lord, for mine eyes are as red as the fire that burns on a dark cold winter's night, my tongue is swollen, O Lord, from crying, my heart feels no more, for it seems like death is coming to me. Not because of something that I did or not because I am sick. For I am your child, Lord. Hear me, O Lord, hear my cry. I come to you not as a man but as a child full of hope and faith. For only you can do what is needed here, my Lord. O Lord, all my life, all that I have known is Mom and Dad, but now they fight like cats and dogs, they hate each other for no good cause. Once, they loved each other and respected each other and worked as one. Neither one of them taking more than the other. They worked together and raised many of my brothers and sisters and made them wealthy and powerful. They watched over them while they slept, they kept them from harm and danger, and nursed them when they were sick. All those things they did as one, but now one must be better than the other. Now all that Mom and Dad do is fight and yell and plot against each other to fail, and meanwhile, me and brothers, sisters suffer. With Mom saying that she should be the leader of this house and Dad saying the same and saying that they have nothing in common, and then they look at me and my brothers and sisters for our approval so that they can go on with their foolish fight of egos and selfish pride and greed. I see my sister, she falls to the ground in tears and grabs her heart and rolls on the ground with her hands to her ears as she cries out. Lord, I can't look at Mom and Dad anymore, help us, O Lord, for I have lost what I thought I would never lose, O Lord, I have lost the very thing that's kept me going, the thing that makes me obey their rules, O Lord, help me for I have lost my trust in my mom and dad, my faith in man, I no longer trust either of them, O Lord, I am so ashamed, help me, O Lord, for every time Mom and Dad fight and say that they have nothing in common, a little piece of me leaves, they put each other down hatefully, O Lord, my heart breaks and my chest tightens and I feel like the end is near when they say those hateful words to each other that they have nothing in common, how can they say that when they have me and my brothers, are they not in charge of us, O Lord, isn't it to watch over us and protect us and feed and clothe us and nurse us when we are sick. They have forgotten, O Lord, the things that matter the most. Come now, Lord, and help us, I see my brother on his knees crying out, they have forgotten to feed us, Lord, it is so bad, Lord, they can't even agree on what to feed the babies that cry for food while they fight among each other, now, my Lord, another has come and whispers in my dad's ear telling him that he is the best one to lead and not to listen to Mom and, Lord, Mom has one that's is whispering in her ear and telling her that Dad is not able to lead this family and she should take over. Lord, this used to be a house of love and caring. A place where great ideas were born, they thought and planned out ways to protect and feed and nurse the young ones. They all worked as one for the greater good, Lord, what has happened to Mom and Dad, will they remember that two or three or even four can be one, as long as they have respect and the same goal, they can be one. Lord, you said where there are two or three touching and agreeing, you will be in the midst, Lord, we need help for the house is divided and a house that is divided cannot stand, Lord, I am a child and I hear the cries of my brothers and sisters. I see their hurt and pain. I feel their suffering, for I am suffering too. Lord, is there no help for us, will you not come for us, will you not send your angels of war and kill the ones that have turned our house into a house of pain and mistrust and lies. Fight for us, O Lord, but I know we must first fight for ourselves first and then you will come for me, O Lord, I will not choose. I will not pick Mom or Dad. I choose my brothers and sisters, together we can stop the fighting and get Mom and Dad together again. I asked you brethren who will help us, will it be you that will help my brother and sisters, will you stand with us and show Mom and Dad that they both can lead. Let them know that one can't exist without the other and put things back the way they were, when everyone had the same chance.

Now, my friends, you have read my little parable, I hope you have been enlightened by the words, because there is no difference in any man, only the ones that we let other people make for us. If you don't believe me, just ask ten people you don't know of different backgrounds, rich are poor, what do they want out of life and what they want for their families, and you will see it is the same as yours, and if we work together like in the beginning when this world was young and put away our own hatred for one another just for a while, we can make the leaders of our world see there's no difference in anybody. Republican or Democrat, we must work together to achieve the goals of a nation, it takes more than one to make a great nation. It will take all of us working as one with different motives but for the same goal. The time has ran out for this book, but it hasn't ran out for you, good-bye, my new friends, I hope the words have fallen on fertile soil. May they grow with you as your faith grows in mankind. Together we can do it. Your friend for life, Terry Lee Vail.

Edwards Brothers Inc.
Blue Ridge Summit, PA. USA
April 13, 2011